Anna Lega ... ... DI
Gillian Mars ... ... of-
all-trades, Anna has been an attorney, legal adviser, a silver-service
waitress, a school teacher and a librarian. She read law at the
University of South Africa and Warsaw University, then gained
teaching qualifications in New Zealand. She has lived in far-flung
places all over the world where she delighted in people-watching
and collecting precious life experiences for her stories. Anna writes,
reads, lives and breathes books and can no longer tell the difference
between fact and fiction.

By Anna Legat and available from Headline Accent

The DI Gillian Marsh series

Swimming with Sharks
Nothing to Lose
Thicker than Blood
Sandman
A Conspiracy of Silence

The Shires Mysteries

Death Comes to Bishops Well
At Death's Door
Cause of Death

———

Life Without Me

CAUSE OF
DEATH

ANNA LEGAT

ACCENT

First published in 2022 by Headline Accent
An imprint of HEADLINE PUBLISHING GROUP

1

Cataloguing in Publication Data is available from the British Library

ISBN 978 1 7861 5990 8

Typeset in 10.5/13pt Bembo Std by Jouve (UK), Milton Keynes

Printed and bound in Great Britain by Clays Ltd, Elcograf S.p.A.

Headline's policy is to use papers that are natural, renewable and recyclable
products and made from wood grown in well-managed forests and other
controlled sources. The logging and manufacturing processes are expected
to conform to the environmental regulations of the country of origin.

HEADLINE PUBLISHING GROUP
An Hachette UK Company
Carmelite House
50 Victoria Embankment
London EC4Y 0DZ

www.headline.co.uk
www.hachette.co.uk

To Steve.

Chapter One

The full moon was their silent accomplice – it shone brightly, illuminating the finer detail of the grand forgery they were carrying out on the ground. It wasn't an easy job. The work had to be conducted on the uneven surface of the south-facing slope of a hill which by day was home to a herd of Friesian cows. A hill covered in cowpats was like a minefield, especially to those who had made the unfortunate choice of sandals for footwear.

Old cowpats pretended to be dormant but once stirred they could explode in a bouquet of unpleasant odour. That became evident when Rumpole, Vera Hopps-Wood's Irish wolfhound, was detected smeared with cow excrement and stinking to high heaven. He appeared as happy as a pig in ... mud, but Vera was inconsolable. No one showed her any sympathy. She should not have brought her pet to work. Forgery was no walk in the park.

The first part of the operation was the painstaking removal of topsoil together with all vegetation and the offending cowpats. That task had been conducted under the watchful eye of the designer and project manager – Maggie Kaye. The whole undertaking was her idea. The loosely organised but fiercely proud community of Bishops Well, in the shape of the Bishops Well Archaeological Association, had rallied round, as they usually did.

Sam Dee had had his reservations, but it was that or desecrating Harry Wotton's wheat fields with crop circles. He had gone with the lesser evil. At least the injured party would be harder to establish. The ownership of the hill was disputed and claims to it were laid

1

by three warring parties: the folk of Bishops Well, local magnate Lord Weston-Jones, and the parish of St John the Baptist.

By midnight the works were in full swing. The forgers were careful to stay within the outline of the shape, delineated earlier by the best art students recruited by Maggie and fellow teacher Cherie Hornby from Bishops Ace Academy. The labour distribution had been thoughtfully planned: the fairer sex was engaged in the finer art of scraping off the soil and staying within the lines (that required attention to detail and a steady hand) while the men carried bucketfuls of soil, grass, and the ever-present cow muck, which required little more than brute strength, to the top of the hill. There they distributed it evenly so that no one would detect it in the morning.

'If Alec knew what I was getting up to, he'd have to divorce me,' Vanessa Scarfe whimpered as she shovelled a stubborn tuft of grass out of existence. 'I had to say I was staying at Vera's tonight!' Her chubby cheeks reflected the ghostly moonlight in all its fullness. Crime didn't become her. And it shouldn't – after all, she was the wife of Detective Chief Superintendent Scarfe, a pillar of the community and a man beyond reproach. He couldn't afford to be linked to a common trespasser partial to forgery and vandalism.

'Good thing he won't know, then,' Maggie assured her. She slunk out of the darkness and squatted next to Vanessa.

Maggie had dressed in a tightly fitting black bodysuit, complete with a balaclava with cat ears. She was channelling Catwoman. Considering that she was a few sizes larger than Halle Berry, she was something closer to a seal than a cat in her appearance. Nonetheless, she was a well-proportioned seal and easy on the eye – in Sam's opinion. Nearby and similarly garbed, toned and long-faced Vera resembled a dressage mare, and Vanessa a wombat.

Sam had no idea where those zoological analogies came from. It must be due to the white horse under construction on the hill, he thought. He lifted his two buckets with a groan and began his ascent to the top. His lower back would pay a heavy price for this adventure.

'Nobody had better find out,' he heard Vera grumble, 'especially not my Henry! What that would do to his prospects at Westminster bears no contemplation!'

Sam smiled to himself. The Right Honourable Henry Hopps-Wood had more skeletons in his cupboard than lay buried in St John's graveyard. The only reason he was still an MP was the fact that the Tories could not afford a by-election. Vera's little transgression paled into insignificance by comparison with her husband's past indiscretions.

Sam passed Mary Nolan and Megan Murphy who were working on the horse's rear. They worked silently, Mary as usual tranquillity personified, Megan fully engrossed in her task under the horse's tail. Megan was the newest member of the AA. She and her husband Ivo, both in their early thirties, considerably lowered the average age of the AA's caucus.

Sam plodded on. Towards the very top of the hill, he found himself short of breath. Age was catching up with him.

'You can run, but you can't hide,' he muttered.

'Someone's thinking of running! Blimey!' Dan Nolan grinned at Sam and his two buckets. It was easy for Dan to laugh, Sam pondered, being a thick-necked bull of a man with the constitution of a Neanderthal.

It was good, however, to see Dan laughing and fully reintegrated into Bishops Well's criminal fraternity. He had Mary to thank for that. After his daughter's tragic death, he had cursed the town and all its inhabitants with it, but Mary had brought him back from the brink and now he was full of beans and mischief like the rest of them.

'Mind if I join you? I'll just get me running shoes on.'

All that Sam could afford in reply was to groan and rub his lower back; he had no breath left in him for much else.

'That bad?' Dan commiserated.

'Worse!' Sam emptied his buckets, making sure that he scattered the soil evenly over the (in his view considerable) extension to the hill. When he was finished he wiped his brow and grinned back at Dan. 'So your work's done for the night?'

3

'Sit down with us,' Dan shuffled along the bench to make room for Sam, 'We're taking a short break.'

The menfolk of the AA had gathered on top of the hill, which featured a sturdy wooden bench, its brass plaque dedicated to *Jenny Gorse-Young 1939-2003*. Dan and James Weston-Jones (who was happily going against his father's interests in joining the AA's cause) were sitting on the bench, while Edgar Flynn had made himself comfortable on his upturned bucket. Ivo Murphy and Michael Almond were standing. With his hands on his hips Michael was performing a bizarre shoulder rotation. He, just like Sam, was feeling his age in his severely tested spine.

Sam slumped on the bench between Dan and James and sighed. A few equally desperate sighs answered him, but men, being men, Sam thought, kept their mouths shut and admired the view. And the view was to die for! Lit by the eerie moonlight, the hill rolled down like a lazy sea and seeped into the flat, sleepy meadow sprawled at its foot. The meadow in its turn trickled into the thickets of Sexton's Wood. All of that was bathed in the silver glow of the full moon.

The night silence was disrupted by the occasional hoot of an owl or cry of a fox.

Then came the drone of a van engine, which died quickly, and was followed closely by Cherie Hornby's commanding voice, hollering, 'Over here, gentlemen! Bring your buckets! This is no time for having siestas! We only have a couple of hours before sunrise. Get your buckets! Get a move on! The whitewash is in the drum at the back of the pickup.'

Buckets in hand, the men obediently got to their feet and shuffled towards the van parked in the dead end of the dirt road behind them. When they reached it, they found a large industrial drum filled to the brim with a chalky whitewash. Sam was impressed to discover that Cherie had thought of bringing a ladle with which to scoop the paint from the drum and into the buckets. She had also secured several large heavy duty brooms. They would be perfect for painting the horse white in no time at all.

★

Painting the horse was a chaotic affair. People were tripping over each other, stepping into each other's buckets, and spilling their whitewash all over their feet. White footprints trailed out of the horse in all directions. It looked as if it was under siege from a squadron of white flies. Any minute now and it would start kicking.

Despite those minor hiccups, by five a.m. the project was completed, the area cleared of any incriminating evidence (fingers crossed), and the gang of forgers were packed into Cherie's pickup to be transported to the foot of the hill.

There they stood in awe.

The sun was rising over the horizon, its first faint rays growing wider and more assured. If the night view was to die for, the image of the sun emerging over the left shoulder of the hill was like a resurrection. The sun hit the image etched into the face of the hill with all its might, and the still wet whitewash glistened and sparkled like liquid silver.

Maggie was elevated. She gasped, 'Our very own Bishops Well White Horse!'

The prototype for the endeavour, the ancient Westbury White Horse, had inspired several other equine carvings across the Shires to welcome the approach of the new millennium. Bishops Well might have been a decade or two late joining the trend, but that's how things were done in Bishops – all in its own good time.

Vera shaded her eyes from the sun and scowled. 'It looks more like a donkey.'

Maggie and Cherie glared at Vera. Sam swallowed a chuckle. The truth was that the blinking horse indeed looked like a donkey.

'The ears are far too long,' Vera continued.

'It's a horse,' Maggie growled.

'A bloody horse,' Cherie verified, 'and that's final!'

'It is a bit donkey-like. There's no two ways about it!' Dan Nolan waded in – unwisely – on the ladies' disagreement, to his wife's chagrin.

'It's a horse, Daniel!' Mary, unusually for her, raised her voice.

James proffered a compromise. 'It isn't *entirely* a horse, I admit, but neither is it a donkey . . .'

Maggie compressed her lips to hold back the trembling. Sam could tell she was close to tears. He couldn't bear it. In a conciliatory tone, he declared, 'Of course it isn't a donkey. It's a mule – Bishops Well's very own White Mule.'

Cherie drove the company to the edge of Sexton's Wood. From there they took the brand new footpath leading to Bishops Well Celtic Museum. The museum was situated in the heart of Bishops Swamp, where only last year the foundations of a Celtic round-house had been unearthed. It was the same place where the remains of Lady Helen Weston-Jones, James' mother, had been found. Helen's body had been deposited precisely where the pitch of the thatched roof of the roundhouse would have been.

Following that historic discovery, the AA extended the dig to find an ancient burial ground containing two relatively well-preserved bog bodies with no twentieth-century add-ons. It soon transpired that two thousand years ago, that part of Bishops Swamp hadn't been a swamp at all, but a small island in the middle of a secluded lake. Accessible only through an impenetrable forest and then by water, the island had been earmarked as the perfect place to build a prehistoric housing estate. The people who had come up with that brilliant idea were identified as the Belgae, a Celtic tribe prevalent in the area on the cusp of the Bronze and Iron Ages.

By the time Bishops' amateur archaeologists drilled into the soggy bottom of what would have been a moat, or possibly a pig trough, their Richard Ruta Legacy funds had run out. Ever resourceful, they did not give up. Based on their major findings, they were able to secure funding from Heritage UK and a few shillings from UNESCO. Experts flocked to the excavation site to authenticate and preserve everything in its original location. A sturdy wooden path, complete with rails and platforms, was constructed over the swamps. IKEA donated a pine log cabin on stilts to accommodate the teams of archaeologists and historians who moved on to the site.

James convinced his father, Lord Philip, to sell the site together with the right of way through his land to the AA for a symbolic penny. With the National Lottery grant that Sam had applied for on an off-chance (and was astonished to receive) they had set up the museum, and Cherie became the curator. The site was quickly becoming one of the main tourist attractions in the local Shires, inferior only to Stonehenge and Avebury. And now that they had their own White Horse, there was no limit to how far they could go.

They briskly negotiated the woods to avoid the Swamp's plentiful mosquitoes. Because they were running for their lives with their heads down and because the thick canopy of July treetops hung over them like a huge green umbrella, they were unable to see the result of their handiwork on the hill. But as soon as they arrived at the archaeological site and their collective gaze travelled northward, they were rewarded with a breathtaking vision – that of their spanking new Bishops' White Horse towering over the plains.

They were spellbound. The birds had begun to tweet their dawn thanksgiving. Cherie was taking frantic snapshots of the scene – frantic because the elusive beauty of the rising sun would last only a few minutes. The photos were intended for the Museum's brochure. Looking at the majestic white stallion bathed in the morning sun, there was little doubt that one of the photos would feature on the cover.

'It still looks like a donkey, I'm afraid,' Vera's voice shrilled, having a cringeworthy effect on Sam. There was no saying what effect it was having on Maggie. Her hands furled into tight, deadly fists, and it looked like she was gearing up to beat the living daylights out of the unsuspecting Vera.

'It's a blinking horse,' Maggie hissed through her teeth.

'Didn't we compromise on a mule?' Ivo tried to arbitrate, but it was too late.

'No, no, no! It's a horse. It's always been a horse. It will always remain a horse.'

'Amen,' Cherie intoned and Vera, thankfully, held her tongue.

That settled, the company went into the cabin where they collapsed in a heap of exhausted middle-aged carcasses and started whining. Michael mentioned pulling his shoulder. Sam complained of a suspected slipped disc. Vanessa still worried about the clarity of her conscience (though that, strictly speaking, wasn't a physical affliction). Rumpole was howling outside – they couldn't let him in because he stank of cow excrement. Mary cried over her mosquito bites, woefully broadcasting the fact that her skin was a magnet for the bloodsuckers. Edgar had wandered into a patch of nettles and was now scratching himself stupid. Dan was counting his calluses and Megan was showing everyone a huge blister under her index finger. Everyone had a wound to lick, but – at least according to the radiant Maggie – it was worth it!

'I'll put the kettle on,' she offered cheerfully. Sam welcomed the idea; he was feeling light-headed and in urgent need of sustenance.

'You do that, Maggie.' Dan too nodded his approval. He whisked a hip flask out of his pocket and took a swig from it. He sucked his teeth – whatever it was, it had to be pretty potent. He passed the flask to Ivo. And so it went, doing its rounds. Maggie abandoned the kettle so that she too could have a turn. Tea simply wouldn't do for her if spirits were on offer, and not necessarily those in their ghostly variety.

A teetotaller, Mary took over at the counter. She carried the mugs to the table where a bottle of milk and a bag of sugar were at the ready. They drank the tea in silence, fortifying themselves with the patriotic beverage before embarking on the business of their War Council Deliberations. And it was at that very moment that the cavalry arrived in the shape and form of Angela Cornish, armed with her unrivalled namesake pasties.

'I thought you could all do with some refreshments.' She carried in two baskets wrapped in the aroma of fresh baking.

'How did you know what we were ... well, what we were up to?' Vanessa blinked her astonishment at Mrs Cornish, who tapped the side of her nose and said, 'Bishops Well is a very small town.'

No one else bothered to find out how the town's chief gossip got wind of their enterprise – they were all too busy stuffing their faces with steaming pasties.

Chapter Two

I have so far failed to mention that the Carving of the White Horse on the hill had a dual purpose. One: it was to enhance the cultural appeal of our budding Museum. Two: it was to obstruct the proposed new housing development.

Let me elaborate.

The hill upon which the White Horse now dwells lies in what the locals refer to as No Man's Land. It is a stretch of ten or fifteen acres comprising the hill, the surrounding water meadows where Mr Wotton's cows persevere with establishing their squatters' rights, and the banks of the River Avon meandering towards Salisbury Plain. To the west sits the town (sometimes erroneously described as a village!) of Bishops Well. In the south-eastern direction sprawls the Weston Estate, buffered on the south by Sexton's Wood. Behind the hill, facing north, stands an eighteenth-century folly which during the last war was requisitioned for an army hospital.

After the war, the previous Lord Weston-Jones, from his deathbed, gifted the folly to the Church of St John the Baptist to be used for charitable causes. The army hospital was transformed into an orphanage. It was in use until the mid-nineties when it received its last contingent of war orphans from the Balkans. That had been organised by Vicar Laurence, who knew the area well having spent every summer at his grandparents' farm in Bishops as a child (his idyllic memories of the place were why he'd returned as vicar after many years in war-torn countries). After that, the building fell into disuse. It now presents a sad picture of disrepair and neglect with its broken windows, rotten floorboards and crumbling walls.

Further to the north, No Man's Land borders the estate of a reclusive horror writer, Daryl Luntz. Mr Luntz purchased the land from the current Lord Weston-Jones in the late nineties and built his ugly neo-Gothic residence there. Allegedly, and it is Lord Philip who makes those allegations, No Man's Land was part of the sale and purchase agreement. That allegation is strenuously contended by Vicar Laurence, who claims that No Man's Land was gifted to the Church together with the folly by the old Lord Weston-Jones.

Regardless of those finer details, and most importantly, we, the residents of Bishops Well, demand our continuing possession of the land to be recognised in law. For generations, we have been asserting our rights to this patch of land by grazing it, crossing it at will, picnicking on it, fishing in the river that runs through it, and in some cases doing all sorts of things there that nobody can name without blushing.

The various parties had been coexisting peacefully in No Man's Land until Daryl Luntz decided to sell it to a property developer in March this year. That was when all hell broke loose. And that is why we carved the White Horse on the face of the hill. It was our way of branding it as our ancient Village Green under the communal dominion of the Bishops Well's inhabitants.

I am proud to say, it was my idea.

Tonight's meeting of Bishops Well Parish Council was open to the public and ardently attended by just about every man and his dog. It was held in the village hall, which resembled a World War Two army barracks complete with a well-established lawn on its sloping roof. Despite its size it was bursting at the seams.

The reason for its unprecedented popularity was a new housing development proposed to be built on No Man's Land. That proposal was to be debated and voted on by our parish councillors. The developer, a company with limited liability, trading as Cinnamon Rock, had already done their homework by surveying No

Man's Land and finding it to their liking. An undisclosed offer was on the table, subject to contract. Daryl Luntz stood poised to sign it in his capacity as vendor as soon as the Parish Council approved the development. This was to be done in two steps: firstly the re-zoning of the use of the land from agricultural to residential, and secondly granting Cinnamon Rock the licence to develop it. Both decisions were to be taken tonight.

In anticipation of a favourable outcome, Cinnamon Rock had architects and landscapers design the estate which, on paper, looked green, tranquil, and village-friendly. Plans, sketches, and mock-up digital impressions were plastered on the walls. They showed eco-friendly, mud-brick mansions nestling on the banks of the River Avon or tucked away on the slopes of Bishops Hill. They looked like they had always been there. The folly was proposed to be extended and converted into a low-rise block of flats under the Affordable Housing Scheme. There would be two playgrounds and one pond.

The pond wasn't there just for the entertainment of ducks. Its primary objective was to act as a reservoir to contain and regulate water overflow from the marshes. The floods frequently inflicted on No Man's Land would thus be consigned to the past — alongside most of its unique wildlife.

The Parish Council consisted of five councillors. The chairman was Howard Jacobsen, the erstwhile headmaster of Bishops Well Lord Weston's CE Primary School. He was a man in his early six-ties, short, corpulent, and oozing zero authority. He had the high-pitched voice of a man in a state of permanent distress calling for backup.

The second in command was the parish parson himself. Vicar Laurence held his Councillor's post *ex officio* – it was not something to which he would dedicate his time and energy if he had a choice. He was a military type, and his past as an army chaplain was still in evidence in his straight back, long stride, and clipped speech. Underneath all of that rigour, though, he was a kind man with a big heart, just like you would expect a country clergyman to be.

The CEO of Bishops Rugby Club, Aaron Letwin, was another councillor. He was known for speaking his mind without mincing his words and for frequently being under the influence. His body could take it though – he was large, and just a couple of years past his prime.

The two representatives of the fairer sex were Michelle Pike and Agnes Digby. Despite her matronly appearance, being endowed with a big bust and usually bathed in the frills of a white blouse, Michelle was a seasoned entrepreneur. She was the proprietor of the Golden Autumn Retreat Residential Home, a thriving business which she had started single-handedly using the divorce settlement from her philandering ex-millionaire ex-husband. Apparently, she had taken him to the cleaners on an industrial scale.

Agnes Digby, on the other hand, was a gentle soul, a widow and an active member of Bishops' Women's Institute. She also volunteered for the Samaritans, and had a suitably calming voice layered with honey.

Finally, there was the long-suffering parish clerk, George Easterbrook. As lean as a sirloin steak, George could normally be found running marathons and cycling incessantly around the county. Unless he was painting or playing the organ. George was an accomplished watercolourist and a virtuoso organ player. He supplemented his income by trying to hold the parish together. Tonight, he sat at his laptop, ready to take minutes, looking like someone who'd much rather be somewhere else.

The main interested parties weren't even there. Daryl Luntz had stayed at home, probably penning his next tale of horror. He was represented by his fat cat lawyer from Sexton's Canning's prominent law firm Ibsen & Morgan. Lord Weston-Jones was away taking the air in the Swiss Alps. His proxy was his son, James, who also happened to be one of the 'White Mule' forgers, a committed member of Bishops AA, and an avid birdwatcher. Wearing that many hats, James had a multi-layered conflict of interests to contend with. Cinnamon Rock was represented by its Operations Director, Alistair Wright-Payne, a big-city boy in an expensive, weather-inappropriate suit. He spoke way too much and too fast, made various wild hand gestures, and glared at people so intensely that many were tempted to pour a bucket of cold water over him. And last but not least, the final party to these proceedings was the good citizens of Bishops Well.

'This development is going to bring prosperity and jobs to this dying area,' Wright-Payne babbled on, flailing his arms like a deranged juggler, 'an area which, let's face it, has fallen behind the rest of the region and is, let's face it, in dire need of the kiss of life. And I mean modernisation, urbanisation – revival—'

'We're very much alive without it!' Dan Nolan bellowed. Someone in the background whooped three times in agreement with Dan.

'But this new development will kill life – wildlife. We have a very fragile population of cattle egrets on the banks of the river. What do you think your bulldozers and irrigations will do to them if not kill them?' James Weston-Jones decided to wear his birdwatcher's hat in flagrant disregard of his family's fiscal interests.

'And what about me cows?' Harry Wotton brought another branch of Bishops' thriving wildlife into the discussion. 'They been grazing up that hill as far back as when me grandad ran the farm.'

'Surely they aren't the same cows! Your grandfather's cows are long dead, Harry,' Agnes Digby questioned his statement but her objection was overruled by Harry in no time.

'Cows is cows,' he spoke his piece and sat down.

'What about badgers?!' someone shouted from the back. 'Where will they go?'

'And otters!' The crowd was beginning to warm up.

'Herons!'

'Newts! Newts are rare, they are!'

'Bats are even rarer!'

'Deer – red deer, at that! At least four of them that I know of!'

'Foxes!'

'No foxes left, matey . . . His Lordship's hunted them down to the last one!'

'I saw a fox the other day, in the wood!'

'I'm sure I saw a beaver, meself. Swimming in the river, it was – building a dam.'

Bishops Well wasn't exactly the beaver's natural habitat. The way things were going, someone would mention a polar bear, and the credibility of the wildlife card would be in tatters. George Easterbrook called for order in the house. His voice was drowned in the commotion.

'Stay out of it, Easterbrook! If you know what's good for you!' someone yelled.

'Whose side are you on, anyway?' someone else enquired of the Parish Clerk.

'Order!' the man insisted, for that was what he was paid to do.

'Shame on you, George! If your poor mother knew how you sold out ...'

George waved his hand and sat down. There was no arguing with George's mother even though she had been dead for ten years. If only I could tell George her spirit was sitting right next to him at that moment, breathing down his neck ...

Wright-Payne trumpeted over the rumpus, 'We carried out an environmental impact study! Rest assured that no wildlife will be affected by the development. You have my word! No animal will be harmed—'

'As if you care!' Harry Wotton pointed out. 'You can't tell a cow from a bullock, I bet!'

There were a few chuckles to that, but the commotion was beginning to die down, possibly because people had run out of protected species to mention.

'Settle down, everyone! Please!' Chairman Jacobsen screeched. 'We have to follow the protocol.'

No one listened until Aaron Letwin roared, 'Silence! Shut up! This is a serious business! You lot go quiet or we'll have the house cleared!'

The riot was – temporarily at least – quelled.

Jacobsen cleared his throat. 'Thank you. Thank you, Aaron,' he nodded to Letwin. 'Right, we want to give everyone a chance to have their say, but we have to do it in an orderly manner. We'll take turns to speak. Put your hand up if you wish to make a statement.'

That was my cue to act. I raised my hand and performed a little leap in the air so that I wouldn't be overlooked — I wasn't the tallest person in the room, far from it.

'Maggie, fire away!' Letwin shouted.

I stood up, rose on my toes, leaned forward, and rounded upon Wright-Payne with a steady and piercing gaze, I fancied. Once I had his full attention, I threw my first curve ball at him, right between his eyes: 'You can't build houses over monuments of historical significance – that simply isn't allowed, is it?'

Wright-Payne blinked his confusion at me, 'What monuments? Where?'

'The White Horse. On Bishops Hill. It's part and parcel of the West Country's unique—'

'Do you mean that clumsy hillside *graffiti* a bunch of pranksters carved into the slope?' The fat lawyer from Ibsen & Morgan enquired with a twinkle of bemusement in his voice. 'You can't seriously consider that part and parcel of . . . of anything, really.' He chortled and exchanged smug looks with Wright-Payne.

'It's our folklore, and it's part and parcel of the West Country White Horse Trail!' I stood my ground, repeating myself frantically, my hurt feelings igniting something bordering on fanatical. At that moment in time, my zeal could have easily rivalled Joan of Arc's. I would not be trampled over by a bunch of misogynists in their Givenchy suits, disparaging Bishops Well's White Horse!

'What White Horse, I ask you . . . It's not noted in any records, and it wasn't there when we surveyed the land,' Wright-Payne pointed out.

'Because it's just a piece of worthless graffiti, as I have already mentioned. And it's hardly a horse – more like a donkey!'

'That's what I said,' Vera mumbled under her breath. She was kicked in the shin by Dan. Rumpole growled at Dan, but not as loud as Vera did. I merely sent her a hurt look.

16

A few people failed to suppress giggles. I couldn't un-hear that. My heart spasmed in my ribcage. I compressed my lips, but I was fighting a losing battle against the tears of defeat.

Fortunately, there was someone ready to take over from me. Cherie thrust her hand up in the air and began speaking before anyone asked her to, 'The horse is beside the point. It's just complementary to the actual heritage site of the early Celtic settlement in Bishops Swamp. It is a protected site. You can't just roll over it with your bulldozers, and your . . . your irrigations are bound to damage the foundations of . . . of . . . and all!'

'We've had the development approved – provisionally, of course,' Wright-Payne squirmed a little, 'pending the Parish Council's decision, naturally . . . But that being well, we've had it pre-approved by Heritage UK. The development will be in an acceptable distance from the site and will pose no threat to it.'

'It's a non-issue, I can vouch for that I carried out the necessary checks for my client.' The fat lawyer from Ibsen & Morgan stretched in his chair, kicked his feet out, and laced his fat fingers on the dome of his stomach.

At this point, Cherie surrendered and joined me in feeling crestfallen and defeated. We stood no chance against those City boys. She sat down next to me. We exchanged forlorn glances. At least, we had tried . . .

Luckily, as it turned out, the game wasn't over yet for we had a secret weapon – our own City boy, admittedly in retirement but still firing on all cylinders. Sam Dee, QC put his hand up and gave a gentle cough.

'Mr Dee,' Aaron Letwin pointed to him.

'There is still the unexplored question of the common law rights of the Bishops Well community to what is known as No Man's Land,' Sam began, sounding as terrifically officious as only he knew how. 'The area has been used for decades as communal space . . . There are the grazing rights of Mr Wotton and then there is the ancient right of way—'

'No, there isn't,' the fat lawyer interrupted him rudely, 'and if any claims are made, they'll be strenuously contended by my client. Mr Luntz purchased absolute title to the land with no encumbrances whatsoever, I'm afraid. It's all black and white in the deeds, no grey areas there. I have submitted the Sale and Purchase Agreement to the clerk in my information bundle. Mr Luntz is entitled to do with No Man's Land what he pleases.' He peered at his Rolex ostentatiously. 'Can we please get on with the vote, Mr Easterbrook?'

Before George Easterbrook had a chance to swallow hard, the least likely ally came to his rescue – Vicar Laurence.

'I don't know what Lord Philip sold to Mr Luntz in the nineties,' he said in a calm and assured tone, 'but it couldn't have been the unencumbered title to No Man's Land. In the early fifties, Lord Philip's father, Lord Nicholas, gifted the folly to the Church of England.'

The fat lawyer opened his mouth to object, but Vicar Laurence silenced him with a simple gesture of putting his finger to his lips. 'I haven't finished, sir. It wasn't just the folly that was gifted – it was also the land upon which the folly stands.'

Wright-Payne could not contain himself, 'But the folly is a ruin! By law, it belongs to the land sold by Mr Luntz to Cinnamon Rock!'

'Mr Luntz can't possibly sell what isn't his. The folly belongs to the Church. In the past, it was used as a safe haven for the orphans of the war in the Balkans, like Ivo Murphy and his sister.' Vicar Laurence sent a benevolent smile in Ivo's direction. Ivo nodded slowly back. The vicar continued, 'It was the old Lord Weston-Jones's intention for the place to be used for charitable purposes, not for commercial ends. And now, the Church intends to restore the orphanage for the next lot of war refugees coming from Syria. I have already started the necessary preparations and soon we'll be receiving the first few unaccompanied minors—'

'This is some kind of a joke, and it's not funny!' Wright-Payne yelled and stomped his feet like a spoilt little brat, at last showing his true mental age. I felt like chastising him and sending him to the Headmaster's office. He was now shouting, 'Daryl Luntz sold this land to Cinnamon Rock! It belongs to us! Am I not right, Mr Morgan?' He drilled the fat lawyer with his spoilt brat's beady eyes.

'Of course you are correct. The parson has no legal claim to the land, rest assured. What he's talking about is the unsubstantiated tale of a dying man's words . . . Nothing in writing—'

'That's where you're wrong,' Vicar Laurence interrupted as rudely as he himself had been previously interrupted. 'I can substantiate it. I can produce written evidence of His Lordship's bequest.'

Both Wright-Payne and the fat lawyer gawped in the fashion of two beached whales. You could hear bones click in Wright-Payne's fingers as he clenched his fists.

George Easterbrook spoke over the ominous silence, the sort of silence you get just before the storm of the century. He said, 'The vote of the Parish Council will be adjourned to enable the Vicar to provide evidence of his claim.'

And that was that.

Chapter Three

I was positively buzzing.

One: No Man's Land was as good as ours — snatched away from the jaws of Cinnamon Rock plc. All thanks to Vicar Laurence! He had managed to get in touch with the two people who had witnessed Lord Nicholas's deathbed bequest and were willing to talk about it. As elderly and frail as they now were, their mental faculties were apparently fine and they had a clear recollection of all the details. The Vicar had set up a meeting with them to take their testimonies down in writing. Gerard, the Weston-Joneses' ancient and fiercely loyal butler, had also heard the old Lord's dying words. Alas, all of a sudden, he appeared to struggle with remembering what exactly had been said. I was sure that Gerard would rather die than contradict his master, the incumbent Lord Weston-Jones, and therefore his amnesia was bound to be wholly premeditated. Luckily, the other two witnesses were long retired from service and could freely speak their minds.

Two: the works to convert my late parents' house into a B&B were finally in full swing. The first task had been to repair the damage done by the recent fire, not of my doing, I hasten to add, but that's a story for another day. The works had to be done sensitively and with the approval of the local authority. After all it was a Grade II-listed building, a Tudor hunting lodge that in its glory days used to host kings and witnessed many an out-of-wedlock liaison and a few treasonous conspiracies being cooked up behind said kings' backs. As soon as the permission was granted, restorative works commenced, subject to numerous conditions, stipulations, and caveats. Every step of the way an inspector would arrive to poke through the walls, checking the authenticity of the wattle and daub. At long last, we were now at the stage of stripping the walls to the bare bones, re-plastering, and re-fitting (duly pre-approved) windows where the chipboard used to be. Then experts had arrived and rewired the whole house and re-structured the layout of the first floor to create four en-suite guest bedrooms; the fifth was the loft room under the thatch I'd shared with my sister Andrea, which was spacious enough to be divided into a bedroom and a lounge, and as such would serve as a presidential suite. It would feature prime views of Bishops' White Horse, erroneously referred to by some uninformed individuals as the White Mule.

Next month, plumbers were arriving to install the bathrooms. Meantime, my wonderful friends had come together to clear the debris left behind by the builders, to tear off multiple layers of old wallpaper, and paint their hearts out under my thoughtful guidance and vigorous supervision.

Vera, assisted by Rumpole, was ripping off wallpaper in the sitting room. This particular task had been created with Vera in mind – she was proficient at tearing strips off people, so getting her claws into wallpaper was exactly where she would excel. Rumpole on the other hand was sprawled on the floor, relishing the comfort of the soft paper lining and inhaling the vapours of fresh paint.

Samuel and Dan were also removing wallpaper but, being men, they couldn't tackle it with their bare hands and felt compelled to resort to external apparatus. Dan was steaming the wall with a bizarre hoover-like gadget while Samuel was scraping the paper off with an oversized spatula. They were arguing a lot and telling each other what to do without taking turns. Division of labour wasn't something they knew anything about. I let them get on with it.

The ever-artistic Mary and ever-so-helpful Vanessa were painting the dining room the colour of blossoming primroses. They were working in perfect harmony, occasionally exchanging compliments and words of encouragement.

Cherie and her partner Lisa had gone upstairs to pull up the old carpets. They are both small but sturdy and compact with muscle and sinew, so I had no reason to doubt their ability. No amount of manual labour would be too much for these two.

The works were proceeding to schedule. Tea was brewing in the kitchen while I was busy arranging on a plate a selection of chocolate digestives, Jammie Dodgers, and the two remaining Jaffa cakes from the pack of twelve. Having concluded that two Jaffa cakes were an awkward number, I ate one of them and placed the other in the centre of the composition.

'Come, everyone! Let's have a little break,' I called out to my workforce.

They flocked to the kitchen in record time.

As we indulged in a touch of sustenance, I reached for the last Jaffa cake. I figured that way no one would have to fight for it. I detected a tinge of resentment in Vanessa's eyes, but she quickly found solace in a Jammie Dodger.

'Have you thought of a name for this?' Dan waved his arm towards the bare walls, the pile of wallpaper, and buckets of paint in the hallway.

'Oh yes, of course,' I said. 'Badgers' Hall, since it is situated on Badgers Lane. Did you know that badgers used to rule supreme around here in the days when this place was a royal hunting lodge? There used to be more badgers here than people – more badgers than any other species, in fact ... So anyway, how does Badgers' Hall sound to you?'

'Perfect!' Cherie spat out a few crumbs of digestive. Rumpole hoovered them up from the floor.

He then raised his head and uttered a low growl, aiming it at the front door. Ivo burst in, looking flustered and sheepish.

'So sorry I'm late!'

'You're not. We've only just started,' I assured him though, truth

22

be told, we had been at the hard graft since eight o'clock and he was indeed over an hour late.

'Vesna had a bad night. We hardly got any sleep. Up and down, up and down – exhausting! Megan won't be coming. She had to stay to keep an eye on Vesna.'

'It's the bloody heatwave,' Vera said. 'I can't sleep a wink myself! I can feel my brain melting inside my skull and—'

'Who's Vesna?' Dan asked. I was glad he did. I wanted to know too. As far as I was aware Ivo and Megan had no children.

'My sister – Vesna.'

'Visiting?'

Ivo smiled ruefully. 'No, not quite. My sister is bedridden. In a vegetative state, more or less. Some days are better, some . . . Brain damage, I'm afraid . . .'

'Of course!' I quipped, and bit my tongue. I couldn't say it out loud, but I realised who the teenage girl shadowing Ivo was. She wasn't one of his lost students, as I had suspected when I had first met Ivo– she was his sister. Her spirit had departed from her bedridden body to keep her brother company in the world of the living. That was much more entertaining than watching flies on her bedroom ceiling. She was a pretty young thing with an abundance of golden hair, tanned skin, and large curious eyes. And the fact that she wasn't quite dead explained why her ethereal presence was so faint.

Ivo peered at me, waiting for further elaboration to my outcry, but since none was coming, he turned his attention back to Dan. 'Yeah, I wish it was just a flying visit and she was going back somewhere to her own home and her family . . . I wish she had a life – any sort of life . . . Oh well, Megan and I are all she has. We agreed she'd stay with us until – until the end.'

'Sorry, man. That was a stupid question.' Dan looked apologetic, which wasn't an expression he sported frequently.

'Nah,' Ivo waved his arm dismissively, but his eyes were dark with sadness. 'Vesna used to be in a mental health unit in Gloucestershire, then a residential home. Last year, we decided it was time to bring her home. Megan is brilliant with her – she knows what she's doing. But then she would – she used to work at Golden Autumn as a carer.'

'Ah, that's where I remember her from!' Cherie interjected, looking enlightened. 'She's always looked familiar to me, since we met, but I couldn't put my finger on it. Of course – Golden Autumn! My mother was a resident there – well, it's nearly three years since she . . . passed away. Golden Autumn, but of course! That's where I'd have seen Megan on and off, go past her in the corridor . . . Her face was so familiar! Now I know why. It's been bothering me—'

'I know the feeling – like you've got something on the tip of your tongue and it just won't slide off,' Lisa expounded on the subject, and illustrated it by sticking out her tongue and tapping it with her finger.

'Exactly that! You hit the nail on the head, darling!'

The two lovebirds beamed at each other. They had first found each other five years ago at a convention of military historians in Adelaide. Since then they had met now and again, at various battle re-enactments all over the world, growing closer and closer together until they realised that they could not live without each other. So, after some squabbling as to who should leave their homeland behind and relocate abroad, it was Lisa who had drawn the short straw. She left her native Australia and moved in with Cherie at Easter and ever since, they had become inseparable. They were still in their honeymoon phase. And they always agreed with each other, which I found puzzling. Cherie, with her tyrannical Napoleonic traits, used to be a natural born leader and a formidable orator. Lisa's entry into her life seemed to have softened her mood somewhat. And softened her brain. And swept her into the lap of domesticity. Since Easter, Cherie had missed two Bishops Well AA meetings. That was unheard of, and it made me a little irate. Perhaps, even though I wouldn't admit it, I resented Lisa a little.

To take my mind off Lisa, I forced myself back on topic, 'So, that's where Megan works? Golden Autumn?' Not that I really cared to know the answer.

'She left to look after Vesna. It's been a year since she left. Nowadays, she may take a shift or two when they're desperate for someone to cover, but it's not often. She has her hands full with Vesna.'

Ivo found his way to the chocolate digestives. He grabbed two at once, but then being young, fit, and slim, he had no reason to watch his waist. I may have the reason but I lack the resolve.

'Tea?' I offered.

'Do you have coffee?'

It was an outrage and plain travesty to take digestives with coffee, but I had seen a jar of instant in the pantry so I couldn't deny him. It was probably out of date. 'Yes, of course. I'll just put the kettle on.'

'Funny that,' Ivo mumbled with his mouth full, 'Megan did a couple of late shifts last week and you won't believe what she uncovered!'

We were all only too keen to find out.

'Well, believe it or not, and even as we speak, Cinnamon Rock are hard at work building an extension at Golden Autumn.'

'No!' Sam exclaimed. He was visibly indignant. 'But that's a clear conflict of interest for Michelle Pike! I didn't hear her declare it at the Parish Council meeting, did you?'

I shook my head, as did everyone else.

Vera added, 'And she was about to vote on Cinnamon's development. If it came to it, she would've voted for it. The woman has no shame!'

'She should've excused herself at the very least!'

'And that's not all,' Ivo had more up his sleeve. 'Through the grapevine, Megan heard that Ms Pike wasn't paying Cinnamon a penny for the works. It was a favour, apparently.'

'A bribe,' I was truly disgusted, 'for her to vote in their favour.'

'We should report this to George Easterbrook,' Vanessa suggested.

'We will,' I concluded.

★

25

We returned to work full of virtuous indignation. Vera was now positively sinking her talons into the walls. Such was her enthusiasm that I feared she might pull off the plaster. I could hear Cherie and Lisa upstairs bulldozing their way through the carpeting of the second bedroom. Even Sam and Dan had stopped bickering and seemed to have found their rhythm.

Ivo stayed with me in the kitchen to help me tidy up before he would start taking the rubbish to the skip outside.

Consumed with curiosity, I could no longer show any restraint, so before I burst, I asked, 'I hope I'm not being a nosy parker,' (Of course, I was! That was exactly what I was!) 'but may I ask what is wrong with your sister . . . Why is she—'

'Brain-dead?'

'Well . . .' I swallowed what would be a heartless *yes*, and squinted at Ivo, ill at ease.

'She wasn't born this way. I remember when we were kids – we swam in the river and dived in from a cliff. She was fearless. She would just jump head first, splay her arms and plummet from a dizzy height, screaming her head off—'

'Her thick golden hair fluttering behind her . . .' I smiled to the image which somehow became quite real and vivid in my mind's eye.

'Yes, she does have thick blond hair. How did you guess?' Ivo's hair and complexion were dark, typically Mediterranean.

'They say I have a sixth sense.'

'Yes, I've heard someone call you Mystic Maggie.'

'Yeah, well . . . Don't believe everything you hear in this village!' I pulled a dignified face.

Ivo chuckled.

'So, what happened to her? To Vesna? Why is she the way – she is? A dive that went wrong?'

'No, nothing as straightforward as that. She . . . tried to kill herself. Not the first time, as it happens. But it didn't go to plan. It was a near-terminal overdose – she was literally brought back from the dead. But she fried her brains, and ever . . .'

26

His voice trailed off. I could tell it was still too raw for him to talk about.

'Do you want to do the washing-up or the drying?' I asked to divert his attention away from the difficult subject. Before he had a chance to choose, I took the towel and handed him the rubber gloves.

Chapter Four

We finished for the day at six o'clock sharp. We were knackered, dusty, sweaty, and cranky. The heat outside was only just beginning to subside, ruffled ever so slightly by a lazy breeze. We emerged into it, which felt like wading through a bowl of cream of mushroom soup. That brought to mind the hunger. We'd had sandwiches for lunch, but that was a distant memory. I couldn't let them go home on an empty stomach if I wanted them to come back tomorrow.

'Well done, everyone,' I gave them all a verbal pat on the back. 'We're going to mine for supper. Quiche Lorraine and salad.'

Lisa fluttered her eyelashes at Cherie, I dare say rather suggestively. I could swear she also mouthed a pouty-lipped *NO*. Cherie took the hint.

'We must be going, Maggie. Things to do! They can't wait . . . We'll report for duty tomorrow, eight o'clock on the dot.'

I couldn't imagine for one second that either of them was capable of *doing things* of any kind this evening. They were way too spent. Then again, you can never say never to honeymooners. I expressed my deep regret, but let them go.

Their departure had a domino effect on the others. Ivo had to dash to give Megan a break. Mary and Dan already had dinner plans (as if!). Vera and Rumpole had an overdue walk to tick off their list, and Vanessa, like a sheep, followed the trend without any valid excuse. In the end it was just me and Samuel left. He opened his mouth to produce his apologies, but I would not have it.

'No, Samuel! You're coming for supper. You can't possibly let me have two quiches all by myself. And they won't keep.'

An alarming and confounding scene confronted me as we arrived at Priest's Hole. Both Sam and I could see his mother, Deirdre, dragging a huge cardboard box across the driveway, from his garage to my doorstep.

But only I could see Alice.

She was like no other spirit apparition I had ever seen. They usually come across as detached and mildly disinterested in the world of the living. They just seem to be inadvertently detained in it through no fault of their own and certainly not because they want to. They exist (kind of) in parallel to us. And that was how Alice, Sam's late wife, normally behaved.

But that day she was going berserk. As Deirdre pulled the box bumping and scraping across the gravel, Alice was running circles around her like a mother hen around a fox stealing her chicks. She was thrusting herself violently at the old lady (unsuccessfully, I should add, but it was the evil intent that worried me). Her spirit zoomed and weaved, and wrapped itself over and around the cardboard box. And her face was terrifying. A scream was frozen on her gaping mouth. Her brows came down and hung, ominously, over her narrowed eyes – very, very angry eyes indeed. The contortion of her whole face could not be produced by a living human being. Frankly, she gave me an almighty fright.

Blissfully unaware of the goings on in the realm of spirits, Samuel dashed to his mother's side and took charge of the cardboard box.

'Let me, Mum! You shouldn't be lifting heavy things, you know that!'

'If I don't do it, it won't be done,' she retorted in petulant fashion. 'You've sat on all this rubbish for years and done nothing to get rid of it . . . If I didn't step in—'

Samuel sighed. 'Where do you want it?'

'I'm taking it to Maggie's to put in the skip. I hear she's got a skip at her parents' house.'

'OK, fine.' Samuel took over from his mother and was carrying the box while Alice screamed inaudible blue murder in his face.

'I've got two more in the garage.' Deirdre toddled behind him. 'It's Alice's stuff, old papers and such. You'd never bring yourself to go through it, or God forbid, to chuck it away. And why, I ask, do you need to hang on to it? For what purpose if not to torture yourself?'

'You're right, you're always right. I'll get the other two boxes and take the whole lot to the skip tomorrow morning. Happy?'

As much as Deirdre looked happy, Alice looked nothing of the sort. She was livid. I had to intervene.

'No, you can't!' I stood in Samuel's way. 'You can't throw any of it away!'

'Whatever do you mean, Maggie?'

'And what business is it of yours what we do with Alice's junk?' Deirdre huffed.

I fixed Samuel with a coded glare. He should know better than to question me. 'It's Alice. She's furious with Deirdre—'

'I beg your pardon!' Deirdre began but I wasn't going to let her stop me.

'She doesn't want her stuff to be lost. That's all I know. She is absolutely beside herself.'

'What is she talking about, Samuel?' Deirdre was disconcerted. 'Could it be the heat? I hope it's not sunstroke! We'd better take her to see a doctor.'

'I think she wants you to keep her stuff, look through it – there must be something there she wants you to find.' As I was saying that, Alice began to settle. Her face returned to its normal, calm and distant self. I half expected her to nod her approval.

'What sort of claptrap is that?'

But Samuel understood. 'I see,' he said and put the box down.

'I don't! What is it that you can see and I can't?' Deirdre slammed her hands on her hips and adopted a combative posture. 'I'm only helping you to clear the mess, son. Take the boxes to the skip. I've been through them – it's just calendars, newspaper clippings, chocolate wrappers, loads and loads of paper, and an old mobile phone. It doesn't even work . . . You can't hang on to the past like that – you have to let her go.' Something plaintive and deeply, deeply despondent crept into Deirdre's eyes. She was trying to do the right thing, to snap her son out of wallowing in the past and bring him back to the here and now.

But for some reason Alice would have nothing of it. Maybe Alice was a bitter selfish soul incapable of letting him go? Maybe Deirdre was right. I dropped my shoulders and muttered under my breath so that only Alice could hear me, if she was listening, 'Sorry, you're on your own,' and I bent down to fetch my house key from under the terracotta pot. I was resolved to stay out of this particular family dispute.

Alas, I had already made up Samuel's mind. He lifted the box from the ground and started towards his garage with it. 'I'll go through it this week, I promise. Then we'll chuck it.'

Deirdre stood, hopeless and confused, in the middle of the driveway. She looked like she had just lost the battle that would determine the war that she had waged on her son's eternal mourning.

'Deirdre, we're having quiche for supper. Would you be able to give me a hand with the salad, please?' I tried to distract her, but she gave me a flummoxed look and waddled slowly back to Samuel's house.

Samuel and I ate our supper in silence. To me the quiche tasted off and the salad was wilted.

In the end I had to say it, 'Sorry for coming between you and your mother.'

'You didn't, Maggie. It was Alice.'

'True. You should've seen her face.'

'I wish I could.'

It was said with such sadness that I had to give him a hug. I rose from my chair, went to him, and put my arms around him. 'It's awful when they're gone and there's nothing we can do to bring them back. All we have is a bit of this and a bit of that – things they used to touch and hold dear. We cherish those things – give them meaning, build stories around them, treat them as if they were relics.' I knew how he felt. I was missing Mum and Dad every waking moment, and I too was trying to keep them alive by clinging on to their house and everything in it. It was just a place but to me it retained their ways, their tastes, their memories. The same as Alice's box of rubbish.

'Thank you, Maggie.' He took my hand and kissed it.

That felt awkward. The kiss, I mean. It threw me out of my comfort zone. I didn't know what to do with that kiss, or what it was for. I wondered how Alice felt about it. I glanced at her. She was poised by the window, her favourite place, looking out, uninterested. She didn't give a fig about that kiss. I bet she thought Samuel was thanking me for helping him to keep in touch with her. On reflection, she was probably right. I withdrew my hand from him, and returned to my chair and my last mouthful of quiche Lorraine.

'I hope Deirdre is all right,' I said. I meant it. She was home alone, stewing in resentment, the poor thing.

'She'll be fine. She's made of stronger stuff than the two of us put together. I'll explain it to her later. I'll have to weigh my words carefully – she doesn't know about you and the dead. She's thinking it was all your idea. Nothing to do with Alice, her being long dead and buried . . . They didn't get along in life, Mum and Alice, and it looks like nothing's changed in death. Both stubborn—'

'She was so insistent! I've never seen her like that before . . .'

'Who? Mum or Alice?'

'Alice, of course!'

'Alice? Yes, that doesn't surprise me,' Sam spoke with affection like a father proud of his child. 'I told you she worked as an investigative journalist, didn't I?'

I nodded – he had. Everything he had told me about Alice was stored neatly in my memory bank.

'Yes . . . when she was well . . . When she was on a case, she was like a dog with a bone – unrelenting. That's why Mum and her didn't get on. They were too much like each other. Only Mum is made of that tough wartime stuff, and it takes a lot for her to fall and not get up. Alice kept falling at every hurdle. After the last one, she didn't get up. It wasn't her fault.'

'No, it wasn't.' I knew that Alice had battled mental illness. She didn't manage it well, but no, it wasn't her fault when she had finally thrown in the towel. It was the illness that killed her. At least, that was the impression I got from Samuel. After all, I didn't know Alice at all.

My telephone ringing interrupted the pensive silence we found ourselves in. I left Samuel in the kitchen and went to answer it.

It was Will.

We had not spoken since we had seen our sister Andrea off at the airport, to go back to New Zealand. It had been a while. I didn't know what to make of this phone call. Will wasn't a man given to casual chitchat. It had to be something serious.

We exchanged polite — if filled with surprise on my part — greetings and enquiries after each other's health and general wellbeing. I quickly ascertained that Tracey and the children were alive and well.

'So, what is it about?' I fired. There was no point beating about the bush — he had something on his mind.

'It's the house, Maggie — my share in Mum and Dad's house.'

'What about it?' My blood began to undergo a sudden temperature drop. Despite the heat, I felt distinctly chilly. I shuddered.

'It's not working for me, I'm sorry—'

I started to speak over Will and over my fears, 'I should be keeping you up to date, shouldn't I? Which I fully intend to do! Well, not to keep you in the dark a minute longer — we're doing well. Better than well! The plumbers are coming next week. Everyone's helping where they can so I'm keeping costs down — really, really down . . . The builders have been!' I was now positively shouting. 'What a transformation! Five en-suite guest rooms! Will, you won't recognise the place when you see it. When are you coming? Soon?' By this point, I was blabbering at the speed of an Austrian yodeller. 'If not, I'll send you your share of their bills—'

'That's what I'm calling about.'

'Ah . . .' It was about money.

Samuel arrived from the kitchen, probably alerted by the volume of my voice – high, and rising. He stood in the doorway, leaning against it and closely watching my face. It was bound to be telling a horror story!

'I'm afraid I'll have to pull out of the project. I'm sorry . . . You see, from September, Aimi's joining Jack at Blackhurst.' I recalled Blackhurst to be a rip-off of a public school somewhere in Berkshire. 'And the fees are going up, so—'

'We could slow down with the works. I will put off the plumbers until—'

'It's not just money, Maggie. I don't think I can ever go back to Bishops.'

'Why ever not! This was your home! Your roots!'

'And I thought that Dad was my father, and I had a lot of things wrong. I don't want to talk about it . . . I don't know how long it will take me to digest it and to get over it. Maybe I never will . . . I want to stay in touch with you, Maggie, and with Andrea, and I want to see the two of you as often as I can, but not there – not in that house . . . I want to get rid of it – sell it.'

'But I don't!' I shrilled and made Samuel jump.

'What's going on, Maggie?' He ran towards me – his turn now to hug me.

'OK, I understand,' Will said in a pacifying tone. 'You do what you need to do, and I will do my thing. I'm selling my share of the house. Of course, I'll pay whatever is my share of the expenses incurred so far—'

'But that will force my hand, and Andrea's! We'll be forced to sell.'

'Don't be overdramatic, Maggie. I already spoke to Andrea – she wants to keep her share. You can keep yours. The two of you could buy me out.'

'Buy you out? How? I haven't got a penny to my name!'

'I don't know, sis. You'll think of something. A loan, I don't know. Like I said, I am sorry. I've tried. I just can't.'

I ground my teeth. 'OK, so you did. How much time do I have?'

'Take as long as you need, but I'd like to close this by Christmas.'

Typical Will! I put the phone down. By this time, my blood was as cold as ice, and curdled. It was over. My dream was over. I knew I couldn't get a loan – I didn't have a regular income. No bank would trust me with a mortgage. I wouldn't trust myself.

Samuel was squatting next to me, looking me in the eye like a faithful hound worried about his mistress. 'What's happening, Maggie? Why are you crying?'

I didn't realise I was crying, but yes, I ran my hand across my cheek and it was wet.

'Was that Will on the phone? What did he say? Is he – is someone ill? Talk to me, please!'

So I talked to him, not expecting this to make any difference, but just to unburden myself. A burden shared is a burden halved, as the saying goes. But as I finished relaying to him Will's decision about putting his share of the house on the market, I did not feel any relief. In fact, the full hopeless picture unfolded before my eyes in all its ugliness.

'There won't be Badgers' Hall. I can't do it on my own. The whole thing – it's going in the bin. And that's that, Samuel.'

I tried to be brave and mature about it, but it isn't my style, so I cried a bit more. A lot more, actually. It took me a while to compose myself.

Samuel sat next to me on the sofa and patted my back as if I were a baby with colic and he was trying to make me burp. I only realised what he was saying halfway through his sentence:

'. . . so as recently as yesterday I was thinking of where to invest that money. Banks give you terrible interest nowadays. Real estate is money best spent in the current climate, I'm told. Investing it in Badgers' Hall would be ideal for me, honestly!'

I think I blinked at him at that point, which he mistook for a sarcastic wink and promptly went on to double reassure me, 'I'm not joking, Maggie! I'm happy to put that money into Badgers' Hall. I'm invested in the project emotionally and on every other level, so why not financially too? Plus, it'll do me good to stay out of my mother's way, but to have a half-decent excuse for it. That's a better excuse than whatever I could dream up!'

'What are you saying?' I did my best not to blink – or wink – so that he would know that I wasn't being silly, just confused.

He inhaled deeply and began again, 'Like I said, with my mother selling up in London and coming to live with me – not that I asked, but I can't turn her away . . . Anyway, she is convinced it's she who is doing me a favour!' He scratched his head with sudden, animated vehemence. 'Are you following?'

I nodded very slowly. I knew the story and I couldn't really blame Deirdre for intruding on Samuel's exile the way she had done – her intentions were pure. Being a native Londoner, she couldn't even begin to understand the joys of country living in blissful isolation from all things large and loud. Upon visiting Samuel a few times and witnessing the tranquillity of what I once heard her call a *middle-of-nowhere-backwater*, she had decided to rescue her stranded son by . . . joining him. At least he would be stranded in the *middle of nowhere* with his mother for company! So she took it upon herself to spice up the provincial doldrums with her suave big city airs and graces. I feared she believed that Samuel's Bishops Well episode would be short–lived, and she wanted to be by his side when he returned home to London.

'And then it's the money Richard left me – again, I didn't see that coming!' Samuel continued. 'I have a small fortune sitting in my bank account, doing nothing. I was thinking of an investment portfolio but—'

At last! I caught up with him! 'You want to buy Will out! We're going to run Badgers' Hall? Together!' I threw myself into his arms. I'm not a hundred per cent certain but I think I heard his ribs crack under my embrace. 'I love you, Samuel Dee!'

We – I – decided, and he conceded, to celebrate in my garden with a glass of champagne and a piece of cake. Quickly, I discovered that I had no champagne in the house and the last piece of Victoria sponge had been polished off by yours truly last night. So, we settled in the garden with a glass of red wine and a box of Jaffa cakes (I do have an unlimited supply of those).

As we sat there sipping our wine and munching on Jaffas, we listened to the majestic organ music being emitted from the church. It was loud and full of pathos.

'Is that George Easterbrook?' I marvelled. 'He's going for it today!'

I don't know much about music and I can't sing for toffee, but Samuel is somewhat of a classical music connoisseur. He had been listening to the tune for a few minutes, and declared, 'Handel's *Dead March*. Exquisite! I didn't know George had it in him.'

We listened and drank. George was pumping it out relentlessly. He was going on a loop.

Then I had a thought. 'Why don't we go and see George, and tell him about Michelle Pike's conflict of interest? It's as good a time as any to get it done.'

'Why don't we,' Samuel agreed. 'Before we forget.'

Chapter Five

The volume of the music rose as they approached the church. When they entered, it became deafening. Usually placid and agreeable, George Easterbrook was going ballistic with the *Dead March*, as if he was rearing up for battle. His eardrums had to be in tatters. As soon as Maggie and Sam entered the side door, so were theirs.

Holding their ears, they climbed the wooden spiral staircase leading to the organ at the back of the church. Maggie tried to speak but whatever it was she attempted to utter was drowned in the cacophony. Her face said without words, 'I can't take it! God help me!'

Sam briefly contemplated going back home and calling Noise Control. Either George Easterbrook had gone bonkers or he desperately needed the services of an audiologist.

When they finally stood in front of the organ, Sam realised it was neither. George Easterbrook wasn't even there. The organ stood still and silent.

The rampaging *Dead March* continued.

'Where is George?' Maggie shrilled through the din. A shadow of panic crossed her eyes.

Sam threw his arms out and shrugged.

'And the music? Where's it coming from?'

They looked around them, turning on the spot, trying to find the source of the noise. It was beginning to feel as though Judgement Day had arrived and Heaven's trumpets would be sounded any minute, raising the dead.

Maggie peered down, over the banister, and shouted, 'Vicar Laurence! Hallooo! What the hell's going on?'

Sam followed her gaze and saw no one.

He clutched Maggie's arm and shouted into her ear, 'He's not there! There's no one there, Maggie!'

She went pale.

They tumbled down the spiral staircase. In the main aisle, the ungodly music was even louder than upstairs with powerful speakers pumping the noise right at them.

They began their search. There wasn't a shadow of a doubt in either of their minds that they were looking for the vicar's dead body.

It wasn't hard to find.

Vicar Laurence was bound to his ceremonial chair, to which he would normally retire during the Readings. The chair was positioned to the left of the altar and flanked by two smaller stools upon which his altar boys would sit. The stools were empty. Vicar Laurence was alone. His mouth was covered with packing tape which had been wrapped around his head several times. The tape had also been used to tether his wrists and ankles to the arms and legs of his chair. If the trussing of his limbs with the tape wasn't enough indignity for the old man to be made to suffer, his killer had gone to the trouble of slashing his forearms and the inside of his thighs so viciously that the fabric of his sleeves was shredded, revealing the bloody gashes beneath.

Apart from the blood on the vicar's body, there was a long smear leading down from the altar and into the aisle. There, by the front pews, stood a slightly disturbed puddle of coagulated blood. The killer had clearly dragged the body to the chair and placed it there for some unfathomable, sick reason. For that same bizarre reason he (or she) had arranged five large service candles around the chair, positioning them on the five vertices of a pentagon drawn faintly and clumsily on the floor with white chalk. And finally, to end on a high note, he had played the awe-inspiring tune of *The Dead March*.

Maggie and Sam found a CD playing in the Hi-Fi system which linked to all the speakers in the church. Maggie pressed the STOP button. The silence that followed fell on them like a ton of bricks.

'My God, what happened here?' Maggie whispered. 'Who'd want to kill the Vicar?'

'I'd better call Alec.' After the two previous incidents when Sam had to urgently seek the Chief Super's assistance, he had stored Alec Scarfe's number in his mobile's speed dial.

Scarfe answered on the second ring. He too seemed to have Sam's details on his phone. 'Sam Dee! Don't tell me you've found another body,' he chuckled. 'What can I do for you?'

'We did,' Sam mumbled at first, but quickly cleared his throat to make himself perfectly clear, 'We've found Vicar Laurence dead in St John the Baptist's church—'

'You're kidding me!'

'I'm afraid not. It looks like murder. We didn't touch anything. You're the first person I called.'

'*We*? Don't tell me – does that mean you and Maggie blinking Kaye? Why is it always the two of you?'

'We didn't set out to look for a body—'

'I know, I know . . . Just your rotten luck! Don't touch anything. I'll send my team over.'

The team arrived within twenty minutes, spearheaded by DI Gillian Marsh and Michael Almond who were there in a matter of seconds. It was obvious from the speed with which they materialised on the scene and from the state of their homely attire that Gillian and Michael had come directly from his house in the village. They must have been called to duty just before hopping into bed.

They took a long while to visually examine the scene of crime by the front pew, then the trail of blood to the altar, and finally the chair with Vicar Laurence trussed up in it with the packing tape.

Maggie and Sam took a pew, as instructed by DI Marsh who had told them to *sit down and wait* – she wasn't finished with them and wanted to have a word before they were allowed to leave. Coming from her, that didn't sound promising. She had said it in that ominous tone of hers that made one feel like the prime suspect with a guilty conscience and no hope of ever clearing one's name. Maggie and Sam sat meekly in the third pew from the front, and waited while eavesdropping on the conversation between Michael and DI Marsh.

'Frantic.'

'It certainly was.'

'Killed over there, by the pew, I take it?'

'It looks like it, yes. Then they dragged the body to the chair.'

'They?'

'The vicar wasn't a small person, and a dead body becomes heavy and awkward to handle. I'd say there were either two of them or perhaps a strong bloke.'

'A woman?'

'An extraordinarily strong woman – possible but not very likely.'

'How did he die?'

'I'll tell you when I've had a chance to examine the body.'

'Come on, Almond, you can venture a guess! Even I can!'

'And what is your guess, Inspector?'

'Judging by the blood loss, he bled to death.'

'Hmmm ...'

'What?'

'I don't know. The lacerations on his arms and thighs seem superficial—'

'But bloody!'

'Yes, but where did the blood come from ... I will have to look at the body, like I said. Unless the killer severed the femoral artery in the groin, I can't swear to anything.'

'Dead for how long?'

'I'd be guessing.'

'Please do.'

'Can't we wait for my gear, Gillian? The team will be here in a minute, and then I'll give you my best estimate.'

'Then you'll give me the actual time of death, now you can give me your *best estimate*.'

Michael rolled his eyes and grunted. 'OK, looking at the blood and how it has already clotted and coagulated, I'd imagine he's been dead for eight to ten hours. That's the best I can give you, and it's not a perfect science.'

The Forensics team rolled in at long last. Michael slipped into his rustling light blue jumpsuit and was finally able to approach the body by the altar. He began instructing the photographer what pictures of the body to take before it was removed from the chair for more thorough in-situ inspection. Another photographer concentrated on immortalising the settings, the pentagon and the candles, and every object en route between the puddle of blood by the pews and the chair by the altar. The explosion of flash photography was enough to send anyone into an epileptic episode.

Forensics issued everyone present with protective gear to pull over their shoes. It seemed a bit too late for Maggie and Sam – they had already caused their share of scene contamination. Nevertheless, they put on the plastic overshoes they were given and remained seated. Maggie watched the goings-on with great interest. Her eyes shone brightly with an emotion Sam would describe as *unhealthy excitement*. That emotion seemed to be intensifying as Maggie's eyes widened. Whatever she was thinking in that pretty head of hers, Sam feared, foretold trouble. Sam was convinced Maggie was concocting her own lines of inquiry into the vicar's murder.

DI Marsh joined them in the pew. 'Mr Dee, Miss Kaye, your turn.' Her gaze was focused primarily on Maggie. 'What's your part in this?'

'We found the body – around nine o'clock – and called Chief Superintendent Scarfe,' Sam answered the question.

However, Maggie had her own ideas about how this interview

should be conducted. She clapped her hands together and began, 'I think I can tell you who may've done it.'

'You think you know that?' DI Marsh didn't appear intrigued – rather, sceptical.

'Well, you see, since Daryl Luntz – he's the famous horror writer . . . You've heard of him, haven't you?'

'Now I have.' DI Marsh knitted her brows, probably wondering – in passing – what Daryl Luntz had to do with the murder under investigation. It was in passing because Maggie was at hand to clarify everything.

'So, you see, I read a few of his books, just to get a feel for our new neighbour . . . Well, I read those I could find in Sexton's library. Gory, nasty stuff, if you ask me! It made my hair stand on end, but then I do enjoy a bit of gore from time to time . . . It's fun.' Maggie's face crumpled in an impish grin.

By this time, both DI Marsh and Sam looked confused. DI Marsh was inhaling through her nose and exhaling, slowly and deliberately, through her mouth in an exaggerated wheeze.

Maggie was oblivious to the reaction she had provoked in her listeners. 'In one of his books – I can't recall the title, but I can find out if you want me to – but in one of his books Daryl Luntz describes a scene of human sacrifice carried out by a Satanist cult. And the funny thing is that it looks exactly like this—' Maggie thrust her finger in the direction of the chair recently vacated by the body of Vicar Laurence. 'I mean – to the letter! The pentagon, the candles, the throne . . . Well, I don't know if that is a throne, but it was in the book. And! And the scene of that sacrifice was at the altar in a chapel!'

'Interesting . . . Would Mr Luntz kill someone in the same manner as he described it in his own book? That's a bit of a giveaway . . .'

Maggie shrugged, 'He probably thought no one here had read his books.'

'OK . . . Assuming that Mr Luntz lacks imagination to that extent, which is at odds with him being a novelist,' DI Marsh fixed

Maggie with a gaze of intellectual superiority, 'but if we go with your theory, what motive would he have to kill the Vicar? Are you implying Mr Luntz is actually a practising Satanist?'

Maggie snorted. 'Of course, not! What I'm implying is that he had a very, I mean *very-very* strong motive. A real-life motive. A motive of a financial nature . . .'

'I'm all ears.'

Maggie paused, pointedly lifting her eyebrows, to make sure that she had a captive audience. Satisfied, she said, 'Vicar Laurence put a stop to Mr Luntz's lucrative land transaction with a property developer. You see, Mr Luntz was planning to sell No Man's Land to Cinnamon Rock, but Laurence had evidence of the land actually belonging to the Church. He was going to present it at the next Parish Council meeting. That'd be next week and that would kill the whole deal. So, thinking on his feet, Daryl Luntz killed the vicar instead.'

'I see. It does seem a bit drastic though.'

'A lot of money is at stake. I suggest you talk to Daryl Luntz and ask him about his alibi!'

'Thank you for that. Meantime, I need to ask you about yours. How did you come to find the body? And can we please start from the beginning.'

Sam opened his mouth to give a clear and chronological account of the day's developments, but once again was beaten to the post by Maggie. She said, 'As a matter of fact we came to talk to George Easterbrook, not the vicar. We found Laurence by pure coincidence! Interestingly, we wanted to report Michelle Pike to George. You see, George plays the organ, and the music was so loud – we obviously knew – well, we thought we knew, but it turned out we were wrong . . . Still, we thought we'd find George here. The music had nothing to do with George. It was the CD!'

'A CD?'

'Yes! The *March of Death*! It was playing when we got here. It was unbelievably loud! We turned it off.'

'The CD is still in the CD player. It's *Dead March*, the actual title, by Handel. We left the disc in the machine. The killer must've put it there. His fingerprints may still be on it.' Sam attempted to elucidate Maggie's chaotic report.

DI Marsh, though still visibly baffled, called one of her officers and asked him to retrieve the CD from the Hi-Fi. 'Bag it with the other exhibits, Miller,' she instructed the man, 'and send it to Forensics for fingerprinting.'

She returned her attention to her hapless 'prime suspects', first addressing Sam, 'Mr Dee, could you give me a succinct account of how you came to find the body, please? I haven't got the whole day for endless digressions.'

Maggie's nose looked out of joint as she turned it up and away from DI Marsh. At last, she decided to assert her right to be silent.

Sam explained about their renovation works at Badgers' Hall, followed by the supper of quiche Lorraine, the wine in the garden, the organ music pumping out from the church, and their finding of the vicar's body. He also explained why they felt obliged to report their concerns about Michelle Pike and her dealings with Cinnamon Rock to George Easterbrook. DI Marsh listened carefully and midway through his account began to nod her head. Things were beginning to make sense to her.

'Thank you, Mr Dee,' she said at last. 'I'll need you both to come to the station to give your witness statements.'

'We'll do that, no problem.'

'Can we leave now? If we aren't under arrest?' Her ego bruised, Maggie contended her freedom of movement. 'This has been a bit of a shock. We both need to go home and lie down.'

'Of course, you can go and do whatever you like. I'll be in touch if I need to talk to you again.'

DI Marsh was already on her feet, heading towards the newly arrived DS Webber.

Shock notwithstanding, Maggie was finding it impossible not to have the last word, 'And DI Marsh? One more thing so you don't waste your time on investigating us – we have a cast-iron alibi for the time of the murder. Since eight o'clock this morning, all the way until six, we've been working on my parents' house, surrounded by several people, including the Chief Superintendent's wife. I am happy to supply you with a list of names—'

DI Marsh flicked her wrist, 'Not now! Tomorrow at the station!' Then they could hear her mutter under her breath, 'Barking mad . . .'

Chapter Six

It had taken Sam a few days to bring himself to sort through the cardboard boxes. They contained Alice's work papers. They were slightly damp and mouldy, and smelled musty. He had kept them, unlike everything else that belonged to her. He'd had no difficulty giving her designer clothes, jewellery, and shoes away to charities and sweeping her cosmetics, toiletries, and lingerie into a rubbish bag. He'd felt no particular attachment to her personal belongings, but he had kept her papers. One day, he had been telling himself, he would wade through them with a clear mind, and learn about the subjects that made Alice tick. And, perhaps, about the reasons that led to her taking her own life.

That day had finally arrived.

No, Sam wasn't quite yet ready for it but his mother had forced his hand. He had promised her he would do it: he would clear the past and make room for the future. She thought it was that simple.

Sam feared it wasn't.

Opening Alice's notebooks and looking at her rushed, almost illegible handwriting – the letters leaning to the right, falling over each other, apostrophes lagging behind their due spaces, doodles of bizarre spider webs, floral patterns, and emoticons – all of that had caused his heart to ache with longing. He had to overcome that pain to finish what he had started. It felt like amputating his own heart, but he had no choice – he had to do it.

Alice had thrived on chaos. Her papers were in a state of dishevelled, artistic disarray. Sam segregated handwritten notes and article drafts from newspaper clippings, which she had torn out and scribbled illegibly over in the margins. He organised her year-to-year diaries chronologically – the last one for the year of her death. With shaky hands he paged through it until he arrived at the day of her death: October the fourth – the day the woman he loved more than anything in this world had chosen to kill herself.

He expected to be confronted with a gaping empty page, followed by more empty pages for all the remaining days for which Alice no longer had any plans. He was however surprised to encounter Alice's jottings indicating a meeting she had planned with someone with the initials *L.D.*, or maybe *L.P.*, the rendezvous place being recorded in shorthand as *Sth Ctle*.

Sam sank in his chair. He pushed emotions to one side and began to think. Alice's body had been discovered on the railway tracks between the stations of Gladestoke and South Castle. Not far from there her car had been found, the key still in the ignition. The police believed that Alice had driven alongside the train line, then abandoned her car and thrown herself under an oncoming freight train. The train driver did not see her, and the moment of impact did not register on his radar – he wasn't aware of what had happened until later. He may have looked briefly away, reached for his lunch box, turned his attention to changing the radio station he was listening to.

Nobody was able to explain what had made Alice throw herself under a train. It seemed so senseless, so random and so irrational that it bore no explanation. An assumption had been made that Alice had gone into one of her lows and given up on life there and then. She had been battling depression for years. It had been an ongoing battle. It would go away, sometimes for years, but it would never go far. It was always there, always shadowing Alice.

Ever since her death Sam had been beating himself up over missing the signs. The signs of her worst ever low looming over the horizon had to be there, but he could not see them. He had failed Alice. He had failed to watch out for her. He had failed to notice that she needed help.

But what if there had been no prior warning – no signs? What if her actions had stemmed from that meeting at South Castle? Who was L.D. or L.P.? Why had he, or she, met with Alice? What was the meeting about? Did it have anything to do with Alice's death?

Sam had to know. He had to identify L.D. or L.P. He had to find them. He had to speak to them. He had to know if that last meeting in Alice's life had any bearing on her killing herself.

He spent the whole day ploughing through Alice's notes and scribbles, studying all the names and cases she had been working on prior to her death. None of them corresponded with the initials L.D or L.P. He reached for her mobile phone to search through her contacts. The phone's screen was crushed – probably the result of the impact. It was dead.

Sam found a charger and spent half an hour pacing the length and width of his study, waiting for the thing to come to life. Finally, he screwed up his courage and pushed the power button, and it did. His fingers slid across the cracked screen. The phone demanded a password. He tried several possibilities. None worked.

He called Michael Almond:

'Michael, I need your help. You're bound to know someone who can unlock my wife's phone. It's very important – I wouldn't be asking otherwise.'

Like a bird aiming for an earthworm, Maggie swooped into his study as he was readying himself to leave. Deirdre followed her, whining as she puffed her way in. 'Well, have a look for yourself! Look at the mess! He promised – you are my witness! He promised to tidy up those boxes and take them to the tip . . . But that's what I get!'

Maggie paused in the doorway and swept the study with a critical eye.

'Oh, dear!' She wrinkled her nose.

To an untrained eye, the study was a tip. It appeared littered with piles of scrap paper, notebooks, and newspapers, plus a collection of paperclips, broken pens, and chewed pencils. But there was a method to this madness. At least, to Sam everything made perfect and logical sense. And right now, he had no time to debate this.

'I'll help you sort it out,' Maggie quipped helpfully.

'Not now, Maggie.'

'Agreed: not now.'

'Why not? There's no time like the present,' Deirdre chipped in.

'I need to do something else first!' Sam and Maggie uttered these words – or something closely to that effect – in unison. Sam stopped there, but Maggie continued, 'We need to go and interview Daryl Luntz. Now. Like you said, Deirdre, and you're bang on: no time like the present. Especially when one investigates murder. You have to strike while the iron is hot.'

'DI Marsh is investigating Laurence's murder, not you, Maggie.'

'The more, the merrier!'

Sam despaired. He was to pick up Michael in five minutes. But Maggie had not finished.

'And I have a plan. Simple but brilliant. We'll confront Mr Luntz when he least expects it. We'll catch him with his trousers down—'

Deirdre glanced at her askance and screwed up her face in disgust. 'Keep me out of it!'

'I wouldn't dream of involving you, Deirdre. I don't think you'd be much help anyway. I was hoping Samuel would be free. I'd feel much safer with him by my side. Come on, Sam. I'll explain everything on our way there. I have this simple but brilliant idea – it can't go wrong.'

Maggie was positively bristling with excitement. It pained Sam to say no.

'Not this time, Maggie. I'm sorry, but as I said, I have something else to do right now. If you'd listened, you'd have heard me.'

Her face dropped. It was a sorry picture. Perhaps he was being too harsh, but then his mind was elsewhere. She had to learn that other people had their own lives to live and things to do, things that didn't necessarily involve her. But, admittedly, there were nicer ways of saying it.

'Sorry, Maggie. If this . . . *interview* of yours can wait, then count me in. Another time, though. I've an appointment I can't miss. And I'm already late.'

She thrust her little chin up and peered at him down her nose, an expression of unspeakable hurt lurking behind her compressed lips. 'No, it can't wait. You go ahead – do your stuff. I'll do mine.' And she breezed out.

Michael introduced Sam to an IT wizard going by the name of Jon Riley. To meet him they had to drive to Sexton's Canning and get security clearance to access the Computer Forensics department where Riley worked. Apparently, he rarely left his workstation and when he did, it was only to go home to sleep. Michael whispered into Sam's ear that the man was agoraphobic and definitely a nutter. But he was a genius. If anyone could help Sam, it was Riley.

Riley resided in an expanded cubicle taking up a ten-foot square corner of the basement. He was surrounded by several computer screens, as well as takeaway trays and remnants of food in various stages of decomposition. Indeed, the cubicle smelled as if something had died in it.

Riley himself was seated, or rather semi-reclined, in what appeared to be an adapted sports car seat. He shook Sam's hand without getting out of his seat. That didn't come as a surprise: the man was huge and fleshy, probably as a result of permanently functioning in virtual reality for which he required no physical presence – or exercise. He had a beard spliced into uneven and unkempt wisps. His long hair was bound into a tight bun on top of his head, held together with two chopsticks.

'So, you want a *post-mortem* on this relic?' Riley turned Alice's phone in his hands, looking at it with bemused contempt. 'They don't make them like that anymore, which is what I call progress.'

'It's my late wife's.'

'Yes, Almond told me. Right, let's get its guts out.'

Riley got down to work, leaving Michael and Sam to float

behind him as he had offered them nowhere to sit. As it turned out, there was no time for that. He had the phone unlocked in no time.

'Here you go.' He handed it back to Sam.

Sam tapped on Contacts and began to scroll down the alphabetical list, pausing firstly on Ds and then on Ps to discover that none of them featured first names starting with an L. He let out a small sigh of disappointment.

'Nothing of interest, I take it?'

'I don't know. I was looking for someone with particular initials.'

'I could try and retrieve deleted items, names and text messages,' Riley offered, and without much ceremony, took the phone out of Sam's hand.

Again, there was a wait, a bit longer this time. At last, he passed the phone back to Sam, saying, 'No deleted contacts, but I found a few deleted texts. All of them from the same mobile phone number, not assigned to a name.' He promptly recited the number from memory.

Sam grabbed the phone. The sequence of brief messages was highlighted on the cracked screen. It was hard to read them.

'Hang on. Let me connect this to my computer. It'd be easier to read on the big screen.' Riley snatched the phone back. He plugged it in with a charger cable and soon the string of texts showed on his computer.

Sam devoured them, reading them in reverse order as Riley scrolled back:

Fine. U can park at the train station. C u there.
No trains going to Sth Cstle. I'll drive.
He's gone now. Won't mind.
I be there. What changed ur mind?
South Castle train station @11am

'That has to be L.D,' Riley commented.

'Or L.P.'

'Is that all you could retrieve?' Michael asked. 'It just seems like it starts in the middle of a somewhat longer conversation.'

Riley glared at him, indignant. 'That's all of the messages. I'd say the messages are a follow up from phone calls. Let's look at the call history.' He switched screens. Indeed, the first text had been sent two days after the last call from that number. There had been twelve calls between Alice's phone and that number, starting the previous year, with the last three coming in the weeks before her death.

Sam felt bile come to his throat. He was nauseous and eerily light-headed. He knew he stood on the threshold of something big. He swallowed the bile, pulled his phone out of his pocket, and dialled the number Riley had given him.

'The number you have dialled does not exist.'

Sam swore.

'It's a dead number, isn't it?' Riley shrugged. 'What did you expect?'

'I don't know. Is that it?'

'I could make discreet inquiries about it, but I wouldn't hold my breath. I bet you a tenner that it was an unregistered Pay-As-You-Go.'

Back at home, Sam endured a late supper with his mother. He hardly touched anything and quickly retreated to his study. He sat there in the dark, thinking. He didn't want to give up. There was still a sliver of hope that Jon Riley could track down the owner of that phone. But if not, certain nuggets of information had come into focus: the train station at South Castle, some sort of intelligence someone was to share with Alice – someone with links to South Castle . . .

The ringing of his phone made him jump. The lit screen of his mobile showed the time as ten twenty-eight. Who would call at this hour? The caller's identity was withheld.

'Sam Dee,' he spoke warily.

'Samuel! Thank God! It's Maggie! I'm under arrest. I'm entitled to one phone call . . . I couldn't think of anyone else . . . Can you come and bail me out? Please!'

Chapter Seven

My prime suspect was that horror-writing lone wolf who lived on a secluded estate in a mansion that could easily pass for the Addams Family house. Daryl Luntz never showed his face in the town, not even on Halloween. Since moving to Bishops Well in the mid-nineties, he had made no effort to mingle with the local populace, treating us with detached contempt. With time, whether by default or design, he had developed notoriety Vlad the Impaler would be proud of. Mothers would chastise their five-year-olds with the threat of Mr Luntz coming to haunt them in the night if they didn't eat their greens.

Luntz wasn't an accessible man by any stretch of the imagination, but I found a way to get to him – I convinced Hannah to twist his arm and see me in my invented capacity as his die-hard fan. Even Hannah was taken in by my act.

I had known Hannah since she was a baby. She was three years my junior and used to be Andrea's best friend until some argument had broken out between them over a boyfriend. I think it was Matthew, now Hannah's husband, who had come between them. Men, I am led to believe, do know how to divide and rule – just take a look at the history of the British Empire. Not that I have anything against Matthew (or the Empire), but I could never shake the impression that if it hadn't been for Matthew dumping Andrea, my sister would have never left Bishops in the first place. So maybe I do carry a small grudge against him . . .

Before he arrived on the scene, Andrea and Hannah had lived in each other's pockets, and Hannah had become like another little sister to me. But then, in the immediate aftermath of Andrea's disappearance, we'd lost touch. I guess Hannah also felt she and Matthew were responsible for Andrea's disappearance and couldn't look me in the eye. Now I had no scruples in using that guilt to secure access to her reclusive employer.

With a copy of Luntz's *Dying at the Altar* under my arm, I marched purposefully down the cedar-lined lane leading to the mansion. To add credibility to my horror enthusiast profile I was wearing a black satin dress (which had belonged to my mother and which she had reserved for funerals) and a pair of black Doc Martens boots (which my sister had acquired when experimenting with being a Goth in her teens). I also sported dark purple lipstick and matching nails.

Hannah opened the door as soon as I rang the bell. She looked startled even though she had been expecting me.

'Bloody hell, Maggie, I didn't recognise you!'

'Sorry if I startled you.'

'I never knew you were into this stuff! When you said you were dying to meet Daryl, I didn't realise it was *that* serious!'

'It isn't *that* serious, Hannah. I've been dabbling in the occult on and off. You could call me a recreational occultist.'

'Is that how that whole *Mystic Maggie* thing started?'

I fixed Hannah with a stern and steady glare that required no further elaboration.

'Lead me to Mr Luntz,' I instructed her.

Daryl Luntz wasn't anywhere near as majestic and piercingly intense as the photos on his book covers implied. In reality he was a small and shrivelled old man. He was as bald as a coot, a fact amplified by his impressive mutton-chop whiskers. I could not escape the impression that I was looking at an egg in a nest made of twigs and feathers. His neo-Victorian appearance matched the dark, mahogany-panelled interior of the room in which he received me.

'Miss Kaye, my pleasure.' He shook my hand. It wasn't a handshake in the true sense of the word – it was more like the paltry brush of a spooked reptile in flight. His hand was cold and bony.

'The pleasure is mine, Mr Luntz. Thank you for agreeing to see me!' I enthused. It wasn't an act. I couldn't wait to begin interrogating him.

'I'll be on my way,' Hannah said. She was all set and ready to go home.

'I'll see you tomorrow, Hannah. Let's make it noon – I've some errands to run in the morning.'

Hannah looked pleased with the idea of a lie-in. She bade us both farewell and tottered away, her footsteps resonating on the chessboard floor.

I don't think I've mentioned that Hannah worked for Daryl Luntz as his secretary. He recorded his books on a Dictaphone at night and she transcribed them during the day. She had signed a watertight secrecy agreement, was not allowed to take any tapes or typescripts home or talk to anyone about works in progress. Luntz was apparently paranoid about people trying to poach his concepts.

I was left alone with him in the smoking room. It had to be the smoking room, as Luntz took out one of those vaporisers and began vaping. It soon formed a fog cloud which drifted towards the window. The heavy, full-length curtains were half-drawn, letting in the red hues of the setting sun. The vapours and the sunset brought to mind the accessories of a crucifix and a clove of garlic which I had forgotten to bring with me. I wished Samuel was here to hold my hand.

'So, Miss Kaye, I believe you're after my autograph?'

'Yes, if you'd be so kind. I'm a great fan of yours.' I smiled keenly.

'Thank you for saying that. A writer – any writer – needs faithful readers just like other people need air to breathe.'

I felt a slight tightening in my throat at hearing that, and gave a cough. The way he said it made me think that he *didn't* need any air to breathe. That, in combination with the smog from his vaporiser enveloping his shrivelled persona, gave me the strong impression that the man wasn't quite human.

Or quite alive.

'Are you all right? Shall I get you a glass of water?'

I waved my arms. 'No, thank you! Just a tickle . . . It's gone now.'

'OK. So which one of my books did you bring with you, Miss Kaye?'

'*Dying at the Altar*!' I passed him the book.

'Would that be your favourite of mine? It's quite old – it came out in the early eighties, one of my first ones . . . but then a good book doesn't age, does it?' He presented a gratified smile, put aside his vaporiser, and switched on a desk lamp. The room filled with bright light which instantly dispelled the vapours and banished the insidious scarlets of the sunset. He slid a pair of reading glasses on to his nose. Their lenses were incredibly thick. I realised that the man had to be partially blind to need lenses of that magnitude. That explained why he needed a secretary to type his work, and it put everything into a human perspective. He no longer seemed supernatural. My irrational fear of him fell away and I relaxed.

He opened the book and held his pen up. He gazed at me, puzzled. 'This is a library book, Miss Kaye . . . It's a book from Sexton's Library, it says here on the stamp.'

'Yes, as it happens, it is,' I nodded.

'I don't think I should be signing a library book. Don't you have your own copy?'

'No. Why would I if I can borrow it from a library?'

'This is most . . . irregular.'

'I'm sure Sexton's Libraries would love to have an autographed copy.'

'You're sure? Do you mean to say you haven't asked their permission?'

I shrugged. 'No. To level with you, Mr Luntz, the request for your autograph was just a ruse so that I could speak to you and ask you a few questions.'

'An interview?'

'Of sorts, yes.'

'I don't give interviews.' He took off his glasses. His eyes returned to their natural size.

I felt compelled to press on before he asked me to leave. 'It's not that kind of interview. I want to ask you about the death of Father Laurence.'

'It's a tragedy.' He stood up. 'But now, I'd like you to leave.'

'I haven't finished.'

'*We* haven't started.'

'But since I'm already here,' I persevered even though he was heading for the door, showing me the way out, 'can you explain why the way the vicar was killed is exactly as you described it in this book!' I thrust *Dying at the Altar* in his face.

He paused and sneered at me. 'Miss Kaye, dear, if I were to kill someone, the last thing I'd do would be to replicate a scene from my own book.'

'That's what everyone would think,' I triumphed. 'But there's the concept of double bluff, isn't there?'

'I don't know what you're talking about. You're raving mad. And why, in God's name, would I want to kill the parson?'

'Isn't it obvious? He had the power to stop the sale of No Man's Land to Cinnamon Rock. That would complicate your life somewhat. How much do you stand to make from that sale, Mr Luntz?'

He stared at me as if he didn't know what I was saying. But he did! He knew damn well!

'You had a motive!' I kept waving *Dying at the Altar* in front of him.

'Leave now, or I'll call the police.'

'I'll leave when you admit the—'

His phone rang. He headed for his desk and grabbed the receiver, 'Luntz! Oh, Alistair, good evening! How are you? Yes, I know, I know . . . Hang on a second – don't go away, I'll be right back!'

He glared at me. I could see raw fury in his face. 'You're leaving now,' he growled and started in my direction.

'Don't bother,' I reposted, 'I can see myself out. Good day to you, Mr Luntz.' I stormed out of the room.

Passing through the massive hallway, I happened to notice a half-ajar door to another room and through that door I saw a telephone. I had a thought. I realised, of course, that Luntz was on the phone with none other than Mr Wright-Payne of Cinnamon Rock. I had to hear what they had to say to each other. It was pertinent to the case.

I dashed to the front door, opened and shut it with a bang. That illusion of my departure successfully created, I tiptoed to the other room and picked up the receiver. I became all ears.

'Mark doesn't think the project viable – considering recent developments—'

'What developments, Alistair? We have a contract!'

'The death of the vicar. You did notice, didn't you? It really complicated matters. Mark doesn't want to bulldoze over his grave and start building. We've our reputation to look after.'

'Just give us time, all right? For the dust to settle. I've got it all in hand.'

'We won't proceed without guarantees.'

'What other guarantees do you want, Alistair? I'm giving you clean title to No Man's Land—'

'Tainted by the death of that clergyman.'

'That's not a legal impediment.'

'But the evidence he threatened to provide would be, wouldn't it?' Wright-Payne was proving himself a right – well, a right pain.

'He didn't have any evidence. Trust me, my legal team have got it all under control. They're working on it. That man's death is in no way—It's unrelated!'

'So you say, but Mark is getting nervous.'

'Leave it with me. A few days is all I ask.'

'I'll see what I can do.' Wright-Payne put the phone down. I could tell it was he who rang off because I could still hear Luntz breathing heavily on the line, then curse under his breath and finally slam down the receiver.

I replaced mine in the cradle very softly.

Just as I was about to really leave the house, I heard Luntz's voice.

59

He was on the phone again. I returned to the small room and, again, sat down to eavesdrop.

'Well, I'm very sorry about the interruption, Larry!' He was seething with sarcasm. 'I, on the other hand, haven't had a chance to think of dinner, so tough!'

I guessed he was now talking to Larry Morgan, his fat cat lawyer at Ibsen & Morgan. Luntz must have interrupted his dinner. My stomach rumbled, reminding me that I too hadn't dined.

'OK, but let's be quick. It's bloody late. This isn't office hours.'

'Can they back out of the sale?'

'Anything can happen until the exchange date, I told you already.'

'I need that money, Larry.'

'I need you to pay my fee!' Morgan raised his voice. The subject of money seemed to introduce the motif of urgency to their conversation. 'On what grounds would they want to terminate the agreement?'

'The vicar's bloody death!'

'That's not—'

'I know! I told Alistair as much, but they want to be sure he had nothing to undermine my legal title to the land.'

'Nothing has been provided. Calm down. Your title derives from Weston-Jones's title. If he sold you a dud, we'll be able to go against him for compensation.'

'I don't have the time, Larry. I need the money now. I've holes in my budget the size of a football pitch. The royalties aren't coming as they used to. I can't wait for the outcome of a legal action against Weston-Jones! This sale has to be finalised now!'

'It will be. There is no evidence to challenge your ownership. If the vicar had something, it died with him, or else the Church's solicitors would've submitted it by now. They have not. The sale is on track. Tell Wright-Payne—'

'Hang on! Wait a minute!' Luntz interrupted him.

I was disappointed. I wanted to hear what he was meant to tell Wright-Payne. I supposed I had to wait a minute alongside Larry Morgan. Unfortunately, it wasn't meant to be.

Luntz and his mutton-chop whiskers appeared briefly in the doorway of my hideaway room. He shot me daggers, but said nothing. Instead he flicked off the lights and shut the door. I heard him turn the key in the keyhole. I was shrouded in perfectly terrifying darkness.

'Mr Luntz! Let me out! I was just going anyway!' I shrieked and stumbled in the dark. I must have tripped over something and fallen, hitting my head against a hard, blunt object. I blacked out.

I was awoken by a policeman, who rather unceremoniously shook me by the shoulder. As soon as I opened my eyes and while I was still lying incapacitated on the floor, he told me I was under arrest on suspicion of breaking and entering.

Daryl Luntz's whiskers hovered above me, bristling with supercilious fury. 'She was posing as a fan, pretended to leave, and then I found her going through my possessions in here!'

'I wasn't going through his things! I was just listening—' I bit my tongue at the last minute. There was no point in incriminating myself any further.

I let the policeman lead me to his car where his colleague was waiting at the wheel. The policeman placed the palm of his hand on the top of my head as if he were to perform a blessing, but only told me to mind my head as he shoved me into the back seat.

Luntz ran out of the house after us, carrying the copy of *Dying at the Altar* I had left behind. He handed it to the policeman, insinuating that I may have stolen the book from the library.

'I borrowed it!' I shouted, 'I've got it on loan!'

We drove off.

At the police station at Sexton's Canning I demanded to make a phone call, to which I knew I was entitled. I called Samuel. I tried to explain everything to him calmly when he finally arrived to bail me out.

Chapter Eight

Maggie arrived late. She presented herself as forlorn and thoroughly hard done by, but she had no choice in the matter: she had to make an apology or else Daryl Luntz would press charges against her. At this moment in his life Sam needed these distractions like he needed a hole in his head, but his reputation was on the line: he had given Alec Scarfe his word that an unconditional apology would be hand-delivered today. It was on that basis that the Chief Super was prepared to pull a few strings and get Maggie released from custody without her having to appear before a magistrate.

Maggie marched into the lounge and slumped on the sofa.

'Do I really have to do this? It makes me look guilty,' she whined.

'You are guilty!'

'What is she guilty of?' Sam's mother joined them in the lounge.

'Nothing, Deirdre,' Maggie told her. 'I did nothing wrong.'

'Nothing except trespassing and—'

'I didn't trespass! I was invited. I'd made an appointment beforehand!'

'Under false pretences! And you overstayed your welcome. You hid in the house and were spying on the poor man's private conversations.'

'I had reasonable grounds to believe he'd killed the vicar. I still do!' Maggie lowered her voice to the level of conspiratorial, 'Daryl Luntz is broke. He's desperate for money – desperate to sell No Man's Land. I know he'd do anything to push that sale through. I heard him say it in so many words to his lawyer – he can't afford to lose that sale . . . I put it to him, but of course he refused to confess. He had a motive to murder Vicar Laurence and he had devised the method. I mean, the method—'

Although Deirdre was listening with great interest, Sam didn't wish to hear it all over again. He was tired of Maggie's busybody sleuthing, even more so because his mind was elsewhere. He interrupted her diatribe without much ceremony.

'Luntz may have a motive, but he also has an alibi. And it is watertight.'

'Who says?' Maggie thrust her chin forward in her typical stance of defiance against all odds – and against every reason.

'The police. I spoke to Alec, Maggie. Without his help, you'd still be rotting in a cell. Anyway, Daryl Luntz is off the list of suspects. They've investigated him and confirmed that he was nowhere near Bishops Well when the murder was being committed. The man was on a plane to Edinburgh!'

'Well . . .' Maggie pursed her lips. 'Well . . .'

'If only you left the investigation to the professionals we wouldn't be in this place right now—'

'What if he got someone else to do the deed for him? A paid assassin?'

'Didn't you just say that he was flat broke? And anyway, Maggie, just think about it for one minute – a paid assassin! This isn't a gangster movie – this is Bishops Well! I've drafted your apology – all you need to do is to sign it and we'll deliver it to Luntz together. It's in my office.'

'I'll make some tea, then.' Deirdre took herself out of the room. Even she wasn't prepared to give Maggie's fantasies any more credence.

Sam drove Maggie to Luntz's house, escorted her to the door, and rang the bell himself. He wasn't going to let her change her mind and evade the task at hand. Once the apology was delivered and accepted, Luntz would withdraw the complaint, the matter would be closed and Sam could return to tracking down L.D. (or L.P.).

Daryl Luntz did not answer the door. Instead, he sent Hannah. She greeted them truculently and fixed Maggie with a resentful eye.

'You're a terrible liar, Maggie,' she said through her teeth. 'I trusted you. You got me into so much trouble – I had to swear I'd had no part in your scheme, and he still didn't believe me. I nearly lost my job.'

For the first time since this whole sorry affair had begun, Maggie looked contrite. 'I'm sorry . . .'

'You'd better be!'

A spark of defiance flicked in Maggie's eyes, 'I was only trying to get to the bottom—'

'Don't!' Hannah raised a cautionary finger at her. 'Don't even think of justifying what you did! Stay here and wait. Daryl doesn't want you inside the house. He'll read the letter and let you know if it's OK. Wait here, I said.'

They waited at the door like a pair of wretched hawkers.

Daryl Luntz took his time keeping them there, probably to teach Maggie a lesson in humility. Sam ground his teeth as Maggie chewed on her nails.

Finally, Hannah re-emerged. 'It's fine,' she informed them and shut the door in their faces.

They drove back in stony silence. Sam was contemplating his next step in investigating Alice's contact. He wasn't having any bright ideas. A phone call from Jon Riley to reveal the identity of the owner of the mystery mobile seemed an unlikely possibility.

'What's with Alice?' Maggie muttered from the back seat. Apparently, Alice was occupying the passenger seat next to Sam and refusing to budge. 'She's acting all fluffed up and agitated and, frankly, so are you, Samuel. What's going on? I know something's going on. You haven't been yourself lately – either of you. You wouldn't come with me to interrogate Luntz, for one! If you had, I wouldn't be in this . . . this untenable position of having to apologise to a potential murderer—'

'He isn't a murderer, Maggie.'

'He looks like a murderer, he behaves like a murderer, he is a—' She sighed. 'Anyway, that's not the point. You are the point! Something's up and you aren't telling me . . . I thought we were friends. I thought you trusted me.'

Yes, Sam trusted Maggie – to make a meal of everything she touched! She was so excitable, so hot-headed, so irascible! But he couldn't bring himself to tell her that. So instead, he shared his dilemma with her.

'It's all wrong, I'm afraid,' Maggie declared. 'You have your timings wrong, Samuel. You've been looking at the cases Alice was working on at the time of her death.'

'What's wrong with that?'

'Can't you see? You're supposed to be a clever man, but you miss the finer detail. You do need a woman's touch, Mr Dee.' He gazed at her, mildly flummoxed at that suggestion. Her cheeks flushed scarlet, and she hastened to add, 'Not *that* sort of touch. What I meant was a woman's insight – you need my insight.'

'OK, enlighten me,' Sam sighed.

'You see, what intrigues me in those phone calls is this – most of them were made the previous year, but the last three occurred just days before Alice's death, right?'

He nodded and began to listen attentively. Maybe she had a point.

'On top of that, someone – a man – is gone by the following year. Read that text message again, where he or she says – *we can talk now that he's gone.* Can you see where I'm coming from?'

Sam nodded again, now more vehemently. 'Go on.'

'It's bound to be about something Alice was investigating the year before, maybe earlier, but with a follow-up a year later when the other person was prepared to talk because "*he*" *was gone and wouldn't mind* anymore. Do you see what I mean? We have to explore Alice's cases from the previous year, not from the time of her death. And only those cases where the subject of her investigation, or the suspect – call him what you will – was somehow *gone* by the following year.'

She was right. She was spot on! Sam grabbed her and squeezed her shoulders. 'Maggie – you are a genius!'

'I know. You don't have to tell me.'

Chapter Nine

For the next three days, Sam and Maggie worked tirelessly. They trawled through Alice's papers, exploring court records in those of her investigative scoops that culminated in prosecution, and sieving through all of the newspaper articles she had written in the year before her death. In the hope that this would lead to the final clearance of 'Alice's old junk', Deirdre had joined in the effort. Her contribution took on the shape of nutritious meals, fortifying snacks and endless cups of tea. Alice too was at hand, supervising their research with calm detachment. They must have been doing her tacit bidding for her agitation had dissipated into thin air and she settled down by the window, looking out.

By Saturday evening, they had narrowed it down to four cases which met their criteria. These cases had been under active investigation in the last year of Alice's life, and the persons of interest were male who had been gone one way or another by the time she died.

The first case pertained to fraudulent dealings over 'golden visas' for foreign millionaires prepared to invest their fortunes in the UK economy. Alice had gone undercover to investigate Damian Miskin, a solicitor she believed was up to his eyes in money laundering via the scheme. Her final expose provided irrefutable evidence, on tape. Miraculously, before the police knocked on his door with a search warrant, Mr Miskin had managed to close up shop and retire to Qatar, from where he could not be extradited. He had left the country four months before Alice's death.

The second of Alice's cases revolved around allegations of

historical child sex abuse against, amongst a few others, John Erskine, a retired Chief Constable. It was a well-publicised case, and Alice was the first investigative journalist to report it, following her broadcast interview with the now notorious Ryan Barrett. Barrett himself had since been convicted for falsely accusing a number of public figures and for perverting the course of justice. However, at the time, everyone, including Alice, had believed the man. Of all the figures falsely accused by Barrett, Erskine was the only person of interest because he had died of a heart attack in the April, six months before Alice's death.

The third investigation was to do with the river pollution in the town of Fisherhead, near Milton Keynes, where farm stock had to be culled in their hundreds, causing local farmers huge financial losses. Again, Alice had been there to bring this catastrophe into the public domain. The contamination had been linked to a meat processing plant in Fisherhead, whose proprietor was ultimately charged with the crime of industrial water pollution and imprisoned a month before Alice died. The business itself, crippled by astronomical penalties, went bust. The proprietor's name was Rahim Patel. There were rumours that he had a handsome sum put away in Swiss banks for a rainy day.

And the final case Sam and Maggie deemed relevant to their inquiries was that of James Watson-Cure, the once governor of Erlestoke Prison. This investigation followed the violent death of a prison warden, one Seamus McCormick. Mr McCormick had been assaulted by a disgruntled prisoner and suffered critical head injuries. He died in hospital a few days later. An internal inquiry followed, which according to Alice's notes was hindered by Mr Watson-Cure every step of the way. Allegations of the wardens working illegally long hours and extra shifts had been made, but in the end it was the recruitment contractor, ForcePlus, who had to take the blame. Watson-Cure had come out of it smelling of roses. The summer before Alice's death, he had left his post as governor and moved on to a private security corporation in the Cayman Islands.

*

'What a bunch of beauties!' Maggie remarked. 'If I had to deal daily with wretchedness of that magnitude in my job, I too would go bipolar – just to block it all out.'

'Alice wasn't bipolar. She suffered from depression,' Sam said.

'That's what I'm saying – I'd be depressed too, big time! Knowing that vile people like that walk this earth gets me down. For the life of me I can't comprehend why Alice chose to do that job!'

'She loved it. Exposing those bastards was where she got her kicks from, and she was damn good at it. Oddly enough, being on a case was what kept her depression at bay.'

'But rubbing shoulders with all that evil must've eroded her here, inside.' Maggie slapped her chest. 'It would've done my head in . . .'

Sam reflected. Perhaps Maggie was right. Maybe when the adrenaline was pumping, Alice was doing well, but when it was over and the case was closed – that's when the strain and emotion would catch up with her and bring her down. An emotional shutdown in the end – suicide – was her only escape.

He offered Maggie a wry smile. 'Mine too, and probably Alice's, in the end . . . I think she was a highly functioning adrenalin junkie, but she was too decent a human being to metabolise all that wickedness and misery and not be affected by it. That's why she killed herself.'

'Well, actually, we don't know that she did kill herself. In fact, the chances are that she was killed. That's why we're here doing this, isn't it?' Maggie peered at him with those sincere, child-like eyes of hers that never failed to remind him of all the good things in life. The tenseness in his muscles subsided and he could breathe without any obstruction in his throat. Maggie had the talent for easing his pain. Irrational as she was, she was his voice of reason.

'Yes, a hundred per cent – that's why we're doing this, Maggie!' He almost saluted her.

'Let's do it, then! Let's split the workload: I'll handle Chief Constable Erskine and Rahim Patel. You can take on the prison governor and that dodgy lawyer, what was his name?'

'Damian Miskin,' Sam said. 'I knew him, actually, when I was at the Bar.'

'You didn't!' Maggie clapped her hands together. 'That's brilliant! You'll have a head start then with all that background knowledge.'

'I didn't know him that well, I just knew of him. He often briefed one of my partners at the chambers.'

'But that's great! We need that sort of intimate background on our suspects . . . I mean, let's face it: none of our main persons of interest either resided near South Castle or sported the initials L.D. or L.P. So we must dig deeper and that means their business partners, employees, family members, their enemies, plus their addresses, and . . . and . . . and hopefully we'll dig something up.'

Even Maggie looked fractionally overwhelmed by the size of their task. She dropped her shoulders and gave a faint sigh. Fortunately, at this very moment, Deirdre waltzed in with a tray full of refreshments, including a box of Jaffa cakes. Maggie's eyes lit up.

Over coffee – for it was coffee that had been served despite the late hour of nine fifteen p.m. – Maggie observed, 'Did you notice, Samuel, how in all of those cases we are dealing with quite powerful individuals? They are all men in positions of authority: a prison governor, a chief constable, a solicitor . . . Are you thinking what I am thinking?' She put her question to him in her usual fashion which required no input from Sam whatsoever. He continued sipping his scorching-hot, black coffee and let her continue on her as yet unclear trajectory. 'This may explain why Alice's death was so readily dismissed as suicide . . . if someone high up there wanted the inquest closed quickly and discreetly. As little fuss as possible. With all those big fish in the pond, they didn't want to make waves. Reading through the inquest records, I don't get the impression that they tried very hard to look for any connections to Alice's cases.' Alice tilted her head and gazed at Sam enquiringly. 'Are you thinking what I'm thinking?'

'I am now.' Sam scratched the three-day stubble on his chin, not only intrigued but also inspired and eager to get started.

★

They returned to work. It was late, but Maggie showed not the slightest intention of retiring to her own house. She claimed the box of Jaffa cakes and took it with her to her corner in the office where, directly on the floor, she spread the paperwork for her first case under review: the case of Chief Constable John Erskine. She took out the first Jaffa cake and, munching on it, began to draw a family tree with the intention of identifying Erskine's relatives who may have offered information to Alice on that fateful day when she died.

Sam started with Miskin. He was scrutinising the list of clients whom Miskin assisted with their Golden Visa applications. Though it seemed like looking for a needle in a haystack, Sam searched for the initials L.D. or L.P. with dogged determination. The letters were swirling before his eyes. He had lost track of the names a few times and had to go back to the top of the list. He was dead tired, and his hope of finding the elusive person had begun to steadily dwindle away. He stole a quick glance at the mantel clock to discover to his shock that it was five minutes to midnight. His eyes travelled to Maggie, who was showing no signs of slowing down. He wished he'd had some of those Jaffa cakes (if she only knew how to share!) Perhaps it was time to call it a day, he mused, rubbing his temples.

'Oh my God, I've got it!' Maggie shrilled from the floor, making Sam's heart jump to his throat. She gathered the sheets of paper and carried them to the desk. 'Come here, Samuel! We've got her – we found L.P.!'

Sam followed her and, squinting in the poor light, tried to make sense of what looked like a family tree drawn by Maggie in a particularly untidy hand. She stabbed her finger at a name in the middle of the sheet, and declared, 'Laura. John Erskine's daughter. Married to Gordon Price. That makes her an L.P. – Laura Price. She's our man – or woman, to be precise!'

'Laura Price,' he pronounced the name in a kind of wondrous trance.

'I found her! I found her!' Maggie screeched and threw herself at Sam, almost succeeding in knocking him down to the floor. 'This calls for a celebration, Samuel!'

71

Just then the mantel clock chimed its celebratory twelve-note tune and Deirdre burst in, looking alarmed. She herself was a cause for alarm in her rollers and with her face covered in an oxidised avocado-coloured facemask.

'What's going on here? I thought someone was being murdered!'

'Quite the opposite, Deirdre!' Maggie babbled, 'We found who murdered Alice!'

'Alice was murdered?'

'I wouldn't go that far,' Sam attempted to restore sanity to this conversation. 'We just found a woman who may have been the last person to see Alice before she died.'

'I need something strong to clear my head,' Deirdre mumbled and sat down in a chair.

'Grand idea! Let's raise a toast to our discovery. What have you got there for us, Samuel? Brandy will do.'

Chapter Ten

Laura Price, nee Erskine, was a good-looking woman in her prime. She was tall, athletic, and endowed with a sturdy bone structure. Her natural light-brown hair was cut in a no-nonsense bob and was pushed behind her ears to stop it from falling on her face. She wore no make-up. She was the picture of health and strength.

She had agreed to receive Sam in her house in the town of Gladestoke. Maggie tagged along. Sam had made her promise to stay in the background and to leave the talking to him. She was to refrain from making any wanton accusations against Laura Price. Maggie had graciously conceded.

'I just want to look her in the eye. There's so much one can tell from a person's body language! So much more than words. Of course, you need a woman's intuition to be able to do it properly.'

'As long as you don't provoke or challenge her in any way, Maggie,' Sam warned her for the umpteenth time. 'It took some convincing to get her to see me.'

At first, when he had telephoned her, Laura Price seemed wary and suspicious of his intentions. She was sorry about his loss, but frankly, her father was dead too, and there was no point picking at old scabs. The past was best left in the past. It'd be too painful to talk about it. But Sam persisted – he could not rest until he had tied up all the loose ends. Laura Price was one of them. Her name had surfaced amongst Alice's papers. He wanted to know why. All he knew was that the two of them had arranged to meet on the day of Alice's death.

That revelation must have swayed her. She told him to pop over on Thursday, at eleven o'clock, and gave him the address.

Although Gladestoke was a grey post-industrial town with a derelict centre comprising boarded-up shop windows and an abandoned red-brick factory looking down on the place, Laura Price lived on an affluent housing estate on the outskirts. It was separated from the dilapidated town by the flourishing greenery of a country park. Mrs Price's house was a detached two-storey white stone building set in its own lush garden. Maggie and Sam's arrival was greeted by a hostile bark coming from inside even before they used the pull-rod doorbell. Mrs Price opened the door, holding a small but cantankerous white poodle who was still yapping. Behind her stood a little blond boy, no older than five.

'Who's that, Mummy? Is that Mr Postman?' the boy was mewling and trying to push by her to take a look for himself.

'Hi! Nice to meet you. I'm Maggie Kaye, Samuel's associate.' Maggie charged forward, holding out her hand.

Laura Price shook it automatically and muttered a reluctant hello, but she shot Sam a questioning glare. No, she clearly wasn't happy about him bringing along an *associate*.

Sam stepped on to the porch to stand face to face with her. She was almost as tall as he. She had an air of authority about her. He did his best to be civil.

'Samuel Dee. Thank you for agreeing to talk to me. May we come in?'

She passed the now growling poodle to the child and said, 'Johnny, darling, go and play in your bedroom and take Whoopie with you. You know how she hates strangers.'

'She'll want to bite your heads off, you know!' Johnny addressed the visitors.

'Oh no! My poor head!' Maggie clasped her hands over her ears and pulled a face of mock terror.

'Don't worry, I won't let her.' The boy, holding the wriggling creature in his arms, began a clumsy ascent of the stairs.

His mother saw him off and turned to face her guests, the warm,

74

loving smile she'd had for her child dying on her lips in an instant. 'Come in. This way.'

She offered them tea and biscuits, which in itself meant nothing in particular. In Gloucestershire as in Wiltshire and further afield in the West Country, even an axe murderer would be expected, as a matter of basic etiquette, to offer his victim a cup of tea before despatching them. The assortment of biscuits was an added bonus. The dismay that instantly registered on Maggie's face could only mean one thing, though: there were no Jaffa cakes on offer. Rich Tea biscuits and custard creams were not Maggie's treats of choice. Her disappointed gaze wandered off the plate and strayed towards the mantelpiece, where it rested on some family photographs: Laura in a full-skirted white chiffon dress, on the arm of a dashing young man with a black beard, wearing a grey tailcoat; Laura again, this time looking tired but contented on a hospital bed, the dashing young man minus the beard but with the addition of a newborn baby in his arms; a young Laura, dressed in a PC's uniform, standing with an older policeman, large and fair, presenting a confident, military appearance, his silver epaulets signifying his high rank: probably none other than Laura's late father, Chief Constable John Erskine.

'So, how did I get implicated in all of this?' Mrs Price asked bluntly.

'As I explained on the phone, my wife – my late wife, Alice – was the journalist who investigated your father's . . . erm . . .' Sam was struggling with choosing the right words, words that would not offend her. 'Well, she interviewed Ryan Barrett who made allegations against your father—'

'Which turned out to be utter fiction, unfounded, untrue, and which totally devastated Dad. He died a broken man,' Laura Price helped him, a steely expression in her face betraying no emotion. Only the word *Dad* caused her voice to momentarily quiver.

'Yes . . . Barrett lied, and Alice believed him.' Sam nodded. 'She couldn't have known—'

'Mr Dee,' Laura Price cut him short again, 'that is precisely why journalists should refrain from sticking their noses into people's lives and stirring up public outcry on the say-so of con artists, fantasists, and attention seekers. Ryan Barrett was all of those things. And he also happened to have been a juvenile offender, and my father was his first arresting officer. Barrett had unfinished business with Dad and he chose his time to strike to perfection. If only the media had let the police do their work without interference, Barrett would've never succeeded in destroying my father's life and reputation.'

'I'm sorry.'

'So am I. But what's done is done. We can't undo what that man did. It's too late. Dad died before the truth came out, before he was vindicated. That I cannot change. That's why I was reluctant to talk to you – I don't want to rake up the past. I want to forget it.' Her tone had morphed into something soft and plaintive. Her pain was still raw. Her mourning for her father had not ended.

'Your father isn't gone, not entirely. He's watching over you, all the time,' Maggie leaned towards her and smiled. Though she was talking to Laura Price and patting her hand, she wasn't looking at her but was gazing over her shoulder. Sam surmised that John Erskine, or at least his spirit, was in the room with them, and Maggie meant every word literally.

Laura Price however knew nothing of Maggie's ability to see the dead. She pulled her hand away and looked sharply at Sam. 'Be it as it may, you wanted to talk about your wife, not my father. How do I come into it?'

'Alice left some notes. Papers and calendars . . .' Purposefully, Sam chose not to mention the mystery mobile phone or the circumstantial trail of calls and messages. As a lawyer, he knew he would not be able to establish any connection between that Pay-As-You-Go account and Laura Price. 'There were some scribbles and a record of a meeting with you in her diary. At South Castle. On the day Alice died.'

He scrutinised Laura's face. Maggie was doing the same. He

could not detect any reaction in it. It was inscrutable. He inhaled and continued, 'You may have been the last person to see Alice alive. You'll appreciate how much I'd like to find out how . . . how she seemed to you. It may help me understand . . . That day, Alice—' He couldn't finish, but he didn't have to. Laura Price knew all about Alice.

'I'm sorry to disappoint you, but I didn't see her.'

'But the meeting?'

'Yes, yes, there was to have been a meeting, but she never turned up. I waited. She didn't come. I'm sorry you came all this way for nothing.'

'I see.'

'I'm sorry, I can't help you. I don't know why your wife did what she did, or why she chose that day to do it.'

Sam found himself in a state of mental paralysis. Laura Price stood up, signalling that the meeting was over. He was feeling defeated. He should have known it would be a dead end: Alice had never made it to South Castle. She had died a few miles short of her destination. He too stood up and opened his mouth to thank Mrs Price for her time.

But Maggie remained seated. He heard her ask in clear disregard for his instructions, 'But why were you meeting with Alice in the first place?'

There was a fleeting moment of hesitation in the woman's eyes, followed by a short-lived spark of anger which she put out promptly with a lame, disingenuous smile. She answered Maggie, still standing in readiness for her and Sam's imminent departure, 'You'd have to ask her that. I don't really know. She wanted to meet – said she had something important to run by me, something that could clear my father's name. She said she had to confirm a few facts with me. I was wary of her but also quite hopeful about that meeting. I never lost faith in my father. You can imagine how much I wanted to clear his name. I'd have met with the devil himself . . .'

'Were you not surprised, or disappointed, when she didn't turn up? Did you try to call her to find out what had stopped her?'

'No. The meeting was her idea, not mine. When she didn't come, I felt ... well, I felt, it was just typical, I don't know ... I wasn't sure about meeting her anyway. I didn't trust her, like I said.'

'Why didn't you mention that at the inquest?'

'I wasn't subpoenaed to the inquest. It had nothing to do with me or my father.' Laura Price looked hard at Maggie. But Maggie didn't as much as flinch.

'But you could've reported it to the police. The investigation into Alice's death was in full swing, at least I imagine it was ... It would've been relevant to let the police know that Alice was on her way to meet you. It would've helped them establish the sequence of events leading up to her death ... It would've helped *you* because you *are* the police, aren't you? Looking at the photos of you and your father ... You know how it works, how important it is for witnesses to come forward. But you withheld vital information – you, a police officer!' Her left eyebrow raised, Maggie looked triumphant.

'I *was* one, well spotted. I left the force when Johnny was born. Anyway, I wasn't involved in that investigation. To be honest with you, I deemed my meeting with Alice Dee irrelevant because it never happened. And there was something else ... how do I explain this to you?' Laura Price bit her lip. 'The link to my father – it was something I didn't wish to advertise to my colleagues. It was too soon, too painful to talk about Dad in the context of ... He was dead by then, but the paedophile label was still stuck to him ... even now. I suppose you could say it was shame.' She groaned, but quickly regained her composure. 'There was nothing to report to the officer who was looking into Alice Dee's case, especially after it was established that the woman had killed herself.'

Sam winced. Laura Price sounded cold and callous. It felt as if she was referring to nothing more than a cat that had been run over by a car. But it was his wife – it was Alice she was talking about. He said stiffly, 'Thanks for your time. We'll be off.'

Maybe he would be, but not Maggie. Maggie had more questions.

'I'm surprised you didn't pursue this.'

'Pursue what?'

'You said Alice might have information that could clear your father's name, and you didn't follow up on it. That is strange . . .'

'I told you – I didn't trust the woman. I didn't believe she had anything. I thought she was fishing, playing me for her own ends – typical heartless paparazzi sniffing around a dead man's grave.' The contempt in her voice was palpable.

'Maggie, let's go,' Sam urged. He was feeling increasingly nauseous and in need of fresh air.

'Please do,' Laura Price was agitated. She gestured towards the front door. 'Please leave my home.'

Reluctantly, Maggie rose to her feet and set off for the exit. But she was still looking over her shoulder and querying her prey, 'So, you were meeting at South Castle train station . . . Why?'

'I suppose she wanted to take a train.'

'But why not Gladestoke station – so much more convenient for you. Closer to where you live.'

'I don't know.' Laura Price rolled her eyes. 'She chose South Castle. You'd have to ask her!'

'But she drove a car. She wasn't taking a train!'

There was no answer as Laura Price slammed the door behind them.

Chapter Eleven

Our volunteers were dropping like flies. Even before we started, half of them had failed to report for duty, only some offering apologies. I was aware of Vera's husband, the Right Honourable Henry Hopps-Wood, returning home from Westminster for the summer recess, and that explained her and Rumpole's absences. Edgar Flynn had taken his mother on holiday to Bermuda – we could only hope this would not be a long-term vanishing act for either of them. Vanessa was visiting her parents in Wales. Mary and Dan simply didn't turn up.

Nevertheless, we had James, Michael, and Cherie and Lisa, as well as Ivo and Megan firing on all cylinders. My dream B&B was taking shape before my very eyes. Now that I had a new business partner, Badgers' Hall had a great future mapped out in front of it. Having just acquired Will's share in the property, Samuel had thrown a bucketload of cold hard cash at it. We had paid the plumbers, purchased paint, sinks, toilets, and tiles for the bathrooms, and still remained solvent. Being a person of means was a novel and satisfying experience for me.

While putting on the first coat of paint in the first-floor guestroom, Samuel and I discussed our meeting with Laura Price.

'You do realise she was lying through her teeth?' I informed him in case he had missed that somehow. Mrs Price's harsh comments about Alice had upset poor Samuel, I could tell. Towards the end of our meeting, he couldn't leave that house fast enough. He had gone terribly pale and shaky. He couldn't slot the key into the ignition and in the end I had no choice but to drive us home in his fancy Jag. Sam was sitting next to me and Alice was on the back seat; she glared at me through the rear-view mirror right through the entire journey, making me feel even more jittery than I already was.

Compared with my trusty Hyundai, every button and every function was on the wrong side of the steering wheel, so I found myself setting the windscreen wipers into motion when trying to indicate, and driving in second gear all the way home. By the time we reached Bishops Well, I was a nervous wreck. It had therefore come as no shock to either of us that when I finally turned into our narrow driveway, one front wing got scraped against a boulder and several lupins were mown down. Samuel hadn't even blinked. He was in a different place altogether. I wondered how much of our interview with that dreadful woman he had actually taken in.

Not a lot, as it turned out, for he said, 'You really think so?'

'Well, of course, Samuel!' I waved my paintbrush at him in sheer frustration. A few drops of the pearl white paint created a Milky Way impression on his navy blue T-shirt. 'Just think about it: she said the meeting was Alice's idea, and that Alice suggested the meeting place. Both lies!'

'Oh, that! Yes, she definitely lied there.'

'We have the text messages to prove it. The location and the whole idea of the meeting came from Laura.'

'True, she told us a few porkies.'

'Serious whoppers, more like!' In my fervour I splashed the paint again – this time, I felt it sprinkle over my own face. I wiped it with my sleeve. 'She tried to make it sound like it was Alice who played her, but it was the other way around. She proposed meeting, and she gave Alice the exact place and time. There was nothing in those texts to suggest that Alice had any information to share with her. It sounded more like Laura wanted to get something off her chest because – how did she put it?'

'"Now that he was gone, he wouldn't mind anymore", that was the gist of it more or less.'

'Precisely! So have you asked yourself, Samuel, why she would

81

lie? Are you thinking what I'm thinking?' I gave him a few seconds to nod, which he didn't. It is quite frustrating when people don't keep up with one's train of thought. It's as if they missed the train altogether and are standing on the platform, hapless, waiting for the next one. I slammed on the brakes for Samuel to catch up, and elaborated, 'Laura Price murdered Alice: she lured her to South Castle under false pretences, and killed her. She had a motive and an opportunity. We just need to establish how she did it. And prove it.'

'Piece of cake . . .' Samuel smiled ruefully. 'I think you may be right, Maggie, but Laura Price used to be a police officer – she'd know how not to leave any incriminating evidence behind.'

'Everyone makes mistakes,' I pointed out to him, 'and so did she. The text messages on Alice's mobile led us directly to Laura's doorstep. There'll be more crumbs along the way. And we'll find them.'

'It's been almost four years, Maggie. I sat through the entire inquest, listened to every testimony, read and scrutinised the transcripts, and I could find nothing to suggest any other possibility than suicide. Alice walked under that train, and that's that.' He had the downtrodden look of a man who had lost the love of his life and had nothing to live for.

I glanced at Alice and, I could swear, she glowered right back at me, as if beseeching me to do something. That was when I understood why she had been hanging around Samuel for so long. It wasn't possessiveness or clinginess. Alice was held back from moving on. She needed to put the record straight: she hadn't killed herself – she loved him and she would never have left him. She had been murdered and he had to know that.

I dropped my paintbrush and walked to him. I pulled the roller out of his hand and put it in the tray. I took his hands into mine, clasped them like in prayer, and I looked firmly into his tear-filled eyes. 'Alice didn't kill herself – she wants you to know that. The evidence you saw was what the killer wanted you to see. Laura Price had the means of pulling all the strings during the police investigation, don't forget that. At that time, no one knew about the meeting at South Castle station – no one explored the possibility of Alice making it there. We only have Laura's word that Alice didn't turn up. But Laura is lying. She's lying about so many things and she's lying about that. We'll get to the bottom of this and we'll expose her. Alice ought to be put to rest – on her terms.'

Samuel's tears burst their banks and rolled down his cheeks. It was heartbreaking to watch a grown man cry. I tried to wipe those tears off but only smeared white paint all over his cheeks. He looked like one of those sad-faced clowns. I realised how deeply I cared about this man. I was going to untangle this awful lie, even if he did nothing to assist me in doing so. After all he had been there for me when I lost Mum and then Dad, and I would have also lost Andrea if he hadn't stepped in with his heroics. Now, it was my turn to be there for him.

'We'll have to go to South Castle and do some serious snooping,' he surprised me with a sudden moment of lucid decisiveness.

'We will, Samuel. We'll go all the way to hell and back and we'll put Alice's ghost to rest.'

A bizarre ringtone resonated in the bathroom next door where James and Michael were laying floor tiles. It was a particularly unpleasant version of a squealing pig being slaughtered. James answered it.

'Dad? Is everything all right?'

That was the only comprehensive sentence he uttered. It was followed by a few exclamations of surprise, grunts, expressions of disbelief and a mild curse. Finally, he said, 'OK, I'm on my way.'

'Is that ringtone exclusive to your father?' Michael chortled.

'It is, actually.'

Samuel and I popped into the bathroom out of concern. Something was the matter and it wasn't a slaughtered pig.

James looked at me apologetically. 'Sorry, guys, I have to run to pick up my father from the airport. Gerard usually does the chauffeuring, but he failed his refresher test last week. It's for the best, anyway. At his age, he ought to be surrendering his driving licence voluntarily. It wasn't that long ago when he reversed Father's Roller into a bollard.'

'Poor Gerard. He must be a hundred, I guess.'

'Not far off. Another five or six years and he'll be receiving a telegram from the Queen.'

James was wiping his hands on an old rag, and chewing on his lower lip. It wasn't hard to see that he was troubled.

'Rather unexpected? Your father returning home from the Alps halfway through the summer?' (I always want to know everything, so I embarked on the fishing expedition right away.) 'What brings him back?'

'Complications. Legal stuff.'

'Oh? Being sued then?' I encouraged him subtly.

'It's a possibility, yes. He wants to avoid it – negotiate a settlement.'

'With who? If you don't mind me asking . . .'

'Daryl Luntz.'

My appetite whetted, I wasn't going to let him out of my clutches until all was revealed. I couldn't give two hoots that his Lordship was waiting at the airport. 'You don't say! Is it something to do with No Man's Land?'

'Precisely that. Apparently, the Church lawyers challenged Luntz's title to the land and presented evidence of an oral bequest made by my grandfather on his deathbed. We thought there wasn't one.'

'But there is? Go on . . .'

'Clearly! Testimonies by *disinterested witnesses* confirming the gifting of No Man's Land to the Church. Father is fuming. Those *disinterested witnesses* used to be in service with the family – Fanny Dawson, the cook, and Robbie, an invalid war veteran grandfather employed as gardener. Out of charity, because the man didn't know a tulip from a marigold. Father is raging: "*That's how they pay us back!*" He thought he could count on Fanny's and Robbie's loyalty, but "*the sods*" have let him down.'

'But they have to tell the truth—'

84

'Of course, they do. You don't know Father, though. He won't forgive them!'

By now, all of us gathered in the tiny space of an en-suite bathroom, transfixed by the news.

'So, let me get it clear,' I continued with my line of inquiry, 'Luntz doesn't own No Man's Land and can't sell it to Cinnamon Rock?'

'It seems that's the case. He's claiming substantive compensation from Father.'

'Dear me,' I commiserated insincerely. I was struggling to suppress an outpouring of Schadenfreude.

'At least the cattle egret will be able to sleep easy,' Michael pointed out.

'That's true. The bogs and wildlife are safe.' James perked up. 'I'd better be going. Can't keep Father waiting.'

'Send our regards!' I shouted after him.

When James was out of sight, and out of earshot, we all erupted in celebratory shrieks, whoops and pats on the back. We had won! Vicar Laurence had won from beyond the grave! No Man's Land was back in our communal hands. Well, the Church owned it, but we were sure that they would share it with us in the good Christian spirit of giving to the poor and needy.

We didn't get a chance to return to work. We were too excited to drive a paintbrush in a straight line. A trip to the Rook's Nest to raise a toast was suggested, but had to be abandoned because of the arrival of DI Marsh accompanied by DC Whittaker. As soon as James drove off, they pulled in and parked in his space.

DI Marsh charged in with her typically charming resolve, resembling a bull in a china shop. Whittaker kept his bulbous nose out of it, closing the rear.

'Is Ms Hornby here?' DI Marsh demanded, failing miserably to offer us conventional greetings and remarks about how the sunny weather was holding up nicely. 'We were told we'd find her here.'

Cherie stepped forward, looking mortified. She must have felt like one of those culprits who had been given the count to ten to come forward and own up before everyone else was made to suffer.

'Yes? What is this about?' It was a polite and sensible question to ask.

Not that Gillian Marsh would care to answer it.

'We need to talk to you. We can do it at the station, or here, I don't mind where.'

'Here.' Lisa stood by Cherie's side, her feet wide apart and hands on her hips. 'It's easier here. We're all covered in paint and dust . . . So, what is it that you want? My partner asked you what it was all about. You didn't answer.'

'It's about her mother's death. Gertrude Hornby. Three years ago,' DI Marsh looked Lisa up and down like some kind of an alien specimen. 'Before your time, ma'am.'

Poor Cherie looked even more mortified than before. She had gone as white as a sheet.

'Is it OK if we use one of the rooms on the premises to conduct the interview?' DC Whittaker addressed me. For a second I wondered why me and then I realised I was the actual premises proprietor.

'Yes, yes . . . Why don't you pop down to the living room? It's fairly tidy down there, unlike here . . . I could get you a cup of tea while you're chatting?'

'No, thank you.' DI Marsh spoke for all.

Cherie looked like she needed something much stronger than tea.

Chapter Twelve

Indeed, by the time DI Marsh had finished with Cherie Hornby, the poor hen was in dire need of a fortifying alcoholic beverage, or several. She came out of the living room looking confused. She was unable to string a sentence together in order to answer our many questions. Lisa, who had been hovering by the door to tune into the interview, was equally confounded. She couldn't make any sense of the snippets of the conversation she had intercepted. We were dying to know every detail of every question the police had asked Cherie, and why. We were also dying for a drink. We still had to celebrate on account of No Man's Land returning to its rightful owners. A collective decision was made to head for the Rook's Nest.

'We'd love to come,' Ivo grimaced apologetically, 'but we must go and check on Vesna. She's been on her own the whole day.'

'Well, check on Vesna, do what you need to do, and come and join us when you're ready.'

'We'll try,' Megan promised, but Ivo said not to wait for them.

So it was just Cherie and Lisa, Michael, Samuel, and I. Five o'clock denoted the first wave of peak-hour traffic at Rook Nest. Patrons were beginning to pour in from the farms surrounding Bishops Well for a well-deserved pint. Terrence Truelove, the publican, saw us enter and waved us to an empty table in the bay window facing the market square.

The first round was on Samuel. We ordered our beverages and laid our weary bones on a cushioned bench. I could feel aches and pains in parts of my body where I didn't even know I had muscles.

The renovation works were taking their toll on me. But I didn't fret – I had a B&B and, evidently, a brand new toned body to look forward to.

Cherie was having a shot of tequila to calm her nerves. Once she downed that, she was ripe for conversation.

'Go on, Cherie, tell us what they wanted,' I encouraged her.

'I've no idea. They asked me hundreds of questions about my mother's death – every tiniest detail: what time I left her room, did I see anyone, did Mother have any packing tape in her room—'

'Packing tape?' All of us, except Michael, chorused. To say that we were baffled would be an understatement.

'But why are they asking you about your mother now? It's been three years since she passed away!'

'Not quite three, but yes – a while,' Cherie sighed. 'Can I have another tequila, please?'

I gulped the rest of my gin and tonic and put my hand up to take care of this round. It wasn't going to be an expensive one. The men, relishing their pints, weren't quite ready for refills, and Lisa was still nursing her glass of white wine.

I pushed my way to the bar. The place was positively buzzing with thirsty clientele. I had to wait my turn at the back of the queue. I tried to remember the circumstances of Cherie's mother's death. There had been a few question marks at the time. The police had been involved – there certainly were doubts whether Gertrude Hornby had died of natural causes. I remembered the handsome and well-mannered detective from Bath – DCI Greyson. He had headed the investigation while Sexton's own DI Marsh was tracking down that terrorist who got stranded in our neck of the woods, Sexton's Wood to be exact. The poor chap, having Gillian Marsh on his back couldn't have been a pleasure cruise for him. Though he'd got all that he deserved for murdering those innocent people on the train.

'What can I get you, Maggie?' Terrence was shouting to me over the crowd. It seemed I had made it to the front of the queue. To spare myself another trip and a long wait at the bar, I ordered a double-tequila for Cherie and a double gin and tonic for yours truly.

'Getting smashed again, lovie?' Terrence grinned. He had big teeth, like a carthorse, which suited the fact that he was altogether a big man with a large frame.

'Not really, Terrence. I always drink responsibly. What makes you think that?'

I winked at him and his dubious attempt at humour, then took the two refilled glasses and carried them to our table.

'Right,' I said to Cherie after she downed this double as quickly as she had downed her first single shot. 'Let's start from the beginning. I thought your mother's case was shelved after the police had found nothing untoward. It was that nice DCI Greyson, wasn't it?'

'Yes, it was, but before he took over, DI Marsh had given me the third degree. She accused me of all sorts.' Cherie exhaled tequila fumes together with her frustration in one long sigh.

'That's so like her,' I seethed, incensed. 'She's such a cow!'

From the corner of my eye, I saw Michael flinch. OK, so she was his girlfriend, but I wasn't going to apologise. She was lucky. I hadn't done my worst. She was more than a cow. Cows are nice. Gillian Marsh is, usually, a bitch.

Lisa groaned. 'I shouldn't have let you go with them on your own.' She gazed tenderly at Cherie who did the same in return. It was touching.

'They wouldn't have let you in on the police interview, anyway,' I disrupted their moment reluctantly but firmly. 'Police have their ways of making people feel guilty and besieged. That's how they get their confessions. DI Marsh is particularly adept at that.' Michael was now twitching and blinking with outrage, but I wouldn't let him interrupt me. 'So, tell us from the start, Cherie. We may be able to help you make sense of it all.'

Cherie laced together her stubby fingers and pressed them to her lips. 'OK,' she muttered, 'So, she asked me all the same questions she had asked before.'

'Like?'

'Like the standard stuff they usually ask, I suppose: did I see any strangers when I visited Mother that day, did anyone act suspiciously, did Mother . . . As if Mother was capable of acting in any lucid way – she was in the thrall of Alzheimer's, bedridden . . . She didn't even know who I was any more! The doctors weren't giving her more than six months to live . . .' Cherie reached for her glass with trembling hands only to discover it was empty. Her chin down, she stared helplessly at it.

'Whose turn is it now?' I enquired. 'Cherie needs another drink.'

Michael stood up and took the orders. He was probably glad of the excuse to leave the table and hear no more abuse directed towards his girlfriend.

'So, she was asking about your visit on the day your mum died?'

'Oh yes! Back to the same old tune, DI bloody Marsh! She didn't believe me then and she doesn't believe me now. I told her it was a short visit because Mother had driven me barmy. She did! I was in tears. I'd hardly walked in when she accused me of stealing from her. Her hankies or knickers – I can't remember what it was . . . She was shouting at me, wanting a different nurse . . . It goes without saying that she didn't realise who I was. Of course, no one was stealing anything from her drawer, but I couldn't make her understand. She started swearing at me. Where she'd got those curses from, I've no idea . . . Mother never swore. Never before . . . I got distraught, telling her to stop. She threw me out. I burst into tears and ran away.'

'So, you explained that to DI Marsh all over again . . . Why is she so interested in that?'

'Because the visit lasted only eight minutes, she says. Not enough for a proper visit, she says, but long enough to kill a helpless old lady.' Cherie sobbed.

Lisa cursed DI Marsh, using language I won't be able to quote here.

Luckily, Michael arrived with the tequila just after Lisa closed her statement. Cherie knocked back her third shot of liquor. I wondered if it was a double. It looked like a double.

It must have been a double. Following that drink, Cherie's eyes bulged out momentarily and her chubby cheeks flushed red. Soon, the impairment caused to her speech had become evident too.

'Was there anything else she asked you? I just can't understand why she'd drag this whole affair out into the light of day now?'

'She . . . the cow . . . She's been on and on about some sodding packing tape,' Cherie slurred. 'Didn't I say . . . Wazere any bloody packing tape in the room . . . Wazere? "What packing tape?" I go . . . She goes, "just answer the blinkin' question, ma'am" . . . I'm not feelin' a hundred per cent.' Cherie burped. We all tilted away from her to give her room to breathe. And in case she was about to throw up all over us.

'We're going home.' Lisa stood up and grabbed Cherie by the elbows. She managed to lift her from the chair with help from Samuel and Michael. Once on her feet, Cherie leaned heavily on her partner and nestled her head under her armpit.

'Take me home, Lisa,' she mewled.

'I am, love, I am.'

They staggered on unsteady, wobbly legs towards the exit.

'Right, Michael! You'd better start talking! What is your horrible girlfriend up to now? Is she accusing Cherie of murdering her own mother? Has she gone mad – or should I say, madder than she already was!' I was fuming. I wasn't going to stand by while Gillian Marsh trampled over one of the best people I knew, someone who wouldn't have the nerve to kill a fly. The gin was burning through my guts and boiling my blood.

Michael twitched some more: his newly recultivated walrus moustache bristled and he cocked his head as if to hear me, and my blasphemy, better. I wasn't taken in by his shocked expression.

'Come on, cards on the table – what's she up to?'

'You know, Maggie, I can't discuss an active police investigation with you. And I do,' twitch, twitch, 'I do object to your attitude towards Gillian. She may be a touch on the brusque side, but she had a compelling reason to re-open Gertrude Hornby's case.'

'A *touch on the brusque side!* Your girlfriend, Almond, has zero empathy and no people skills. Is she even human?'

'And that's coming from you, Maggie! Your people skills leave a lot to be desired.'

My blood turned into vapour and began to steam through my ears. I consider myself – and I know I am right – to be the very archetype of a people person, the life and soul of the party, if I put my mind to it.

Michael wasn't finished. 'Yes, Gillian can be a little brusque and she isn't exactly the life and soul of the party. But, if you must know, it's nothing to do with her social skills – it's something altogether different, something that goes with the pressures of her job – and therefore, none of your business. She has an excuse. What excuse do you have, Maggie?'

My top blew off. I stood up and seized him with a vexed glare. He stood up too and instantly dwarfed me with his large frame and his massive moustache. I wasn't budging. I didn't know how many beers Almond had in his bloodstream, but I'd had three potent gins.

Samuel stood up as well and stepped in to hold me back for I was ready to give Michael Almond a good thrashing.

Samuel said, 'Sit down, you two. You're making a spectacle of yourselves. Let's get it sorted out in a civilised way. I will speculate and you, Michael, you will nod if I'm right or shake your head if I'm off the mark. That way, you aren't saying anything about the ongoing investigation. You, Maggie – you just sit down and listen.'

I snorted, and sat down. So did Almond.

'It's to do with the brown packing tape,' Samuel began.

Almond nodded.

'When we found Vicar Laurence, he was bound to the chair with packing tape.'

'He was!' I concurred. Samuel shushed me. It was rather unnecessary but I swallowed my pride on this occasion.

'I'm surmising that the same, or similar, packing tape was somehow involved in Cherie's mother's death? How?'

Forgetting that he wasn't to speak, only nod, Michael Almond answered the question. I must say Samuel hadn't lost his barrister's knack for getting people to talk.

He said, 'The *same* tape, according to Forensics. In Gertrude Hornby's case we found her lips sealed with the same tape. It wasn't the cause of her death, it hung loose – she had been smothered, probably with a pillow, which was then propped under her head and puffed up. The tape was only … ornamental, and the then SIO, Greyson, didn't know what to make of it. In the end, we had no suspects and the weight of evidence pointed to assisted suicide. The whole thing was swept under the carpet. Gillian was convinced the Chief Super had his hand in it, but for once she didn't want to challenge him. Because she is *quite* human,' Michael rounded on me with a resentful glare. 'She thought it was for the best and not in the public interest to pursue a grieving daughter for murder, even if she had helped her sick mother to end her life. Anyway, back then Gillian was dealing with another, more pressing case. But now, she has no choice. She has to re-open the Gertrude Hornby inquiry because there's a possible link to the murder she's investigating. A very disturbing link – the blinking packing tape. We could have a double killer on our hands.'

Well, that was a lot to say for someone who was only to nod his head, or shake it. Undoubtedly, Michael had been dying to tell us and, after all, needed little encouragement. Or perhaps, encouragement of a different kind than the one I had offered when accusing his girlfriend of being a sociopath.

'Sorry, Michael,' I mumbled, 'I was out of line.'

He blinked, as if coming round from a trance. 'Yeah, me too,' he nodded (as he was supposed to do). 'But now that you've got it out of me, it *cannot* go any further. I didn't tell you anything. Is that clear?'

'Of course, sir.' I hiccupped. 'We wouldn't dream of losing you your job, or your lovely girlfriend.'

Chapter Thirteen

Holed up in his office since dawn, with the door bolted from inside, Sam was engrossed in his research. He had bolted the door after his mother had brought him the third morning tea in as many hours. If that wasn't enough interfering, she had also offered to clear the litter from the floor since today was the paper-and-cardboard bin day. Gently but firmly, Sam had led her out of the office and slid the iron bolt into place.

He hadn't slept all night, his mind swarming with trains, train stations, and railway tracks. A couple of times, just as he had begun to drift off, he would be jolted into sweaty, wide-eyed alertness by the image of Alice walking head on into a fast-approaching train. He couldn't take it anymore. Without washing, shaving, or having breakfast, he had locked himself in his office and commenced a methodical investigation into train lines and schedules.

His findings made his skin crawl. It was the sobering realisation that Alice *had* been lured to her death.

Gladestoke was one of the main stations on a busy commuter line between London and Bristol. South Castle was not. It lay on a non-electrified railway line used primarily by freight trains. To get there from London, one had to change at Gladestoke. There weren't many passenger trains stopping there: three to five a day, and none of them arriving at approximately eleven a.m. on the day of Alice's death. It didn't make any sense for her to choose South Castle over Gladestoke station if she were to travel by train. But, as Maggie had pointed out, Alice had driven there. It had been Laura Price's choice of date and time. Sam could not shake off the conclusion that she'd had it all planned.

Sam returned to his computer to ascertain the freight trains passing through South Castle, and their timetable on the fateful day. It was a freight train carrying fertilisers that had mowed Alice down. Had that train been on schedule? Had the killer – assuming it was Laura Price – had access to that schedule? How easy had it been for her to obtain freight train times and routes? How meticulously had she planned it and how well had she disposed of any evidence pointing to her? Was it really she who did it? And most importantly, was Alice's death really a premeditated murder?

The stern face of Laura Price hung before Sam's eyes, stubbornly refusing to go away. Maggie had sown the seed of doubt in his mind. Maggie was a hot-headed amateur sleuth running around in circles and looking for trouble, but she wasn't stupid and – as she would frequently remind Sam – she had a woman's intuition at her disposal. When everything else failed, she could rely on her sixth sense. Not to mention consorting with the dead, including Alice.

'Oh, Alice,' Sam whispered to the empty four walls of his office, 'Maggie's right, isn't she? You didn't leave me. Not in such a violent, mindless way. It wasn't your style . . . That woman murdered you, didn't she? How? Just tell me – say something!'

'Samuel!'

Sam clutched his chest. His heart must have stopped for a few seconds and his blood drained from his brain.

'Samuel, are you there?' The door handle was being shaken with impatient ferocity. It was Maggie. 'Open up! We need to talk. I've got it all cracked.'

No, Maggie's breakthrough had nothing to do with Alice's murder, despite her earlier promise that she would dedicate all her powers of deduction to solving that case. Maggie was heart and soul on a different trail – that of the vicar's killer.

She pushed in past Sam and flopped into his chair, accepting Deirdre's offer of tea and 'a small bite to eat' along the way.

'The murderer used the same unorthodox weapon, packing tape of all things, twice! The first time at Golden Autumn! That was an eye-opening revelation, don't you think, Samuel?' She fixed him with eyes full of fearsome excitement. 'You must be thinking exactly what I'm thinking!'

Sam hadn't been thinking about that at all. It took him a while to divert his thoughts from Alice to Vicar Laurence via the incongruous packing tape route. When he finally grasped the subject matter of the conversation, he exhaled with unconcealed impatience, 'So, what exactly are you thinking, Maggie? Be quick though – I've got something on the go.'

She paused in her tracks to frown at him. She didn't like being fobbed off when she got into her *thinking* mood. She shook her head. 'You know what I'm thinking, Samuel, surely! You aren't as inane as you look.'

The things he was learning about himself from dear Maggie! He should be tearing his hair out, except that right now he had neither time nor inclination to care. He blew out his cheeks with ostentatious indifference.

She frowned even more. 'Come to think – you do look bad! And what on earth are you wearing?'

Sam was dressed only in his pyjama boxers and a faded T-shirt. That's how he slept. When he had rolled out of bed this morning, changing his clothes and doing his daily ablutions had been the last things on his to do list.

'Sorry, Maggie, I wasn't expecting you. I've been working on Alice's case since dawn. You see, the trains—'

'That will have to wait.'

He opened his mouth to contradict her, but she thrust her hands at him, her palms flat out in his face, and continued, 'We'll deal with that in due course. Alice isn't going anywhere, are you, Alice?' She peered over his shoulder and gave a tiny salute to the wall. 'But here, in Bishops, we have a serial killer on the loose. You know who I mean!'

'No, not a hundred per cent. You'll have to—'

'Michelle Pike, of course!'

So, Daryl Luntz was off the hook . . .

'Think about it. We had our suspicions about her even before we found out how Cherie's mother was killed!'

Sam recalled their unfulfilled mission to report Michelle Pike to George Easterbrook on the day they had found Vicar Laurence's body. The works carried out gratis by Cinnamon Rock on the extension to the residential home owned by Michelle implied a clear conflict of interests. True, Ms Pike ought to have declared it and excused herself from casting a vote on the rezoning of No Man's Land. But surely that wasn't a plausible motive to murder the clergyman!

'You're overreaching, Maggie.'

'Am I? Am I? Come on, Samuel – think! The same packing tape was used to murder an old lady on the premises of the Golden Autumn Retreat three years ago and now again to truss up poor Vicar Laurence after he was lethally stabbed – doesn't that make you think? It's the same killer! Even the police believe this to be true. So who? Who is the common denominator here? Michelle Pike – that's who! She owns Golden Autumn – she has easy access to all its residents. As for the vicar, he stood in the way of her expanding her business at no cost to herself.'

'But why would she kill old Mrs Hornby? *She* was no threat to the business. She was one of her clients, paying good money for her accommodation . . .'

'Oh, Samuel,' Maggie growled. 'I don't know *why* Mrs Hornby! That's what we need to find out. But you know,' she pressed her index finger to her lips and adopted a pose of deep reflection, 'she has always struck me as one of those dark angels—'

'Dark angels?'

'Yes, dark angels. On the one hand, she's a brutal businesswoman – God knows, she took her ex to the cleaners big time . . . On the other hand, she put her – well, his – money into a care business . . . But that's not the same as *caring* for people, is it? Maybe she goes around bumping off elderly residents for money? A sort of angel of death. With a monetary agenda. We must look into this, Samuel!'

'I can't, Maggie. I'm sorry, but as you know I'm dealing with Alice's death. I've got a new lead I must follow. In fact, you put me on to it and you promised—'

'I know, I know, and I will.' Maggie pulled a desperate face, her eyebrows quivering on her forehead and her little lips dropping round the edges. 'But for now, at least, just one thing – just for me: can we at least speak to George Easterbrook about this, like we were going to do in the first place . . .'

'It would make more sense to share your suspicions with the police than the parish clerk.'

'What! With DI Marsh? You know how she feels about me. And you damn-well know how I feel about her after she mauled poor Cherie! I'm not talking to her and she won't listen to me anyway. But she may take George Easterbrook seriously. Ex officio . . . We must bring him on board. You aren't going to leave me to this on my own?'

Sam drew in his shoulders and covered his face with his hands. He looked as if he were expecting a punch to the stomach. He knew that if he didn't humour Maggie he would never get rid of her.

'OK, let's go and see George. But after that, I will have to leave you to it. I've got other things on my plate.'

'And I'll help you with those, Samuel. Just as I promised.'

Chapter Fourteen

Just like the first time, they didn't find George in the church. The church building and the cemetery were off-limits to the public, the police tape criss-crossing the entrance. The two gates leading to the graveyard had been padlocked. It had been a month since the last Sunday service had been held. No one had been tending to the graves of their loved ones in that month. Cut flowers placed in vases and jars were long withered. The place was well and truly dead.

Maggie and Sam headed for George's cottage in Bog Lane. It was at the end of a terrace of three eighteenth-century cottages with overwhelmingly huge thatched roofs and underwhelmingly tiny windows. The front door opened directly on to the road as there was no front garden. The door wasn't locked and nobody answered when they called. They let themselves in. George wasn't in. It didn't take much time to ascertain that. The place was minute – you couldn't swing a cat. But it was charming with its aged black beams and an impressive chimney breast occupying the best part of the sitting room.

They discovered George in the garden, painting. The fact that there was no front garden was compensated tenfold by the vast stretch of green foliage dwarfed by several huge chestnuts which probably remembered the reign of King John. Walking into that garden from the matchbox of George's cottage felt like walking through a wardrobe into Narnia.

'George, hello there!' Maggie waved and led the way.

George squinted against the sun to identify his guests, and waved back. The summer was holding up in all its golden glory – its last stand before it gave way to the inevitable downpours of the autumn. George was hard at work. His easel was set up on the lawn and facing a climbing wild rose which he was busy immortalising in watercolour. He resembled one of the French Impressionists. It was partly to do with the shock of his greying hair electrifying not only his head but also his chin. Primarily though, it was his oversized grey shirt splattered with the full range of colour from his palette.

Maggie stretched her neck to take a close look at his painting. 'It is so beautiful!'

'That's a kind thing to say, Maggie.'

'It's not kind – it's true. Anyway, I was thinking – could we possibly commission your services for a watercolour of the Bishops Well White Horse?'

'Could *we?*' Sam murmured more to himself than anyone else. He was trying to figure out when and how the *we* crept into this commission.

'It'd be perfect for our promotional material.'

'What are you promoting?'

'Our B&B. Samuel's bought into the business. *Badgers' Hall* we called it. I – we – need a recognisable image to go with it. We thought of you.'

'It'd be my pleasure. When do you need it by?'

'Well . . . I'd love you to capture it now, in the late summer, as the sun sets in all that rich colour and light . . .'

Sam began to think that he had misunderstood the purpose of their visit to George Easterbrook. He was sure they had set off to report Michelle Pike to him. Either he had misheard Maggie, or she had a very cunning plan up her sleeve.

It soon turned out it was the latter.

'It sounds interesting. I'll give it a go. I'll charge you only if you like it.'

'I've no doubt we'll love it. We've got a deal, Master Easterbrook.' Maggie shook hands with George. She then turned to Sam, 'You see, I told you, Samuel – leave it to me.'

100

'Would you like to come inside for a drink? I've got homemade lemonade. My great-great-grandmother's recipe.'

'That'd be grand!' Maggie enthused. She was in fact in need of urgent rehydration.

Seated in the tiny sitting room, sipping lemonade, Maggie at last touched on the subject which had brought them there in the first place.

'Terrible thing about Vicar Laurence ... We've lost our spiritual guru. He was so good to me when my parents went. I could go and talk to him at any hour of the day or night. He'd always make time for me.' That sounded genuine and heartfelt, but what followed was cold hard business, 'And the parish council has lost a councillor. Do you have a replacement yet?'

'Yes, awful business.' George shook his grey mane. 'I hear through the grapevine that a new vicar has been appointed and will be starting at St John's before Christmas. I don't know who he is, but he'll join the parish council automatically – as of right. All vicars do.'

'As they should,' Maggie agreed. 'It's their parish. They should have a say in how it's run. And they have the integrity to run it in our best interests.'

'Quite,' George nodded, looking at Maggie questioningly. He was beginning to wonder where she was going with this conversation. He didn't have to wait long.

'Of course, you may not realise, but not all of your councillors are beyond reproach. In some cases – in one case in particular – I personally would have serious doubts about that person's true intentions ...'

'What? Who are you talking about?'

'Michelle Pike, I'm at pains to say.' And Maggie ventured into the full ins and outs of Ms Pike's suspected shady dealings with Cinnamon Rock and her alleged motive to kill Vicar Laurence. 'So, you see, we thought you had to be informed about such ... issues.'

'Such as?'

'Well, her conflict of interests for one. Has she declared it?'

'No.'

'She should have, don't you think?'

'Perhaps . . . Now that you mention it, it was irregular of Michelle to withhold information about her pecuniary interests prior to the vote, but . . .'

'But?'

'But that is a far cry from a motive to murder Laurence!'

'That's what I said,' Sam backed up George, unwisely.

Maggie groaned. On reflection, she should not have asked Samuel to assist her with this highly sensitive mission. 'Well, I disagree with your assessment. She'd vote for the new development to save herself a small fortune in building costs and Vicar Laurence was just about to ruin her scheme . . . He had evidence that the land belongs to the Church and if he produced it, the whole project would be at an end, including the extension to Golden Autumn—'

'Not exactly,' George attempted some clarification, but wasn't given a chance to elaborate.

'Yes, yes, yes! Didn't you hear? There was evidence – there *is* evidence, and the Church have already claimed No Man's Land back from Daryl Luntz. Successfully, may I add, because now Daryl Luntz is suing Lord Philip for compensation—'

'I know that,' George started again. 'But the Church has every intention of allowing the development to go ahead.'

Maggie stared at George, and then at Sam, in the vain hope that he would ride to her rescue and say something clever to contradict George. Sam was as gobsmacked as Maggie however, and as speechless.

That gave George a chance to finish his point. 'There's a provisional agreement between the Church and Cinnamon Rock. As it happens, Cinnamon Rock is still buying the land, all except the Folly and its immediate surroundings. They're going to upgrade and renovate the Folly so that Laurence's idea of housing Syrian child refugees can go ahead – sort of Laurence's legacy. He was very keen on it . . . The rest of the land is to be sold to Cinnamon Rock for the new development, provided, of course, that the land is rezoned for residential use and there are no other legal impediments.'

'So they're still building on No Man's Land?'

'An extraordinary parish council meeting is called for September the third. It'll be open to the public, just like the first one. So, in essence, the whole consultation process hasn't been halted by Laurence's death.'

'But three weeks ago it was a different story altogether! The person who killed him wouldn't have known that this would happen,' Maggie persisted. She was a stubborn old girl. 'Michelle Pike is still a suspect!'

'I'll bring her potential conflict of interest to the attention of the Council. Maybe I'll start by having a quiet word with her on the side before I do that. She may just excuse herself.'

'But what if she killed Laurence – not to mention Cherie's mother?'

George blinked at her without comprehension. Sam stepped in before Maggie could throw more libellous allegations at a powerful businesswoman who wouldn't take kindly to them.

'We can't make wanton accusations, Maggie. Neither can George. He said he'd raise the question of Michelle's eligibility to vote on the new development, but it's not his role to conduct criminal inquiries—'

'Someone has to, and I guess it will have to be me.' Maggie compressed her lips and said not another word on the matter.

Sam felt obliged to apologise to George for putting him in an awkward position and asked him quietly, out of Maggie's earshot, if he could forget her ravings about Ms Pike. George promised not to make anything of it.

They left soon after. Marching along Bog Lane with the view of the hill to their right in all its White Mule glory, Maggie sniffed. 'It'll be the end of an era when they build over that hill and the marshes . . .'

'Who said we won't fight them?' Sam assured her. A spark of mischief twinkled in his eye and he added, putting on Churchill's voice with an amazing exactitude, 'We shall fight them in the Rook's Nest, we shall fight them at the White Mule and in Sexton's Wood, we shall fight them in the market square, we shall never surrender!'

'We shall?'

'Why not? I'll look into it as soon as I have sorted out that business with Laura Price.'

She beamed. 'And while you're after Laura Price, I'll sort out Michelle Pike.'

Chapter Fifteen

Sam had driven to London, to his and Alice's home in Richmond. He parked in Lions Gate Gardens, a few houses away, and strode towards his old address. Another family lived there now. They too had two children, a boy and a girl. Sam could easily imagine them playing in the small garden at the back. Maybe the tree house he had built for Abi and Campbell was still there. Maybe the kids who lived there now had just climbed the rope ladder to the trapdoor, to hide inside and sit out the rain.

This was something Sam preferred to do on his own. The memories of his beloved Alice, his pain and his guilt, were all too personal to share with anyone, even Maggie. Not for one second did he begrudge her abandoning Alice's cause to embark on her solo undercover operation against Michelle Pike. In a way, he was glad that Maggie had left him to deal with this alone.

Sam had not brought his umbrella with him. He stood in the drizzle, which quickly transformed into a downpour. The puddles on the pavement were as bad today as they had been before he left. It was due to the large tree roots burrowing and twisting underground and pushing some of the paving stones out of place. Annie and Desmond at number sixty-one had once floated the idea of having the trees culled, 'to sort out the pavements, unblock the gutters, and let some sunlight through.' They had met with fierce opposition from just about every resident in the street, with Alice leading the rebellion. They would rather break their ankles tripping over the uneven paving than lose the trees. The trees remained, well-rooted and immovable, and somewhat bigger and denser.

Sam was soaked to the bone even though he had taken shelter under the thick foliage of the elm in front of his old family home. When they had bought it nearly thirty years ago, Sam and Alice had made a pact to live there until they were both dead, to bring up their kids, retire, and look after their grandchildren there. They had never contemplated one of them dying way before their time and leaving the other with only ghosts and memories. Sam could not keep his end of the bargain – he could not stay there without Alice.

He was glad of the rain. He didn't have to keep wiping his tears. He sheltered under the tree until the sky began to clear. A faint patch of pale blue broke through the clouds in the west and began to sail towards him. He stepped out into a puddle, and laughed heartily under his breath. His trainers took in water and squelched all the way to his car. He got in, started the engine, and drove off.

He was going to take the exact route Alice had taken on the day she died. It would be his own reconstruction of events – painful, no doubt, but hopefully it would reveal something new and enlightening.

It was raining again when he entered the single-carriage road that ran parallel to the train line between Gladestoke and South Castle stations. It had been raining the day Alice died. Her body had been found seven miles from South Castle, on a sharp bend of the railway track where the line joined, like a river tributary, the other tracks going to the main station of Gladestoke.

Sam parked in the same wide lay-by where Alice's car had been found with its driver's door open and the key left in the ignition. Unlike Alice, Sam did lock the door and slipped the keys into his pocket.

From the lay-by it was a short but tedious walk through thick blackberry bushes to the tracks. He struggled to push through the brambles and got viciously scratched by the dense thorny branches. There was no clear path through that wild tangle. On the other side of it, wiping blood from his cheeks, he wondered how Alice had

106

managed to negotiate it unscathed. And why? Why would she have chosen this route? There was no clear pathway leading to the railway tracks. He could not even see them from the lay-by. Neither were they visible from the road. How did Alice know they were there? She was not familiar with this area. Had she been sitting in her car, feeling defeated and crying before she heard a passing train and learned about the proximity of the tracks that way? Was that when she had got the idea . . . Was that a plausible explanation?

Of course, it wasn't.

By now Sam knew that that explanation couldn't be plausible – it was a total non-starter – because Alice had not killed herself. It wasn't easy to shake off those old doubts that had been churning over in his head over the last few years, rehashing Alice's motives, guessing, speculating, and agonising over it – all of that on the false premise that she had taken her own life. It had to stop. Alice did not kill herself! But she must have come here – her car had been found in the lay-by. She had not made it to South Castle. Why? What had stopped her?

He climbed the bank and stood on a sleeper between the two smooth metal rails, facing the way from which the freight train would have come – the same way Alice would have been facing before she was hit. The buffeting wind brought a lash of rain and a few dead leaves with it. One of them, brown and slimy, stuck to his face. He peeled it off and released it. It didn't go far. It drifted and settled on his shoe. Sam swallowed the lump that had come to his throat, somewhere from inside his ribcage.

He had never been to this place before. He hadn't had the strength to face it. Now, as he stood here, it hit him with its remoteness, loneliness and a sense of inevitability. It felt like a plughole to nowhere.

Alice would not have done it – had not done it. He was certain of it. She had been pushed under that train, but why here?

He turned to look the other way – towards the branching of railway tracks that splintered in several directions. There was a pole by an overhead bridge with a set of lights and triangular signs used for semaphoring the railway traffic. Why hadn't the lights turned red and stopped that freight train in its tracks, thwarting Alice's killer in her plans? Maybe this particular location was random. Maybe Alice and Laura Price had met at South Castle station and come here together in Alice's car.

But why here?

In the distance he saw an approaching train, moving so fast that within seconds it had doubled in size. Sam jumped off the tracks. The powerful draught created by the carriages screaming over the bend of the tracks threw him back. He fell and was caught by the prickly tangle of brambles. Cursing, he disentangled himself and returned to his car. He was heading for South Castle station. Alice might have gone there too.

'Can I help you, sir? If you're wanting a train, there aren't any until tomorrow morning, I'm afraid.' A man approached him on the platform. He was dressed in a white work shirt, black trousers, and a cap with the Great Western railway logo. He had a radiophone attached to his belt and a set of keys. He looked and acted officious.

'No, I'm not waiting for a train. I'm travelling by car.' Sam smiled at the man and extended his hand to him. 'My name is Sam Dee.'

Left with little choice, the man shook his hand. 'Andrew Wilkins, station manager. So, what *are* you doing here?'

'I'm following in my late wife's footsteps, so to speak. Trying to work out what happened to her. Her name was Alice—'

'Alice Dee? The woman that killed herself four years ago? Threw herself under a train at the Bridge Pass junction?'

'Er, yes, that'd be her – my wife.'

'That was tragic. I'm sorry for your loss.' Andrew Wilkins's tone had softened. He was nowhere near as officious and suspicious as he had been a minute earlier.

'Thank you. It's been a while. It's taken me this long to come to this place.'

'You haven't found it. This isn't where she died. The Bridge Pass junction is a few miles east. Just follow the—'

108

'Oh, I've been there already. That's where I've come from. No, I want to . . .' Sam paused. He hesitated about how to explain himself without sounding overdramatic or deranged. 'I am investigating her death. I know the police did that already, but you see, they may have missed a few clues . . . For example, I don't think they knew, at the time, that Alice was heading for this station – South Castle. She was meeting someone here.'

'Was she?' Andrew Wilkins appeared intrigued. 'And did she make it here? Did they meet?'

'That's what I want to find out.'

'Is that gonna make some difference to . . . you know . . . to how she died? The Coroner's finding was suicide. I remember. It was all over the papers. Are you hoping to have that overturned?'

'Maybe.'

'To be honest with you, Mr Dee, as far as I can remember the police did a damn good job investigating it four years ago. No stone unturned, as they say.'

'What makes you say that?'

'Oh, they were all over the place. They searched every square foot between here and Gladestoke. They came and got volunteers to comb the area around Bridge Pass, and all that. The line was shut down for a week. More than a week. Ten days, I think it was . . . If they were to find anything, they would've found it then. You may be wasting your time, Mr Dee. But I do understand – it must be hard on you . . .'

'Yes, it's been hard to face up to it. It took me a while. But I've been looking into it with a fresh eye, and . . . And it bothers me.'

'What does?'

'The fact that Alice was coming to this station and no one checked it out. Well, the truth is, the police didn't know this at the time, so they couldn't have followed this lead—'

'But they did!' Mr Wilkins was pleased to give Sam this reassurance. 'They did come to investigate. A detective constable, at that, came asking if we had any CCTV footage from inside the station and of the platform and that. She wasn't in luck though – some local hooligans had sprayed over the cameras, as it turned out, when we went to view the recordings. We found nothing. Mindless vandalism – we have our share of it in South Castle. The youth – they've got nothing to occupy themselves with. Boredom and no opportunities in this backwater.' He sighed. 'But yes, they did come, asking questions.'

Sam felt light-headed with anticipation. 'You said it was a *she*. The police detective. Do you remember her name?'

Andrew Wilkins scratched his head. 'Hmmm . . . let me think . . . She didn't have much to say to me, mind. It was my predecessor, Stan Pollock. He was the stationmaster then. I was Assistant Stationmaster, then got promoted when he . . . went. Anyway, back to the policewoman, Mr Pollock showed her around, and they checked if anything had been caught on camera, and that's when we became aware of the vandalism . . . We were hoping, of course, we could get their faces – the vandals, I mean – before they'd done the deed. But there was nothing – the bastards had been very careful, worn balaclavas and done the damage in the night, in poor light. And they had painted over both cameras, at each end of the platform. The detective lady said nothing could be done, in fairness, to track them down. I've got her name on the tip of my tongue . . .'

'Could it be Price? DC Laura Price?'

'Right you are!' Wilkins beamed, pleased as Punch. 'That was the name – DC Price! I remember her now, like it was yesterday! Tall and powerfully built for a woman. Could give any bloke a run for his money, she could!'

110

Chapter Sixteen

Wilkins — Andrew, as he insisted on being called — invited Sam to his office at the back of the station for a cuppa. The rain had intensified by then. The roof over the platform offered no protection against the raging wind. Andrew was at the start of his eight-hour shift. He was alone. There were no other staff due to cutbacks. The ticket booth was no longer manned, 'what with all those self-service machines taking over, and that.'

Andrew made 'proper tea, from the pot, with real milk from the fridge,' as opposed to the 'polyester piss from the vending machine,' which could be found in the waiting room. He was a talkative chap, happy to bend over backwards for you as he put it himself. He had given Sam the full account of his working life, including a timeline as well as detailed cross-references to his personal life, including the missus and their three adorable children, raging in age from fourteen to four in descending order.

Sam let most of it go over his head. His mind was on DC Price. How diligent she had been in covering her tracks! How thorough! There wasn't a shred of doubt in his mind that it was Laura Price, not some local hoodlums, who had vandalised the two cameras in preparation for what was to come. There would be no recordings, no evidence of her meeting with Alice, and of her crime.

'Did DC Price inquire about anything other than the cameras?' Sam asked Andrew Wilkins. There could be more clues to be found by examining Price's clean-up operation.

'I couldn't tell you that. She came asking about the CCTV

footage and I took her to Stan. They chatted for quite some time. First, he showed her what footage we had up to the moment when the cameras had been sprayed, but I don't know what they talked about when they went to his office. You see, after I helped Stan inspect the cameras – I held the stepladder for him – I went back to my duties, so I don't know what the conversation was about from then on.'

'Where is Stan? I think it'd be useful to have a word with him.'

'Stan Pollock! Didn't I say? You can't talk to him, I'm afraid, on account of him being dead. When he topped himself, I got the promotion to Stationmaster. Come to think, hardly a year had gone by since your ... your wife's suicide, when Stan hanged himself. They found him swinging from the bridge and that, over the river, in the park. He had it coming – it wasn't a big surprise ... Gambler, he was. Big stakes – big wins and even bigger losses. He put Marion through hell with his antics. Marion, that's his missus. She'd stuck with him through thick and thin ... They had come this close to losing their house a good few times.' Andrew illustrated his point by drawing his index fingers within an inch of each other. 'Then, he had that big win – he bought himself a brand new Audi, in cash. And just months later he was swinging from the bridge. Rumour had it that he'd suffered another loss and didn't know how to break it to Marion. You hear so much these days about the scourge of the gambling addiction. It's a disease, they say, like drugs. Yeah ...' Andrew Wilkins gave a pensive nod.

'I see.' Sam was disappointed, but not prepared to give up. 'I wonder, perhaps I could talk to his widow. Marion Pollock, did you say?'

'Marion, yes ... But what would Marion have to tell you? What does she know about anything? She was a stay-at-home mum, now she lives off her widow's pension. Sold the Audi, of course. What good was it for her? She doesn't drive, but she can travel free by train ...'

'I don't know. Maybe there's something Stan told her?'

'Oh well, if you insist. She's nice enough – she will talk to you . . . I can point you in the direction of her bungalow. You can see it from the car park.'

They left Andrew's cosy office at the station and emerged into an open car park. It wasn't big, thirty or forty parking spaces and one parking meter. Sheltering them ineffectively against the rain and wind with a large umbrella, Andrew guided Sam to a narrow footpath hidden behind a stone wall. From there, he pointed towards a tiled roof, 'That'd be Stan's bungalow. You can follow this path to get there.'

Sam thanked him for all his help.

The wind tried to snatch the umbrella from Andrew's hand, and almost succeeded. Andrew folded it. 'It's no use in this weather,' he shrugged and hunched instantly under the onslaught of heavy rain. 'Well, good luck with your investigation, Sam.'

As Sam watched him jog back to the station, his eye was caught by a camera mounted on the wall, just above the sign which said *SOUTH CASTLE*. The camera was monitoring the car park. Sam set off after Andrew.

'Andrew, wait! One more thing!' He caught up with him. He was out of breath. 'That CCTV camera over there,' he pointed, panting. 'Was it there four years ago?'

Andrew looked up and nodded. 'Yes, it was.'

'Had it also been vandalised, like the ones on the platform?'

Andrew scowled, thinking. At last he said, 'No, I don't think so. We didn't get this one replaced so it can't have been sprayed like the others.'

'Did DC Price check it too when she—'

'Nah, she was just interested in the CCTV on the platforms. She never said anything about the car park and that so we didn't mention it, either.'

'So, might you still have the footage from four years ago from that camera?' Sam was buzzing with excitement. His fingertips were tingling. He was on to something at long last.

'That's possible, yes. But you'd have to ask the IT people at HQ in Gladestoke. If anyone, they'd store old footage from four years back – if those new GDPR rules allow it, that is. They do my head in, those privacy laws, and such.' Andrew screwed his face with dismay.

Sam was filled with – more than that – he was *bursting* with optimism. Just like Maggie had predicted, Laura Price may have made another mistake. She had missed the car park camera. It could be nothing, but if Alice had made it to South Castle station to meet with Laura, she would have parked here, in this car park. The CCTV footage, if still in existence, could prove it. Sam would be able to see Alice park the car, walk into the station, come out again, get into her car, and drive away. He would be able to establish the mood she was in. Her body language, her pace, her general demeanour could shed some light on that. Perhaps she would be walking arm in arm with Laura Price, which would conclusively place the two of them together on the day of her death! This could be the breakthrough he had been searching for.

He ran in the pouring rain towards Stan Pollock's bungalow. He was on a roll. Fingers crossed, Marion Pollock would harbour a few more precious nuggets of information that she would be willing to share with him.

The front garden was well maintained and featured petunias in clay pots lined up alongside the picket fence. Several terracotta frog and gnome ornaments sat around a small pond. The rain bombarded the surface of the pond, causing it to bubble like a boiling pot.

Sam found a doorbell. He rang it, and waited.

Nobody came to answer the door so he knocked, just in case the bell was broken. But still, nobody answered. It looked like Marion Pollock wasn't home. She may have popped out briefly. Sam decided to wait for a few minutes. After half an hour, the rain was showing no signs of relenting and Marion was nowhere in sight. The nearest dwelling was some two or three hundred yards down the road, but it was shrouded in darkness. Nobody was home there either.

Sam glanced at his phone to check the time. It was eight twenty.

He had over an hour's drive home on a dark, wet, and windy night. Marion could be away on a holiday, or visiting relatives in a different town. There was no point waiting without being sure of her return. He reluctantly resolved to head for Bishops Well. In any event, he would be back. A trip to Gladestoke was on the cards to view the car park CCTV footage. After that, he would swerve by South Castle and try Marion Pollock again. It was just a matter of time and patience before he had all the pieces of the puzzle put together to form the full picture.

Chapter Seventeen

On initial assessment, my undercover operation had the promise of being a walk in the park. The surroundings were idyllic. The Golden Autumn Retreat was wrapped in beautiful grounds with manicured lawns, mature trees, and smooth footpaths suitable for wheelchair and Zimmer-frame traffic. The park was dotted with box hedges and seasonal flowerbeds. There was a centrepiece fountain featuring a large fish spewing cascades of water. Around it stood wooden benches arranged in a sociable circle. Birds were tweeting overhead to complete the picture perfect.

The main building used to be a stately home in its illustrious past and, though converted to cater for the needs of the elderly and the frail, it had retained all of its Grade II-listed characteristic fixtures and fittings. The unsightly extension works were being conducted at the back of the building, although on my arrival no works or workers were in evidence. The building site was secured with bright orange net fencing – an eyesore in this calm and tranquil environment.

I entered the reception area. It was designed to please and put your mind at ease: fresh flowers, pastel-coloured full-length curtains, drawn back to allow maximum light, an inviting couch and matching armchairs, a coffee machine discreetly tucked away in the corner, and a table with the latest edition of *Hello!* magazine. If you had any doubts about installing your dearest elderly relative in this establishment before walking away, they would be instantly dispelled by this apparent oasis of tranquillity. You would feel assured that your loved one was in good hands.

I was greeted by a smiling lady who was seated behind a computer. I smiled my widest smile back in return.

'Hello there! I'm looking for some casual work and I understand you have a vacancy?' She stopped smiling, asked me to wait, and left. I waited patiently and with quiet confidence. It is common knowledge that residential homes struggle to attract and retain staff. I was right. Within minutes a portly woman with an air of authority about her came out to see me. She was in her fifties and in a suit two sizes too small for her. I felt sorry for her bust, which was crying out for air and bursting from the straightjacket of her suit. As she trotted towards me, she was busily wiggling her bottom and pulling down her tight skirt which had hiked its way up to her upper thighs and refused to come down.

She extended her hand to me, 'Mrs Robson.'

'Miss Kaye,' I reciprocated, and offered her my brightest smile.

'You're looking for a position?'

'Yes, I'm not afraid of hard work and I'm desperate for money, as it happens.'

'Great!' Mrs Robson enthused, seemingly delighted by the declaration of my fiscal embarrassment. 'Do you have any experience in care work?'

'No, not professionally, though I do have a caring nature and I do work hard when pressed.'

'When can you start?'

'Now. I'm ready and willing – I can begin right away.'

I think she liked me and my work ethos, for at last she smiled and asked me to follow her to the office. There, she took my personal and bank details, and requested contact numbers for two referees. I thought of Samuel and Vera. Neither of them had direct links with Golden Autumn. She made me complete forms, grant all manner of consents, and more or less sign away my soul.

'We'll have to wait for your DBS clearance before you can work

117

directly with clients. That'll take a few weeks . . . I'll put you in for First Aid training. Until then, you will take on cleaning duties.'

I sincerely hoped I wouldn't be around that long, especially as I had my job at Bishops Ace Academy starting again very soon. I imagined clearing plugholes blocked with hair and gunge, and fishing dirty underwear out from under the residents' beds, and swallowed hard. The things I was prepared to do in the line of duty! It took strength of character and sheer determination to get down on my knees and go for it. Luckily, I had both in bucketfuls.

Mrs Robson issued me with a uniform which could under no circumstances be described as flattering. I put it on and morphed into an old Tesco plastic bag, with white and blue stripes: a misshapen old bag overloaded with groceries. I had to calm my nerves by reminding myself that nobody I knew would ever see me like this.

'Perfect!' Mrs Robson was happy with how I looked in my Tesco bag. 'Let's get your tools.' She showed me to the cleaners' cupboard, where I was confronted with a wanton abundance of liquids, powders and detergents, cloths, mops, rubber gloves, and utensils which looked like tools of torture to an untrained eye. I stared in horror.

'Am I going to need a saw and a hammer?' I enquired timidly, ready to turn tail and run.

'Oh no, don't be silly, Miss Kaye. The cleaners share the storage room with our caretaker. I must warn you that he's very particular about his tools. You'll be well advised not to put your hands on them.'

'I wouldn't dream of touching his tools,' I assured her.

Armed with a mop, bucket, and a bottle of antibacterial agent, I followed Mrs Robson upstairs. She instructed me to start with the bathrooms and finish the day on the high note of vacuuming. I could do that, no problem.

I had gone through the motions of scrubbing and polishing the second floor in the record time of two hours, twenty minutes. It was eleven o'clock when I bundled my cleaning apparatus into the lift and pressed the button for the first floor. I had established earlier when interviewing Cherie that her mother had been staying on the first floor, room thirty-one. That would be my starting point. My intention was to carry out an inspection in situ and hopefully to talk to a few residents who remembered Gertrude Hornby or who could enlighten me on the death rates at Golden Autumn. I was also planning to search the premises for the packing tape. Finally, and that task depended on a propitious chance, I wanted to look into their records. For that, I had to carry out a full and thorough reconnaissance involving office hours, staff rotas, and the whereabouts of archives and computer passwords. This could entail a few more days of cleaning the toilets and pulling hair out of plugholes. But it had to be done.

I crept straight to room number thirty-one, and knocked on the door. A firm and commanding female voice answered me, 'Enter!'

I did and found myself in the company of a presence larger than life in more ways than one. The occupant in question was wider than she was tall, sported several layers of chin, droopy cheeks, and doleful eyes underscored with bags of loose skin. She reminded me of an overweight bloodhound.

'May I clean your bathroom?'

'You're new here.' She didn't grant her permission so I remained standing in the doorway, my mop at the ready.

'Yes – I just started! I'm Maggie.'

'I'm Mrs Reznick White. Hello, Maggie ...'

'Nice to meet you.'

'Let's see how long you'll last.' She gave a small humph and returned to her task at hand. She appeared busy with knitting.

'What are you knitting, Mrs Reznick White?'

She peered at me with a critically appraising eye. 'Can't you see that I am not knitting. I am unravelling.'

'Did it go wrong?'

'No, dear. I made a baby jumper, but I've no babies to give it to, and I don't have any wool left. I'm unravelling it so that I can make it again. That's how it goes in this place.'

'Ah!'

'Ah, indeed.'

'How long have you been staying in this room?'

'Three torturously long years, my dear. I wouldn't wish it on my worst enemy.'

'My friend's mother had this room before you – Gertrude Hornby. You may've heard of her. She died here—'

'That doesn't surprise me in the least, my dear,' she interrupted me. 'We all come here to die, and sooner or later we do.'

I didn't know what to say to that. I was collecting my wits when a feeble voice behind me demanded my immediate attention.

'I've been ringing the bell. I can't wait any longer. I need to go. You'll do.' I felt someone pull the sleeve of my Tesco bag. I turned around to find a tiny little lady leaning on her walking stick and looking at me with a mixture of plea and panic in her eyes. 'I can't wait, I said . . .'

I wasn't supposed to deal directly with the residents' pressing needs due to my not being CRB cleared, but I gathered there was no time to explain that to the desperate little lady and to call for backup. I dropped my mop and followed her to her room. There, by the window, I encountered a gentleman of indeterminate age, with a small moustache, wearing an RAF uniform, old-fashioned, WWII-style. I wondered, but only briefly, why he wouldn't help his, well, his mother, was my best guess. She couldn't be his mother, I realised. He was just a ghost. Probably her sweetheart, or husband. Maybe he had been killed in the war, or perhaps he died several decades later in his own bed but liked his war hero image so much that he chose to revert to it in the afterlife. He was hanging about, biding his time on earth until she joined him. It made perfect sense.

'What are you staring at? I don't want to pee myself.'

I assisted the lady to her bathroom.

'Just give me an arm to hold on to, and lower me – slowly, mind,' she instructed me.

I was successful with depositing her upon the toilet seat without major incidents. I left her there to do whichever number nature called her to do. I heard her flush the loo and call me to come and fetch her.

At last, we were back in her room, she in her rocking chair, me on a stool.

'I'm Maggie,' I said, even though we were already on quite intimate terms considering our joint toilet excursion.

'Mrs Fallon. Thank you.' She looked both relieved and apologetic. She had messy, wispy hair, most of which had fallen out of her thin bun. Her face was heart-shaped and her eyes very pale and interminably baffled.

'Don't mention it!' I meant it. I didn't want Mrs Robson to find out I had been handling her clients.

'You were talking about Gertrude,' she changed the subject suddenly. 'I heard you.'

'Yes, I was. Her daughter, Cherie, is a friend of mine.' I perked up. At least I'd be rewarded for my patience. 'She sadly passed away, here as it happens, at Golden Autumn.'

'The room next door, that's where she died, poor Gertrude. Well before her time.' Mrs Fallon confirmed.

'Do you remember when that happened?'

'How could I forget! It wasn't natural, I tell you, it wasn't . . .' She twisted her face. Her pale eyes bulged.

'Do you mean to say that Gertrude was killed? Did you see anyone?'

'Oh, I did! There were spacemen everywhere, like the ones who went to the Moon,' she whispered. 'Cherie ran away in tears. She left Gertrude to the wolves!'

'Wolves?'

'They howl in the night. I can hear them.'

It occurred to me that maybe Mrs Fallon wasn't in full possession of her faculties. She was wearing a hearing aid, but it could be malfunctioning. Her eyes were becoming more and more distant, glazed over with something dreamy and unreal.

'Did you see Michelle Pike? She owns this place. Did she come that day to see Gertrude? You'd have seen her if she had.'

121

'Only at night.'

'She came at night? Mrs Pike?'

'The wolves. And not every night, mind.'

Were the wolves some kind of veiled metaphor? I was puzzled. She seemed to be drifting away from me, into an eerie world of wild beasts and full moons. I had to bring her back down to earth.

'How long have you been here, Mrs Fallon? Have you seen other residents die, like Gertrude – in suspicious circumstances? Do people get killed here?'

'Do they?' She was blinking at me nervously.

'Yes! I mean, Gertrude was smothered in her bed.'

'I knew that! I knew! Oh, dear Lord!'

'Do you think that there may be an angel of death killing off the residents? Easing their way into the afterlife?'

'I don't want to die!' Mrs Fallon screeched and pulled her cardigan sleeves over her hands. She pressed them to her lips. 'Don't let them kill me!'

'No one's going to kill you,' I tried to calm her down. 'I'm just interested in your neighbour, Gertrude—'

'I don't want to die!'

'You don't have to. Take your time.' I was bumbling in the dark by now.

'I want to live! Go away! Go away!' She kept screaming.

I had no means of containing her. The ghost of her sweetheart, or husband, glared at me. His lips formed into an oval and though I couldn't hear him, I was in no doubt that he too was telling me to GO. I fled.

Chapter Eighteen

Shaken by Mrs Fallon's tantrum, I put my head down and redoubled my cleaning efforts. I tried to avoid any more human – or ghost – contact that day. There was a bitter taste of despondency in my mouth. I knew exactly how Cherie must have felt when her mother had accused her of stealing.

I had to reconcile myself with the prospect of not getting much sense out of the residents of Golden Autumn Retreat. I would have to sieve fact from fiction, sometimes alarmingly outlandish fiction and sometimes the sort of fiction that could easily be mistaken for the truth.

Where did the wolves come from, for example?

Was something untoward going on at this place under the cover of night?

Was it related to Gertrude Hornby's death?

What was the overarching motive linking her death to the murder of Vicar Laurence?

I had to know. I had come here to find out and I wasn't leaving until I did.

My plan was simple but brilliant. I carried on with my duties until four thirty p.m., with an hour's break for lunch, the lunch being on the establishment. It was one of the unexpected perks of the job. I was offered fish pie and an apple, followed by a pear and cherry compote for pudding. I enjoyed that tremendously. My opinion of Golden Retreat sky-rocketed for the whole of one hour. I didn't have a chance to speak to the kitchen staff as they were run off their feet serving lunch and bitching bitterly about such and such resident who complained about the quality, and the quantity, of the fish in the fish pie.

Having eaten, I departed and sauntered outside. I strolled around the grounds. There was still no sign of builders from Cinnamon Rock, I was intrigued to discover. I was also pleased to find an entrance into the premises from the building site at the rear of the property. Judging by the still present sign above the doorframe, it used to be a Fire Exit. It appeared that the door had been temporarily taken off its hinges and put away safely, pending the refurbishments. I stored that information at the back of my mind. It would facilitate the implementation of my brilliant plan later.

I was exhausted by my reconnaissance. After a morning of hard labour and with my tummy full and weighing me down, I lay on the lawn. I found a secluded spot behind a box hedge which would serve as a shield from the wind building from the north-west. I folded my hands behind my head and promptly fell asleep.

What woke me up was a barrage of rain. I cowered under the relentless bombardment. The raindrops were heavy, large and bullet-like. I gathered myself up from the soaked ground, thanking the Lord for my plasticky Tesco bag uniform which was keeping me dry. I leapt to my feet and sprinted indoors, using the back entrance. Once back inside, I was shocked to discover that I had slept for two solid hours – it was a quarter past three! I had to create the impression that I had been hard at work all that time. I dried my hair under the hand dryer in the staff toilet and gave it a brush with my fingers. It bounced back into place and I looked just like my old self. I located my cleaning tools outside the cafeteria, grabbed the mop in one hand and the bucket in the other, and thus armed rattled down the stairs to the reception hall.

'I'm done with all the bathrooms,' I told the lady at the reception desk. It wasn't a lie – I was done with them, which wasn't the same as saying that I had done them all. 'I need to get the hoover out.'

'It's in the cleaners' cupboard.'

'I remember it being locked. I don't have the key.'

'Neither do I. I've nothing to do with the cleaning staff.' Unlike her original smiley self, the little madam now spoke with contempt. 'Speak to Mrs Robson.'

I knocked on the office door and was called in. Mrs Robson had by then eased herself out of the constriction of her jacket. Her ample bosom appeared to thrive on fresh air – it looked even bigger and wobblier than before and it was making the frills of her blouse ripple.

'How are you getting on, Miss Kaye?'

'I'm sailing through it,' I enthused. 'I'm done with the cleaning. I think I'm supposed to do the vacuuming now.'

'I like your spirit. Let's put away the bucket and get the hoover out.' She picked up a key from her desk drawer and handed it to me. 'This is the master key. You can open just about every door with it. Do you remember how to find the cleaners' cupboard?'

I nodded.

'Good. The vacuum cleaner is in there. When you're finished, bring the key back.'

I was hoovering with a song in my heart. I had the key to this whole place. My plan was taking shape even faster than I could contrive it. I took special care hoovering under the reception desk in the hope of uncovering the computer password. The long-nailed, long-lashed receptionist rolled reluctantly in her chair to give me access to every nook and cranny around her feet. By the time I finished, her computer went to sleep. I held my breath and watched her wake it, committing to memory her every key stroke.

1-2-3-4

Her long nails tapped in her unimaginative password. I had it!

With the reception area now spotless, I was forced to move on to the lounge next door. I could not blow my cover – I had to keep up appearances. I encountered a couple of elderly gentlemen in the lounge. They were having a heated discussion about some political matter. I say *heated* because their voices were raised, but that could also mean that they had to speak up because of the hearing deficiencies typical of their age. My suspicions were confirmed when I plugged in the hoover. It was one of those rather loud models which tend to swallow all the sounds in their vicinity. I for one couldn't hear myself think, but the two gentlemen continued talking – over the vacuum cleaner's noise and over each other.

When I finished the room and switched off the machine, I heard Mrs Robson say from the reception, 'Goodbye, Natalie. See you tomorrow!'

'Bye, Fiona! Have a lovely evening!'

Mrs Robson had left the building. I retained possession of the master key. I was in business!

A respectable quarter of an hour later, which was at four forty-five (time had flown so fast that I managed to clock up some overtime on my first day!), I rolled the vacuum cleaner into the cleaners' cupboard and took off the dreadful Tesco bag. I slipped the master key into my pocket and waltzed out of the building, bidding the obnoxious Natalie a friendly cheerio. Thereafter, I crept to the back of the building, negotiated my way amongst the rubble left by the absent builders, and re-admitted myself on to the premises through the missing back door.

I had a room lined up for myself on the second floor. When cleaning, I had found that room uninhabited: it was empty, free of any memorabilia of the sort that most residents there seemed to find indispensable, and the bed was stripped. I threw myself on the bare mattress and awaited the arrival of darkness.

At ten thirty the whole place became virtually dead: lights went off and silence descended, interrupted only by occasional snoring emitting from some of the rooms. I rose from the bed and stretched my aching bones (a decent day of physical exertion and I felt like I had run a marathon). I part-limped, part-tiptoed downstairs. Despite my debilitating weariness, I chose not to use the lift – even though a night curfew seemed to be in place, there was bound to be a skeleton staff operating on the premises. A night watchman. A carer or two, maybe a duty nurse. I didn't want to alert them to my presence.

The reception hall was lit dimly with just enough light not to stumble over the furniture. That was serendipitous for me as I didn't know the layout and would have likely bumped into things, tripped and hurt myself while on my mission. I stole into the corridor behind the reception desk. The second door was Mrs Robson's office.

I tried the master key and it worked.

I was in.

I shut the door behind me and switched on the lights. I sat at the desk and pressed the power button on the computer. It came on, displayed a *Welcome Fiona!* message and straight away demanded a password. I smirked under my breath and keyed in *1-2-3-4*.

Password incorrect.

Try again?

Hint: favourite colour

I thought back to Mrs Robson and the colour of her straitjacket. It was bluish-green.

I typed: *blue.*

Password incorrect.

You have two more attempts. Try again?

'Ahhh, all right, you evil thing,' I hissed at it. 'Let's have a gamble. What do you say to *green?*'

I tapped g-r-e-e-n.

Password incorrect.

You have one attempt left.

Try again?

'No,' I told the treacherous bastard. I was wary of its reaction if I got it wrong. Flashing lights and wailing sirens could kick in and a great big cage could fall on me from the ceiling to entrap me. I tore myself away from the useless, uncooperative machine.

I tried the filing cabinet on the wall under the window. Locked. The master key wouldn't fit into the hole. I embarked on a search for the key to the cabinet. I wouldn't be easily deterred by a blinking lock. That cabinet could harbour the most damning records – possibly evidence of unusually high death rates at Golden

Autumn, a copy of a compromising contract with Cinnamon Rock, and God knows what else.

I remembered Mrs Robson taking the master key from her desk drawer – the top one. I pulled the drawer and it opened: just like that: no keys, no passwords. I fumbled at the back of the mess, feeling for anything metallic and shaped like a key.

My jaw dropped.

Brown packing tape was staring me in the face.

I picked it up. It was nearly all gone.

The door flew open.

I dropped the tape into the drawer.

'Maggie?'

'Bloody hell!' I exhaled, relieved. 'You gave me a fright.' It was Megan Murphy.

Megan didn't appear as relieved as I was. Her eyes narrowed. She remained rooted in the doorway.

'What are you doing here?' She managed to construct a question.

'I work here. Casually. I just got the job – Mrs Robson . . . She just needs to run a few checks, but yeah, I started today.' I pushed the drawer closed with my knee just in case Megan misunderstood and accused me of stealing. 'And you?' I smiled nonchalantly. 'What brings you here?'

'I'm on duty. I was offered a night shift. They're short-staffed. Nobody told me about you . . .'

'You know how it is – they forgot.' Quick on my feet, I executed a sharp turn in the direction of our little dialogue: 'So how's Ivo?'

She didn't take the bite. 'So, what exactly are you doing here?'

'Cleaning,' I nodded with vehemence to give more credence to my statement.

'In the middle of the night? Are you having me on, Maggie?' Megan came towards me and looked down on me with a critical and disbelieving eye. I don't mean *looked down* – Megan wouldn't – we are friends. She looked down because she is rather taller than

128

me, some five foot ten to my five foot three. I felt totally dwarfed. I think I might have blushed with guilt.

'OK, Megan, I don't want to lie to you.' I put my cards on the table, keeping only a couple up my sleeve. 'I was looking for something. For evidence . . . I don't have it yet and I don't want to make accusations without it.'

'Evidence? What kind of evidence?'

'Evidence of Michelle Pike's crime,' I spat it out.

'What did she do?'

'As I said, I don't want to speculate . . . Not right this minute. Oh dear, this is hard! I think there's something seriously wrong going on here, and it may lead me to the vicar's murderer.' I gulped and kicked myself for saying that.

'Wow, that is serious . . . And you think it's Mrs Pike – she's got something to do with that? Why don't we call Vernon?'

'Who's Vernon?'

'The nightguard. He could help you find—'

'NO! No, no, no . . . I don't want anyone to know I was here. I don't know who may be involved . . . I'd like to continue working undercover. If you don't mind, Megan, just forget what I said. How about I pop over to yours on Thursday after work and explain everything. I may have something concrete by then.'

'OK. If you think it's better this way.' She scrutinised me warily, and added sternly, 'I hope I can trust you, Maggie.'

'Of course you can! If you can't trust me, who can you . . . I mean, great! Wonderful! I'd better be off. Thank you, Megan.' I pushed by her towards the exit. I didn't know what I was and wasn't supposed to be saying to her. I felt like a thief in the night, caught red-handed. Flustered.

'No problem. See you, Maggie.' Megan raised her hand in a restrained, uncertain gesture of goodbye. She was probably having second thoughts about letting me go. I could see it in her stifled smile.

'And please, don't tell Mrs Robson you found me here!'

'As if I would.'

★

129

The next morning, hoping for the best, I reported for duty at nine a.m. Mrs Robson was waiting for me. This time she was wearing a mauve jacket, and this one was only one-size under par. Maybe mauve was her *favourite color*, I speculated inwardly. Or maybe it wasn't, there was a whole rainbow of colours and only three attempts.

'Good morning, Mrs Robson!' I chirped.

'Follow me to my office, Miss Kaye.'

That sounded ominous. I shadowed her along the corridor, deflecting Nasty Natalie's smug smirk with a hostile glare of my own. What the heck, if I was going down, I'd go down in style! Still, I harboured some optimism. Perhaps Mrs Robson wanted to discuss the date of my First Aid training, or something equally harmless.

No, she didn't.

'I will have to let you go, Miss Kaye. Effective immediately.'

I must say I was disappointed in Megan. I'd had faith in her. She had promised. Clearly, my trust was misplaced. That aside, I still had some fight left in me. I wasn't going to go, pushed out by Megan-bloody-Murphy's betrayal. I decided to defend myself.

'I was lost. No! I was tired, I think I worked way too hard, trying to prove myself to you, Mrs Robson – I fell asleep, you see. I . . . I overslept and, and . . . and then I thought I would return your key before going home . . . I had no other intentions than to just return your—'

Mrs Robson jutted her chin forward and shot fireballs of her burning fury right at me, 'YOU! You waltz into Mrs Fallon's room without invitation. You put the fear of God into her! You threaten to kill her! I could have you arrested. But I won't. I don't need a scandal on my hands. I just want you to leave the premises – now!'

'Oh, so it was Mrs Fallon? I only helped her to the loo. And she asked!'

'Out!' She thrust her forefinger at the exit.

'Right!' I conceded defeat.

'And I'll have my master key back, please!'

'On your desk, Mrs Robson. That's what I mean – I came to return your key last night—'

'Whatever do you mean?'

'Nothing. Nothing. It's a different story. Please pass my apologies to poor Mrs Fallon.'

'I won't be mentioning your name to her. Ever. Good day to you, Miss Kaye!'

Chapter Nineteen

Sam and Maggie left their respective homes in synchronicity on the dot of eight a.m. and bumped into each other on their shared driveway. Maggie presented herself with rare professionalism, wearing a pale pink blouse, a black pencil skirt, and a pair of wedge-heeled pumps. Sam was impressed. And he was delighted to see her. He hadn't laid his eyes on her in a week – not since they had visited George Easterbrook together.

'Good morning, Maggie. You look smashing. What's the occasion?'

'The start of the new school year, I'm afraid. Bishops Ace asked me to supply for another two weeks, possibly a whole term. They weren't able to appoint a new English teacher over the summer holidays, after the previous one had bolted for the second time only a week into his phased return. So, here I come, Thomas Moore!'

'Who's Thomas Moore?'

'One of my students – a tortured soul, and a pain in the neck, but I think I can handle him. Harmless, really … Anyway, I must dash! I can't be late on my first day …'

'See you later!'

'Oh yes – that, of course … We have to get together later, Samuel. I've so much to tell you!'

'Me too. Are you coming to the parish council meeting tonight?'

'I wouldn't miss it for the world!'

She wiggled her fingers in a quaint gesture of cheerio and teetered away on her wedge heels, resembling a drunken heron. She was patently unaccustomed to heels as she tripped and yelped in pain twice by the time she had made it to the road. She bent down to massage her ankle and glanced back at Sam. There was a plea in that glance.

'Samuel, are you driving somewhere?' She must have spotted his car key dangling from his thumb. 'Would you be a darling and give me a lift to the school – if it's on your way? These damned new shoes will kill me if I have to walk all the way there.'

Sam was going to see Alec Scarfe. His house was on the other side of town and nowhere near Bishops Well Ace Academy. He had a feeling however that Maggie didn't want to know that.

'Yes, of course. Hop in.'

Maggie bundled into the passenger seat (she had either elbowed Alice out of the way, or the two of them didn't mind sharing the space next to him). Keeping an eye on the road – sporadically – Sam admired Maggie's shapely knees and a few inches of her lower thighs as she babbled on about her failed undercover operation at the Golden Autumn Retreat.

'That's twice in one month that you broke the law of trespass,' Sam was exasperated.

'At least I wasn't arrested this time.'

'Lucky you! If you were, it'd be on a much more grievous charge. Threatening to kill a helpless old lady, I never . . .'

'I didn't! Mrs Fallon totally misunderstood me! Anyway, that's not the point. I still haven't got the evidence I need . . . But my cover is blown, I'll have to get someone else to finish the job.' She peered at him imploringly.

'Not me, Maggie. Definitely not me.' Sam would not be swayed.

She looked disappointed but wouldn't admit it. 'I wasn't going to ask you, actually,' she snorted. 'I've a plan – I will get Megan to do the snooping for me.'

'You mean to say that as well as yourself you'll get Megan into trouble so she too can get the sack?'

'That's me, then!' she trilled, clearly disinclined to confirm or deny his accusation. 'I'll get out here. Thank for you the lift, Samuel.'

He watched with relish as she tottered on her wedges until she disappeared inside the school gates.

Alec was expecting Sam but he didn't know what it was that Sam wished to discuss with him. All that Sam had told him was that he had a favour to ask. When Alec found out what it was, he wouldn't be too pleased. What high-ranking police officer would be happy to re-open an investigation into another police officer on the say-so of a civilian with an axe to grind ... Nevertheless, Sam would give it a go.

Alec and Vanessa lived in a converted barn tucked away on the easternmost periphery of Bishops Well. Their driveway was off the pothole-infested country lane leading to Little Norton. It was an isolated spot. One could just about see the outline of Nortonview farmhouse – their closest neighbour.

Sam parked in a muddy courtyard – the recent downpours had turned the surface clay to sponge. He pulled the bell – a massive wrought iron thing which made a deafening noise. A couple of blackbirds took off from the roof. A large tabby cat materialised by his side and began rubbing itself against Sam's legs. As soon as the door was opened, the cat shot inside.

Vanessa beat Alec to the door. Sam could hear Alec's voice behind her telling her not to bother – he would get the door, he was expecting someone.

'Sam! Lovely to see you. Come in.' Vanessa was as sweet as honey. It was surprising she didn't have a permanent cloud of bees hovering over her head, or better yet, a halo, Sam reflected. She was the most virtuous, kind-hearted person he knew. It was a wonder how she had managed to preserve her innocence being married to a hard-nosed police executive.

'Vanessa! Back from Wales? How was your trip?'

'It was fantastic. I met with a gang of old school friends. We had a blast raiding every cake shop in St David's. You can probably tell by my waistline.'

'Tell what?' Sam pleaded ignorance. Vanessa was on the chubby side, but that was her charm. 'And your parents – in good health?'

'Getting on, I'm afraid. Every time I visit them, they seem to shrink a little more . . . But enough of me and my parents! Where are my manners? Come inside.'

Alec was standing behind her, a large square man to his small round woman. He was dressed casually in shorts and a T-shirt. On the phone he had told Sam he would be at home as he was on leave; he always booked his holiday at the start of September when the days were still warm and long but kids and pesky teenagers were back in school, leaving the streets and parks for the mature citizens to enjoy in peace.

Oblivious to the challenge Sam was about to present, Alec expressed his delight at seeing him and ushered him through the house and on to an open deck in the back garden. Vanessa offered something to drink and Sam requested coffee. While she was gone, he jumped on the opportunity to accost Alec with his appeal for help.

'Alec, I know this may be irregular, but you are my only hope.'

'Oh dear Lord, this sounds serious.' Alec stopped smiling. 'What is it about?'

'It's about my late wife, Alice. There was a death by suicide verdict at the inquest, which at the time, I accepted at face value.'

'And there's a *but* coming, isn't there?'

'Yes. New evidence has come to light which may implicate one of your own.'

'A policeman?' Alec's body language changed from a relaxed, reclined poise to his pulling himself up in his chair and leaning stiffly forward.

'A policewoman, no longer a serving officer, mind, but still . . . Um . . . And that's not all. She is the daughter of John Erskine—'

'The late Chief Constable John Erskine?'

'I'm afraid so.'

Vanessa returned with the coffee. Sam paused. He didn't feel it would be appropriate to involve her as well. Neither did Alec. He got up and started fussing about with the cafetière and setting up

135

the cups and saucers. It was obvious he was flustered and uncomfortable.

'You sort the drinks, then,' Vanessa said to him. 'I'll get the cakes.' She left.

Sam resumed. 'Let me explain how the two of them come into Alice's death,' and he gave a precise and unemotional account of Alice's ill-fated investigation into the child abuse case against Erskine, his subsequent death after a heart attack, and finally Alice's meeting with Laura Price on the day she died.

Alec listened, occupying his hands with pouring the coffee, and interrupting Sam twice to firstly offer him sugar and then milk. Sam shook his head in response to both offers, which demonstrated his own unease because normally he took both milk and sugar in his coffee.

'You see, that meeting never came to light in the original investigation. We found out about it by pure chance—'

'*We*?'

'Maggie and I. I was clearing away old boxes with Alice's possessions – Mother's orders, don't ask! Maggie was helping . . . We found text messages on Alice's mobile phone.' Sam didn't elaborate on how he had managed to have those texts uncovered – he didn't want to compromise Michael or, even more so, Jon Riley from Forensics.

'Maggie Kaye – a finger in every pie!' Alec sucked his teeth. 'But never mind Maggie Kaye, do go on.'

'We confronted Laura Price with that information. She admitted that there was to be a meeting, but assured us it hadn't happened. Allegedly, Alice didn't turn up, and Mrs Price didn't feel it was significant enough to report it to the investigating team. But, oddly enough, she had made the effort to check that no cameras had been in operation at South Castle train station. That's where she had asked Alice to meet her . . . Mrs Price, then DC Price, interviewed the stationmaster and looked through the CCTV footage from the platforms. Why would she have done that if not to cover her tracks?'

'Doing her job, perhaps?'

136

'She wasn't assigned to that case. And she didn't report any of that to the SIO. There is no mention of that in the files. I read them all back to back.'

'OK. Let's assume for one minute that she was covering her tracks. Was there any CCTV footage that she would have to conceal?'

'Yes and no. The cameras on the platforms had been vandalised so there was nothing there to conceal. I think she had made sure of that herself and was just double-checking. But that's where things get interesting. She may have overlooked another camera – the one covering the car park outside the station. I spoke to the station manager. There just may be CCTV footage showing Alice arriving at the station. That would prove Laura Price lied about not meeting Alice . . . Talking to her.' Sam bit his lip. It pained him to make accusations without clear and unequivocal proof. He was a lawyer – it wasn't his style. But he was also a grieving husband, and that was where rules didn't apply. He continued, 'I could tell how much she hated – still hates – Alice. She blames the press, Alice in particular, for falsely accusing her father and destroying his life.'

'He died of a heart attack.'

'Yes, but that followed that child abuse scandal he was implicated in—'

'And which turned out to be total fantasy. I knew John . . . Of course I knew him. I remember the whole affair like it was only yesterday,' Alec reflected. 'I didn't believe that bastard-fantasist . . . what was his name? . . . Barrett! I didn't believe him for one minute. John was a good man – beyond reproach . . . But we were pushed into a corner, after the Savile fiasco . . . We had to take the bastard seriously even though we knew he was lying through his teeth. The press were on our backs . . . Your wife was one of the reporters who started it?'

'Unfortunately. And I don't think Laura Price forgave her for that. I think she killed Alice and covered it all up.' Sam wrung his hands in discomfort. 'I may be wrong, I understand that, but I must make sure . . .'

'How can you make sure?'

'That CCTV footage from the car park. It may show that Alice had arrived to meet with Laura, or it may conclusively show that she did not. I must see it. And that's where you can help, Alec. I wouldn't ask you if there was any other way of me getting my hands on it. It's held in Gladestoke, Great Western's regional HQ. They won't let me view it, not without a warrant.'

Alec raised his hands in a gesture of despair. 'I can't request a warrant for a closed case! It would have to be re-opened! And on what grounds? Not to mention that I'd have to rake it all up and raise doubt about the integrity of a fellow officer — a man I knew and respected! Especially after what Laura's been through . . . I'm sorry, Sam — can't do it . . . Sorry . . .'

'Of course you can.' It was Vanessa. She had been standing behind them with cakes on a plate pressed against her stomach, listening to their conversation.

She carried the plate to the table and put it down. She sat down in a chair facing her husband and fixed him with firm and unflinching eyes. 'It's your duty to help. Your job isn't to protect your pals. Have you forgotten why you became a copper in the first place?'

'You don't understand, Vanessa. Laura Price is not my *pal*, but she's got no case to answer. It wasn't even an open verdict — it was deemed to be death by suicide. According to the coroner who weighed up all the evidence—'

'Evidence that he saw,' Vanessa interrupted him. 'What about the evidence that Sam has found? The coroner hadn't seen it when he delivered his judgment. Are you going to sweep it under the carpet? You can't do that. This man — and his dead wife — they deserve justice. It's your job to deliver it.'

Sam watched their exchange, speechless and spellbound by this small, sweet lady laying down the law and wagging her finger at her macho husband. He may have been used to wielding a stick over others but he cowered before his wife. There was more steel to Vanessa Scarfe than her cuddly exterior implied.

Alec pursed his cleft lip and ran his fingers through his hair. He looked like he was close to tearing it out. But he didn't. He sighed and said, 'OK, you're right. I'll make discreet – informal, mind – inquiries. I don't want to charge into this, all guns blazing, only to find there is nothing for that woman to answer for.'

'I understand. I'll sit tight and wait for a word from you.' Sam was keen to agree with him – to show he was putting his trust in Alec's methods. It didn't matter how he got his hands on that footage as long as he did.

'You'd better. You mustn't do anything. You, or Maggie Kaye.'

'Understood.'

'I'll view those CCTV tapes from the car park and I'll let you know. If there's anything suspicious, I'll request a formal warrant. Until then—'

'There,' Vanessa offered him a soft pat on the shoulder. 'It wasn't that hard. Now, how big a piece of cake for you, Sam?'

'Oh, I shouldn't,' he tried to protest.

'Yes, you should. I can't indulge in it all by myself. Alec won't touch sugar. He's no fun.'

Sam surrendered, 'What the hell, all right then . . . I'll have a small piece. And thank you, Vanessa. Thank you, both.'

Vanessa cut a slice for him. Alec watched her with a deeply troubled expression on his face – an expression that implied: *that cake can kill*. His annual leave lay in tatters.

Sam left at eleven and made his way from the Scarfes' to the Weston-Joneses'. He had another meeting – and potentially another cake – coming. He was meeting not only James but also his father, Lord Philip, who had just flown in from Switzerland. This time, Sam hadn't instigated the meeting. They had. James had called him last night requesting his presence for lunch, and asking how much he charged per hour.

Chapter Twenty

The crowd had gathered in large numbers at the extraordinary Parish Council meeting. The air was heavy with suspense and it presented all the hallmarks of a catastrophe in the making. It was a large and angry mob. Many interested parties had missed the earlier meeting. It had been cunningly set to coincide with the school holidays, during which time a great proportion of Bishop Well residents relocated to the south of France or the Costa del Sol. On this occasion however, they were all back, reinvigorated, sunburned, and thirsty for blood.

To enhance the spirit of confrontation, a line had been drawn in the sand and the two warring camps set up on opposite sides of the village hall. In the left-hand corner sat Daryl Luntz with his legal team led by Larry Morgan of Ibsen & Morgan. They were suing Lord Weston-Jones for damages and hefty compensation for the loss of profit that No Man's Land could have generated for Mr Luntz had it been sold to him unencumbered. The defendant, Lord Philip, was seated in the right-hand corner. Both sides were vitally interested in the outcome of the vote on rezoning No Man's Land for residential development. If the change of use was approved, the commercial value of the land would go through the roof, thus adding several zeros to Mr Luntz's claim. If, on the other hand, the rezoning fell through and the land use remained confined to serving the needs of Mr Wotton's cows and a few city-dwelling ramblers, then its value would plummet, to Lord Philip's immense relief.

People's livelihoods hung on the outcome of the vote.

Neutral in the matter, Alistair Wright-Payne, representing Cinnamon Rock plc, made himself comfortable right in the middle between the two warring parties. He didn't care from whom Cinnamon Rock bought the land as long as the corporation was free to build on it.

Before it all came to the crunch, procedural and other miscellaneous matters had to be addressed. The whole gathering gnashed their teeth and twiddled their thumbs impatiently as the Parish Clerk, Mr George Easterbrook, opened the meeting and read out the agenda, which happened to be full to the brim. There were endless standing items as well as items carried over from the previous meeting, such as issues of hedge maintenance and urgent funding for resurfacing the part of the High Street where several citizens had their car suspensions wrecked and threatened a collective action against the Council – the list went on. The vote on No Man's Land and considerations ancillary to it was fifth on the agenda.

All Councillors were present bar Ms Michelle Pike. Mr Easterbrook conveyed her apologies – she was apparently unable to attend the meeting due to *unforeseen circumstances*. Her absence would not hinder the voting, Mr Easterbrook assured the House. It would go ahead as planned as the required quorum was in place. That included the Chair, Mr Jacobsen, his deputy Mr Letwin, Mrs Digby, and –

After a dramatic pause, Mr Easterbrook introduced the new vicar, the Reverend Quentin Magnebu.

He, the new vicar, smiled benevolently at the crowd. He clearly didn't have a clue about the bloody war zone he had just walked into, but he seemed well equipped for battle on the physicality front. He was a large man, over six feet tall, with well-pronounced but handsome features, and a big smile to go with his big frame. He was no more than fifty, which in comparison with the average clergyman these days rendered him a spring chicken.

'Officially Vicar Magnebu will take the post at St John's on December the first, but he has flown from Mombasa specifically to join us for this meeting and to ensure the Church's interests are properly represented,' George Easterbrook informed the gathering. This announcement sounded faintly ominous.

Howard Jacobsen sprung up to welcome Vicar Magnebu with open arms – after a fashion. He enthused about the dedication of the new vicar – 'Flying over here, away from his flock in the distant Congo—'

'Kenya,' Vicar Magnebu corrected him.

Jacobsen pretended not to – or indeed did not – hear him.

'With the sole purpose of saying hello to us here, in our humble town of Bishops Well!'

The *humble* didn't go down well with many of those present and a few voices of dissent were instantly vented by way of, 'Not so fast!' and, 'Who's humble?!', not to mention a, 'Let's get on with it!'

Quentin Magnebu rose to his feet, dwarfing Jacobsen in the process. He shook the Chair's hand, which briefly disappeared in his huge palms.

'Thank you, Howard, and thank you, George! I already feel like I am at home, a member of the family.' The man spoke with a strong African accent, his voice well-conditioned to deliver sermons: erudite and brimming with pathos. 'I realise I'm stepping into a big man's shoes—'

Sam mused that such would be a perfect fit.

'I heard a lot about Laurence Ramsey, and his work, when I was an aspiring young deacon. I then met him and became one of his greatest fans. His relentless dedication to saving children from war-torn places and bringing them to safety inspired me and many others in our missionary work. I would like to assure you that Laurence's legacy will be respected. I will personally carry the torch. I intend, with my superiors' blessing, to continue with his noble projects – particularly, the Folly Orphanage. The folly itself and the accommodation building will be refurbished – works are already underway – and by Christmas we will receive the first shipment of Syrian child refugees from camps in Turkey—'

'Hang on a second!' It was Councillor Aaron Letwin. He stood up and rounded on the impassioned new vicar with an icy glare.

'When did we agree to that? We are deliberating the rezoning of No Man's Land for residential use, but no one's said anything about re-homing refugees! With all due respect, you, *Vicar*, have no idea what we went through when that Afghan refugee went on a rampage—'

'He wasn't a refugee,' Agnes Digby pointed out.

'It's just semantics, Agnes,' Letwin scolded her. 'I'm raising this point on your behalf, to protect voiceless people like you – the elderly, the children – you know, the vulnerable in our community—'

Agnes squinted and pursed her lips, tacitly objecting to being referred to as *vulnerable* or, worse yet, as *the elderly*. 'We don't know what those refugees are capable of! We know nothing about them! Some of them ... a lot of them aren't even children.'

'How would you know?'

'I've seen it on TV. I've heard—'

'Sod all,' someone shouted from the floor. 'You've heard sod all, Aaron!'

Within seconds, the village hall was buzzing with combative exclamations, accusations and declarations of *Shame-on-you!* and *Why don't you mind your own business!* Quentin Magnebu was staring with blinking eyes, befuddled. Howard Jacobson's shrills were lost in the cacophony. Aaron Letwin sat mute in veritable indignation. In the end, it was down to George Easterbrook to stand on his chair and holler over the rumpus in a voice worthy of Goliath, 'Silence! Everyone be quiet or I'll have the room cleared! Shut up!'

And everyone paused to see who had been so rude. Quizzical eyes descended on George.

'Thank you,' he said quietly. 'This discussion is NOT on the agenda, and will not be entertained. How the Church uses the Folly is the Church's business. The Parish Council has no say in the matter, and frankly, this fracas is highly irregular and an embarrassment and a disgrace.'

Sheepish looks were exchanged among members of the public and heads were hung low. George wasn't known for his oratory qualities, but nobody could have put it better. However he was now

143

painfully aware of the high-flying tempers and decided to make alterations to the order of the meeting.

'We'll leave the standing items on the agenda until the end, so as not to keep everyone waiting. The public are here for the vote on the rezoning of No Man's Land which was carried over from the last meeting. No Man's Land has changed hands since then.'

Daryl Luntz snorted at that and shot daggers at Lord Philip, who looked back at him down his nose.

'However, I have been advised that the new owner, the Church of St John the Baptist, is willing to continue with the sale of the land, less the Folly, to Cinnamon Rock, who in their turn, are still willing to proceed with the residential development as proposed originally.'

Alistair Wright-Payne nodded his agreement.

'This means that the change of use from agricultural to residential usage needs to be considered by the Council. As the Church has a direct pecuniary interest in the matter, Vicar Magnebu is not eligible to vote. That leaves us with the quorum of three-fifths: Mr Jacobsen, Mr Letwin, and Mrs Digby.'

'Let's vote, then,' Aaron Letwin declared without being asked. 'We all agree that it will be in the best interests of our town, it'll bring new jobs and public facilities—'

'What about the public consultation we were promised?' Mr Wotton queried, visibly incensed. He had come armed with his own lawyer's advice.

'That took place at the last meeting. Today, we vote,' Howard Jacobsen squeaked semi-authoritatively.

That was the turning point. Sam stood up to speak. He had been sitting quietly next to James Weston-Jones and his father, biding his time. Lord Philip shifted in his plastic chair, transposed his legs elegantly by putting his left one over the right one, and smirked. He wasn't looking at Sam, but vaguely in the direction of the ceiling. He knew exactly what hand grenade Sam was about to hurl into the proceedings, and he was relishing the prospect.

'Mr Chairman, I have information pertaining to the restrictions on the use of No Man's Land which has bearing on the matter. These,' he raised a bundle of documents, 'are the true certified copies of the Weston Estate deeds. I have highlighted stipulations on the use of the parcel of land commonly referred to as No Man's Land. You will find that ancient covenants between the Westons and the free town of Bishops Well grant the townsfolk certain rights over the land, which include the easement of the right of way and unobstructed grazing rights. Cinnamon Rock may want to reconsider their purchase of the land in the light of those restrictions. Respecting those rights will not go hand in hand with developing the land. Terminating them and compensating the town may prove too expensive, I'd suggest.'

'Restrictive covenants?' Wright-Payne jumped to his feet and intercepted the bundle of documents before it reached Mr Jacobsen. 'May I?'

'Of course. I've extra copies.' Sam was rather enjoying this.

Wright-Payne thumbed through the pages, focusing on the text highlighted in yellow. Every man, woman, and child in the hall waited for his verdict.

At last, he lifted his bewildered eyes from the pages and fixed them on the Parish Clerk. 'Mr Easterbrook, on behalf of Cinnamon Rock plc, I request that the vote be adjourned until we've had a chance to peruse these documents.'

And so it was done.

Chapter Twenty-one

After the aborted vote, Sam, James, Michael, Ivo, and Edgar headed to the Rook's Nest for a pint. A small libation was in order. Before they left the village hall, Sam searched the crowd for Maggie. In vain. She was nowhere to be found. He was marginally disappointed.

He would have loved her to witness his moment of glory, and she would have loved it too. He wondered what might have held her back from attending the Parish Council meeting. She had been dead keen on being there in person and on raising hell to stop the development from happening.

Sam concluded that Maggie, being Maggie, must have forgotten what day of the week it was, never mind remembering the meeting. Teaching a class of stroppy, foul-mouthed teenagers could have been a contributory factor. Maggie was probably knackered. She would have staggered home in her uncomfortable shoes and passed out on the sofa in her lounge. Sam would have to catch her tomorrow morning and bring her up to speed on the latest developments.

The five men ordered today's special. On Thursdays it was bangers and mash, complete with fried onions. TT bullied them into getting a large bowl of seasonal veg to share. Apparently he was determined to look after his patrons' diet and wellbeing. Fortunately, alcohol was still allowed. Five pints were soon delivered to their table and raised in a toast.

'You threw a spanner in the works!' Michael slapped Sam on the back, his face radiant with relief. He was a reserved man and generally came across as someone who couldn't care less about the town's future. But beneath his big moustache simmered a true and ardent devotion to Bishops Well. 'My bet is Cinnamon Rock are going to back out.'

'If they don't, we'll just have to give them more encouragement,' Sam grinned. 'They won't be able to buy us all out.'

'Are you sure Wright-Payne won't try to bribe our valiant councillors?'

'For what ends? To surrender the town's rights to No Man's Land?' Sam pondered the possibility.

Michael nodded. 'Take Letwin. He could do with a wealthy sponsor for Bishops Well RFC. He'd do anything for the club. He could easily sell out.'

'He may try, but he won't succeed. I've my beady eye on all of them. Did you notice Michelle Pike wasn't there tonight?'

'"Unforeseen circumstances", I believe was her excuse?' Ivo added.

'Yes, as in a conflict of interests. Maggie and I reported her to Easterbrook after you told us about Cinnamon building new extensions for her.'

'Ha!' Ivo slapped his thighs. 'Good old Ms Pike! She's no stranger to shady dealings, I'd bet my bottom dollar on that!'

'You'd do well out of that bet,' Sam agreed. 'There's something about her I don't like . . . Maggie is convinced she had her hand in the deaths of the vicar and of Cherie's mother, three years ago.'

'How so?'

'That damned packing tape – it was used in both cases. Michelle Pike had a motive to do away with Laurence, and she was linked to Cherie's mother.'

Michael frowned at the bandying about of his valuable inside information.

'What sort of links?' Ivo asked.

'Gertrude Hornby was a resident at Golden Autumn—'

At that moment their bangers and mash arrived, followed closely by a bucketful of steaming vegetables. They ordered another round of beers. Their mood was jovial and their tongues loose. Sam half-reflected that perhaps he shouldn't have referred to the packing tape, but promptly concluded that by now, bearing in mind Bishops Well's gossip-mongering notoriety, the packing tape was probably public knowledge.

'Gillian too has thought of it – of the connection,' Michael offered this gem of information, unsolicited. 'The first thing she did was to check Michelle Pike's alibi for both deaths.'

'And?'

'Nope,' Michael's moustache drooped and he shook his head. 'Pike couldn't have done it. Three years ago, when Gertrude Hornby was killed, Michelle Pike was in New York.'

'And the time of Laurence's death?'

'All morning in a business meeting. Guess who with?'

'Cinnamon Rock?' Sam ventured.

'Top marks, Sam! She was with Wright–Payne – a meeting followed by lunch in Sexton's.'

'A dead end, then?'

'Well, Gillian isn't one to give up on a lead. Her team are looking into the background of all employees at Golden Autumn – you never know what they may dig up.'

'Someone with links to both Vicar Laurence and Gertrude Hornby?' Ivo tapped his front teeth with his forefinger.

'That's a long shot,' James said. 'It won't be easy, I can't imagine. A village vicar and an elderly woman who hardly knew each other ... What could they have in common?'

'And yet the police suspect their deaths are connected ... So DI Marsh is looking for a link between them – something that would give a rational person the motive for killing both of them?' Ivo kept musing over the matter. 'Interesting ...'

So far Edgar Flynn hadn't said much, remaining focused on demolishing his bangers and mash. When he had finished his meal, he spoke. 'It's all relative. It depends on what goes through the person's mind. I don't think the killer is rational, though. Just because he has a motive doesn't necessarily mean that he has a logical reason or a clear plan.'

'What makes you think that?'

'Well, there's an element of brutality, even frenzy, in both murders. Of course – that's the very nature of the crime. But you can kill calmly and with premeditation, using less direct and physical violence. In these cases, however, the killer was – how shall I put it? – *hands on.*'

'But he didn't use the same method,' Michael pointed out. 'Gertrude Hornby was smothered and Vicar Laurence stabbed.'

'True,' Edgar nodded slowly. 'But there is a common denominator that points to the same perpetrator. It isn't always the method. In these two cases, it is the killer's behaviour and a high level of incoherence in his actions: first, he kills brutally, frantically and with their own hands, but then they go to the trouble of . . . erm, setting the scene, for the lack of a better phrase.'

'A scene?' Ivo asked.

'That's how it feels to me: a scene is set up. Gertrude Hornby is tucked away in her bed, her pillow – possibly the murder weapon – is lovingly puffed up under her head, the duvet drawn up to her chin, her hands folded together on top of it . . . Now, to the Vicar. He is placed in a chair, candles are lit . . . His body is heavy and hard to move and even harder to place in an upright sitting position, so it is taped to the chair. It's almost as if the killer is trying to afford them a level of dignity in death. But it seems like an afterthought – it is done after the frenzy of the uncontrolled killing. I mean, Laurence had been stabbed and slashed multiple times, and then, out of the blue, the killer lit candles for him . . .'

'That *is* illogical. Contradictory, even . . .' Sam observed. 'What does it say about the killer?'

'It does say something, doesn't it?' Edgar smirked, giving the impression of someone who was enjoying himself. The murders must have provided a good dose of professional excitement for him as psychiatrist. 'My bet is that the killer suffers from mental illness. I don't have all the facts before me, but I would guess some form of paranoia – the dissociative personality disorder springs to mind.'

'Do you mean, multiple personalities?' Ivo asked.

'That's another name for it, yes.'

'So we have a madman serial killer in our midst? Blimey!' James reached for his pint.

Sam's mobile vibrated in his pocket. He pulled it out and checked the caller's ID. It was Alec Scarfe. Sam answered with a pounding heart. The voice on the other end of the line was crackly and indistinct. The noise of the cheery clientele of the Rook's Nest warming up for happy hour could not be overcome.

'I must take this call. It's important.' Sam bade farewell to his friends and charged out into the street. He pressed the phone to his cheek.

'Alec? Bear with me. I'm in the pub – I can't hear a word. Don't hang up – I'll step outside.'

The cold damp night air washed over him. He turned up the collar of his jacket and sought shelter from the wind. He found it in the dark alley between the pub and the stationery shop next door. The walls of the neighbouring buildings insulated it against the noise. Black rubbish bags were piled up against the back door of the Rook's Nest. The door was shut.

Sam was just about to put the phone to his ear when he heard someone pad softly behind him, approaching from the street. The footsteps seemed light. A child? What would a child be doing in a dark alley at this hour? Sam held his breath to hear the heavy, rhythmic panting of his suspect companion. He spun on his heel, ready to defend himself.

'Rumpole?'

Vera's Irish wolfhound gave a jolly yelp and a fervent tail wag. Vera, who followed hot on his heels, appeared, giving Sam a markedly less enthusiastic greeting.

'Oh, it's you . . .' she muttered. 'We thought it was one of those buggers from Sexton's Wood scraping through rubbish bins for food.'

'The homeless people?'

'Yes! They've been at it of late, tearing open rubbish bags, overturning wheelies, rotting stuff strewn everywhere, inviting vermin.

The town's facing rat infestation if this doesn't stop. We're putting an end to it.'

'We?'

'Rumpole and I. We've been patrolling their usual hunting grounds at night, deterring the buggers from crime.'

'Crime? What crime?'

'Well, anti-social behaviour – call it what you will,' Vera shrugged. 'Come on, Rumpole. It's only Sam.' She tagged at the dog's leash and, obediently, he turned tail and followed his mistress to carry on with their vigilante business.

Satisfied that he was alone and that no one was listening, Sam spoke into his phone, 'Are you still there, Alec?'

Chapter Twenty-two

Despite his gallantry on the last day of school in July, Thomas Moore wasn't going to roll over and let me tickle his tummy at the start of this term. Oh no! He chose to make an unbearable nuisance of himself just to prove the point that he would not be tamed, or domesticated, or simply behave like all the other students.

He had started by waltzing in late to my lesson – his trademark behaviour. He then murmured something unsavoury to my greeting and mild admonishment for his lateness. Trailed by a whiff of nauseating odour (cigarette smoke at best, but in all probability weed fumes, I assessed at first sniff) he slumped at the back of the class and went to sleep. In his state of altered reality, he would proceed to make intermittent oinking and snorting noises.

I surmised that he was dreaming of being a wild boar, or a warthog. He wasn't far off, for he certainly looked like one. I had to combat the urge to drive a skewer through him and turn him into a hog roasting on a spit. I was doing my best to 'do him no harm', as Ivo had advised last term, but it wasn't easy because I was at the very end of my tether.

By the end of the day, I was emotionally drained and physically exhausted, as if I had spent my working hours in a mine, chipping away at hard, black seams of coal. I needed to lie down, but I had promised Megan that I would pop over to hers today to explain my manoeuvres in Mrs Robson's office on Monday night. In addition, I wished to enlist her to my cause and get her to act as my eyes and ears at Golden Autumn. From Megan's, I was planning to head for the Parish Council meeting, where I had a few things to say. My evening was full to the brim. I couldn't afford a late afternoon siesta.

I was hoping to catch a lift with Ivo, but he had left earlier to attend a secondary schools' cluster meeting for SENCOs in Sexton's Canning (SENCO being a Special Educational Needs Coordinator, if you were wondering). Off I trundled on foot towards the Holbrook estate. I was forced to cover the insurmountable (it seemed to me) distance of two and a half miles to Ivo and Megan's house at Holbrook in my new shoes.

The Holbrook estate is a brand spanking new residential area by Bishops Well's standards – built in the early eighties (of the *twentieth* century, I should add). It comprises a mix of owner-occupied and social housing. It had started as a small development of forty houses on the north-eastern boundary of the town, but soon it sprawled further afield, crawling insidiously down from the hills and towards the riverside flood plain. Its new additions sit half under water whenever we have a spell of torrential rain. Fortunately for Ivo and Megan, their house was situated in the older part of the estate.

By the time I knocked on their door, I was a barefoot wreck with bleeding blisters and a nasty cut on my left big toe, courtesy of some drunken delinquent who had scattered pieces of broken bottle on the pavement. And I was still bruised after my first round in the ring with Thomas Moore.

'Blimey, Maggie! Your feet are – a bloody mess!' Megan exclaimed as soon as she laid eyes on me.

'You can say that again! I should be grateful I still have them!'

For a brief moment she appeared reluctant to let me in. Maybe she was concerned about her carpets. I had already made two scarlet footprints on her doorstep. In the end the nurse in her won the battle of wills. She said, 'Come to the kitchen. I'll have to see to your wounds.'

She was very kind and gentle. She washed my battered feet with warm water and cleaned the cuts, painstakingly removing pieces of gravel with a pair of tweezers. She then bathed my wounds with an antiseptic spray and bandaged my feet from toe to ankle.

'OK,' she evaluated her handiwork with a nod, 'that's done then. Would you like to come to the conservatory and meet Vesna?'

As soon as I saw her, I recognised her. She was the faint presence of a young girl I had seen floating about Ivo. She wasn't a young girl anymore — rather a woman in her forties, very pale, with her skin withered and beginning to sag around her jawline, but her younger self was lurking in the shape of her large eyes and the sinuous curve of her lips. I had been seeing her in Ivo's company from time to time, but not always, not like with the dead. Vesna wasn't technically deceased, but she was as good as dead on many levels. She had a vacant look in her eyes, as if she wasn't really here — at least, not in spirit. Her long hair was honey blond, with a few streaks of grey. It was shiny, lovingly brushed and plaited. The thick plait weaved over her neck and rested on her chest. She couldn't have done her hair herself — it had to be Megan.

'We have a visitor, Vesna,' Megan stooped over her wheelchair, took her sister-in-law's hands in hers, and looked her deep in the eye to elicit some response or at least recognition. 'This is Maggie.'

I said hi, and did what Megan had done: stooped over Vesna and tried to shake her hand. It felt warm and soft, a bit clammy. Her fingers curled in and closed over mine. I could sense her desire to squeeze hard — to greet me. I told her I was glad to meet her. She didn't look at me. Her grasp loosened. A dribble of saliva glistened on the side of her chin.

Megan wiped it with a piece of tissue. 'She's somewhere in there,' she said to me. 'I know she is, but she doesn't often come out to play. Not anymore.' A doleful smile undulated on Megan's lips.

'So, she hasn't always been like . . . this?'

'No, 'course she hasn't. She wasn't born this way. She was born perfectly normal and healthy. Isn't she beautiful? She looks just like Ivo, doesn't she?'

'Yes, there's a similarity.' I agreed, not to be nice but because it was true. Vesna and Ivo had the same exotic, smouldering quality to their appearance: their golden skin and the same intensely green eyes. Although hers were inattentive and vacant.

'And they have similar personalities – they both care about people. They'll listen and try to understand you. That's why Ivo studied psychology – to understand and help people. Vesna is the same. I knew her before she became like this. We go back a long way, don't we, Vesna?' Megan patted the woman's knee.

'How did she end up in a wheelchair – if you don't mind me asking?'

'It's self-inflicted. She tried to kill herself. Several times. Never quite succeeding, I'm sorry to say, for her sake . . . But then she was young – she didn't know how to go about it. She did her wrists – that didn't work. She did this and that . . . In the end, her foster family couldn't deal with her. She was a danger to herself. She landed in the ATU in Heysham. That's where we met, the two of us, didn't we, Vesna?' Another pat on Vesna's unresponsive knee. 'I've been looking out for her ever since. We've been looking out for each other, come to think of it. She cares about me, I know she does. The same way I do about her. She always listens. She still does underneath all that dribble and . . . silence.'

'ATU?'

'Assessment and Treatment Unit – the one in Heysham, in Bristol. Like I said, she was a danger to herself – determined to end her life no matter what. She couldn't cope with the nasty memories, you see.'

'Her childhood memories?'

'What else? From Croatia – from that horrible war over there . . . Those memories haunted her, and she was too young to face up to them. She witnessed her mother being raped and then killed by Serbian militia – right before her eyes.'

'Oh my, that's awful!'

'It's true . . . She told me about it. I don't know if she told Ivo. He was only small . . . She and Ivo were hiding under the floor-boards. She saw it all. She saw her mother's eyes looking at her through the gap between the boards, mortified, scared – not for

155

herself, but for her children, for Ivo and Vesna. She heard her mother whispering, *shhh . . . shhh . . . shhh . . .* just before they finished her off. She was telling Vesna to be silent. *Shhh . . . Don't make a sound . . . don't let them find you—'*

Vesna stirred and whimpered. Her eyes rounded and her lips formed a fraught shape as she joined Megan, 'Shhh . . . Shhh . . .'

'It's OK,' Megan touched her knee again in a gesture of reassurance. She looked at Maggie, 'I told you she was a good listener, didn't I? We had a lot of late-night talks, didn't we, love?' Megan addressed Vesna, who didn't look in her direction, but I had the impression that yes, she was listening. 'She had a good few things to get off her chest . . . No one else would listen. Vesna used to say they – she meant the staff – weren't paid to listen. Some of them would tell you off for complaining, for telling the truth. They didn't want to know. Upset, she was. It'd made her so angry when people told her to shut up. It made me see red too!'

'Shhh . . . shhh . . .' Vesna hissed.

'Yes, love, I'm just explaining to Maggie here. Stop lying, they'd say, because they just couldn't imagine it was God's honest truth – It was easier not to listen. Anyway,' Megan sighed, 'it takes a good listener to understand.'

'You're so right – people hear you, but they rarely listen,' I reflected rather eloquently, I thought.

'I wish they had listened, the lot of them. It doesn't cost much to listen. Are you a good listener, Maggie?'

'Well,' I started, and paused for thought. Maybe I wasn't. I probably wasn't. No, I definitely wasn't. In my defence, it had only just occurred to me that I was more of a talker, not so much a listener. 'Not really.'

'There you go then! But you're honest about it,' Megan laughed. 'And frankly, you don't have anybody to listen to, living alone, never married . . .'

'I've friends,' I stood up for myself.

'I don't know what I'd do without Vesna and Ivo. They are all I've got. Did you know that it was Vesna who brought us together?'

'You and Ivo?'

'Yes. I'd never imagine, not in my wildest dreams, that me and someone like Ivo could meet and fall for each other, that our paths could ever cross – me, a West Country girl and him, a boy from the Balkans ...'

'Life's full of surprises,' I delivered another nugget of meaningless wisdom. I was on form.

'Not always nice surprises – not for everyone. Take Ivo and Vesna. They came over to the UK as refugees. Vesna was fourteen and Ivo, just six. Eight years between them ... They were separated.

'Being the younger one, and a boy, Ivo was adopted by a nice family. Well-to-do and good people on the whole ... Patty and Vic Murphy. They love Ivo – you can tell just by looking at them. They gave Ivo everything: a good education, a good start in life, all that ... But they didn't give him his sister – you know, they separated the siblings. It was only Ivo they adopted. Vesna went from one foster home to another, until she ended up in ATU.

'Seven years ago, Ivo found her. He was fortunate they have this rare family name: Dobranec. There aren't many Dobranecs knocking about, so it was easy to trace Vesna. By then she'd taken that nasty overdose – it'd fried her brains and she'd become like this,' Megan gestured towards her sister-in-law frozen in her wheelchair and unresponsive.

'At least she had you,' I said.

'I was the only one who could tell Ivo anything about his sister when he found her – things, you know, about what had gone on in her life since they were separated, and such ... He wanted to know every detail, even the worst bits.

'We cried together. We cried a lot. He didn't want Vesna to stay in that nasty place. They'd lost twenty years, he said ... So, when we got together, we decided – straight away, no ifs and no buts, we decided to take Vesna out of that place to come and live with us.'

'It must be helpful that you've got the skills to look after her.'

'I've got the skills and all the will in the world, haven't I, Vesna?

And I know, Maggie, that if it was the other way around, she'd do exactly the same for me.'

A series of beeps erupted from the kitchen.

'The dinner's ready. You'll stay for dinner?'

'I shouldn't – I can't,' I protested, though my resistance was as thin as a sheet of tissue paper. 'I only came to—'

'I won't take no for an answer. It'd be too much for the two of us. Ivo is in Sexton's so he'll stop by at his parents' – they're bound to feed him. There's a spare meal. And it's chicken lasagne – it won't keep.'

My arm was instantly twisted. I love lasagne.

Chapter Twenty-three

I helped Megan dish up and together we made a quick salad – a few leaves and tomatoes. We set the table in the conservatory. Vesna struggled to carry her fork to her mouth with her trembling hand, but Megan let her make a bit of mess instead of feeding her like a baby. She had a napkin at the ready to occasionally wipe Vesna's mouth.

I devoured my lasagne in record time I slowed down strategically to tackle the salad, thus letting Vesna and Megan catch up with me. I am a fast eater – that's how I usually end up eating twice as much as everyone else. But no seconds were on offer. This was an auspicious moment for me to speak rather than eat. I had promised to explain to Megan my raid on Mrs Robson's office.

'About my snooping at Golden Autumn,' I began. 'Yes, I was snooping. I was looking for evidence.'

'Evidence of what?'

'Of crime, of course! I may need your help with this since I've been banned from there . . . Let me start from the beginning – I have grievous suspicions about Michelle Pike.'

'Yes, you did mention that. What do you suspect her of?'

'Where do I start!' I sighed. 'I think she's in cahoots with Cinnamon Rock—'

'The property developers?'

'Yes, that lot. She's got a deal with them to expand Golden Autumn in exchange for her using her influence to push through the rezoning of No Man's Land for them to build on. I'm sure there's evidence of that deal somewhere, if one knows where to look . . . I suspect there are links between them—'

'Natalie could be one of them.'

'The receptionist?'

'Yes, Natalie Guthrie. She's married to the foreman, Gavin, and Gavin works for Cinnamon.'

'Ha! You don't say?'

'It's true! Natalie started at Golden Autumn just as the builders came to do the extension. She followed Gavin, him being the man in charge. I don't like either of them. He's a bully and she's—'

'Such a pompous cow, isn't she?' I concurred with Megan.

Megan chuckled. 'So, she got under your skin too?'

'Oh, yes! I've had the dubious pleasure of making her acquaintance. Her bad side, that is.'

'She doesn't have a good one. It's all bad as far as Natalie goes. I stay out of her way.'

'I wouldn't give her the satisfaction of having the last word. If I had a choice . . . But Mrs Robson fired me. It's a long story, and a whole bunch of totally unfounded accusations. So I hope I can rely on you, Megan, to gather some intelligence for me.'

'Well, I'll do what I can. If I can . . .'

'Great! I knew I could count on you. Here's the story: I think Michelle Pike is behind the vicar's death. He stood in Cinnamon's way and Michelle wanted him out. And that's not all. She has killed before – at least once, at Golden Retreat, on her own turf.'

'Really?'

'Remember Cherie's mother, Gertrude? Were you already working there when she died? About three years ago. Mrs Hornby? Well, Mrs Hornby's death wasn't—'

I did not finish that sentence. I was taken aback by Vesna suddenly doubling up and banging her forehead on the edge of the table. It bounced back like a large ball and fell down again. Her body stiffened and her head went up, her eyes rolled, the whites flashing as she shook in violent convulsions.

Megan jumped to her feet and pinned Vesna's shoulders firmly to the back of her wheelchair, desperate to prevent her from smashing her head on the table again. Vesna's forehead was already bleeding. She was flailing her arms, resembling a puppet on tangled strings. Her sleeves rolled up revealing multiple old scars of horrific self-harm. Although a tall and strong woman, Megan could hardly contain Vesna's tremors, resulting in both of them being gripped in a series of violent spasms.

And then it all stopped as suddenly as it had begun. Megan wiped foam from Vesna's gaping mouth and told her that it was nothing, not to worry her pretty little head, it was nothing. She then used the same tissue to clean the blood from her forehead.

I just stared. I wished I knew what I could do. The best thing for people like me is to do nothing – minimum harm, I concluded, and continued staring.

Megan looked in my direction as soon as she had contained the bleeding. She said, 'An epileptic episode. It doesn't happen often. It has been a while ...'

'I'm sorry ...'

'It's not your fault. But I'm worried about that cut on her forehead. A doctor should take a look at it ... I'll call Ivo. Stay with her, please.'

She fetched her mobile and came back to the conservatory with the phone to her ear. We waited.

'Damn it, he's not answering! I can't drive ... I don't know if I should call an ambulance. It isn't an emergency, but I want someone to check her over ...' She was flustered. Her cheeks were burning, her lips dry.

'I'll drive you. Let me get my car.'

I flew home on the wings of nothing but pure adrenaline and wearing nothing by way of footwear but the bandages Megan had put on earlier. Luckily, Priest's Hole is not light years away from the Holbrook Estate, so it was a twenty-minute sprint to the door of my garage. I jumped into my trusty Hyundai and slammed my bloodied, bandaged foot on the accelerator. I yelped in pain, but kept my foot down.

Megan and I led Vesna to my car, slowly, one step at a time, and strapped her into the seat belt at the back. She was bewildered and alarmed by being dragged out of the house, but she let us guide her. Megan sat with her on the back seat and was comforting her as I drove, breaking all the speed limits in town and on the open road to Sexton's Canning.

We burst into the A&E Department. Vesna was seated in a wheelchair that we found abandoned in the hospital car park. We used it as a battering ram to give the slow revolving door a little help. From there we were catapulted before a gloomy nurse who looked like she hadn't slept for a week.

We explained about Vesna's epileptic fit and her bashing her head on the edge of the table. She agreed that Vesna had to be seen by the duty doctor. She then pointed to my feet, 'And what's the story with your feet? Walking on hot coals?'

'Well . . .'

'You want a nurse to see to that too. Just look at the trail of blood you've left behind! I'll have to get someone to clean that up.' She muttered something else under her breath and told us to take a seat.

After waiting for three hours I had given up hope of ever making it to the Parish Council meeting. I took out my mobile to let Samuel know, but we were called in before he answered. A nurse told me to turn off my phone when we reached the cubicle where a young doctor, who looked no more than twelve, awaited us.

He peered at me, and my bandages now trailing behind me like some Morris dancer's ribbons, and told me to pop over to the nurses' station to have those sorted out.

I found three nurses in the middle of their light supper.

'Make yourself comfortable on that bed, love,' the one who appeared most senior instructed me. 'I'll see to you in a minute.'

The minute extended to half an hour and my treatment took another five minutes. My feet were cleaned and re-bandaged, plus

I received some sort of injection in my bum and a pair of hospital slippers. Thereafter I was sent on my merry way.

Megan was waiting for me in the reception area.

'They are keeping Vesna in for observation,' she informed me. 'I still can't get hold of Ivo. The phone's just ringing.'

'He's probably at the Parish Council meeting. You know how loud that place can get . . . Let's go home. I'll drive you.'

After dropping Megan off, I headed for the creature comforts of Priest's Hole. I was more knackered now than I was before. I was so tired that I felt neither thirst nor hunger. I collapsed on the sofa in my sitting room, in front of the television. I must have dropped off instantly.

I was awoken by a frantic knocking on my front door. Forgetting the sorry state my feet were in, I stood up and cried in agony. It felt as if gallons of water had been pumped into my soles, so much that my skin was at breaking point.

'Maggie!' I could swear it was Deirdre's voice. 'Call 999!'

Chapter Twenty-four

It was nearly eleven when Sam arrived on the doorstep of his house. The lights were out. His mother was asleep and he didn't wish to wake her. He didn't want to explain his lateness and listen to her grievances about him not ever telling her anything. What he wanted was peace and quiet, and the space to mull over Alec's revelations.

He unlocked the front door and crept inside, feeling his way in the dark. He proceeded to the kitchen to prepare a mug of strong coffee for himself. When he switched on the lights, he found the kitchen table set for two: one unused plate, and one with the knife and fork neatly aligned next to untouched pork crackling. Deirdre loved pork crackling but her teeth weren't up to it these days. She had left it on her plate. A pot on the hob had some mashed potato left in it; another one housed a few soggy broccoli florets.

Sam felt a slight pang of conscience. Mother must have waited for him with her favourite supper of pork chops but in the end had to be content with her own company and eat alone. He should have called her if only to tell her not to wait.

The saddest thing was that she had come here to save him, from his self-imposed exile and loneliness. She instead found herself exiled and alone in her son's house while he went chasing ghosts without a word of explanation. Everything she knew and held dear she had left behind in London: her friends, the parks and restaurants she favoured, and even Sam's children – her grandchildren. She had opened her home to them when Sam had suddenly upped and gone to Bishops. She had given them all that Sam, gripped with grief, could not. But as soon as they stood on their own feet, she had parted from them and followed her son to do what she considered her first duty – that of a mother.

She had put him first, and he paid her back with reticence and rejection. No, he hadn't asked for her charity but he ought to have the decency to show her some gratitude for it. When this was over, he would whisk her away on a holiday to remember, somewhere exotic, with warm weather, beaches and palm trees.

It was almost over.

It seemed he had reached a dead end. It was either bashing his head against a brick wall to get through to the other side, or letting the brick wall stand as it was. He had stayed away from Alice's papers all these years, as if they were holy relics – not to be touched, not to be disturbed. Had it not been for his mother's nagging, he would not have gone near those boxes. With time, he would get over the pain and the guilt, and the anger. His self-recriminations would fade away as he built his new life on the ruin of his old one. It would happen. People said, time was the best healer.

Whatever possessed him to reopen the past?

He carried his coffee mug to his study, closed the door quietly behind him, and sat at his desk. A narrow shaft of light from the lamp illuminated his mug, his hands and his forearms propped against the desk. He thought back to his conversation with Alec. He replayed it in his mind, making the effort not to miss anything important.

'So, I watched the car park footage from that day, the Tuesday,' Alec had said, his voice loud and clear in the vortex of the dark and silent alley. 'There was absolutely nothing on it. Nothing suspicious. No sign of your wife or Laura Price.'

Sam's heart had sunk to his stomach. That was the end of the road. He didn't feel relief, only a monumental failure. A small but nasty doubt would forever niggle at the back of his mind, like an itch that he couldn't scratch.

'OK, thanks, Alec. Thank you for trying. Much appreciated,' he had spoken woodenly and probably sounded ungrateful.

Alec hadn't noticed his tone. He had said, 'I watched it three times, just to be sure. I looked for angles and perhaps those blind spots, you know, which the eye of the camera may not have quite got to. Then my attention was drawn to one of those racks with free newspapers. The *Metro*. The rack was stood on the pavement, facing the camera. With a glass lid, so you can see the title page.'

Sam had felt a surge of excitement. He had no idea where Alec was heading but there was promise in what he was saying. He wouldn't be saying it otherwise, would he?

'I got our IT technician to zoom in on those papers – to enlarge the image. I don't know what made me do that. Copper's instinct, I suppose, or just doing a thorough job . . . So anyway, he was able to magnify the picture and clean it a bit – enough for us to read the headline. I had my team check that. The headline was about the Tory conference and their plans for post-Brexit. That was a head-line from the Monday, not Tuesday. Tuesday's headline was about a hurricane bearing down on Haiti.'

Sam was too baffled to follow or see the significance of Alec's words. 'What are you saying, Alec? Take me out of my misery. Tell me what that means!' he shouted into the phone.

'Isn't it obvious? Well, we then watched the CCTV footage from the Monday. It was possible that perhaps an old paper had been left on the rack, and it was still there on the Tuesday, you see . . . I wanted to be a hundred per cent sure.'

'And?'

'And no. There were no papers left over from Monday. It was the same coverage – the *same coverage* for Monday as for Tuesday. Someone had transposed the Monday footage on to the Tuesday tape.'

Sam had cursed Laura Price under his breath, and followed that with another profanity.

'Don't get too carried away. This doesn't prove anything. The fact that we do not have the Tuesday footage doesn't mean that there was anything conclusive or compromising there. It simply means that there is no recording.'

'It had to be damning if it was erased!'

'It could have been an error. A technical hiccup.'

'Do you really believe that?'

'No. I've already asked my best man in Forensics, goes by the name of Riley, to see if he can retrieve the original Tuesday recording. If it had been there in the first place, he can, but he can't vouch for its quality. It may be just a blur. He called it a *ghost*.'

Sam had clutched at straws, raving like a madman, 'She deleted the tapes! That proves it – in my eyes, it proves her guilty as hell!'

'Laura Price had no access to those tapes. She didn't see them. I don't think she knew about them. In any event, there was no request from the police to view the footage at the time of the investigation, and nobody – no officer, DC Price or anyone else – came to take them away. The tapes never left Gladestoke.'

'She did it, Alec. I know it! I don't know how she did it, but I know it was her. I'll get her one way or another. It was Laura Price, it was her!'

'What you should know, Sam, is that as an officer of the law we don't act on hunches. I'll follow this up and I'll let you know if Riley comes up with the goods. But, like we agreed, you let me do my job and stay out of it.'

Alec had rung off.

In his mind, Sam was replaying snippets of his conversation with Alec. Laura Price's guilt was beyond doubt in his mind – she had caused Alice's death in some way or another, and then she had gone methodically about disposing of all the evidence. She had a hand in the obliteration of the Tuesday car park footage. If she hadn't done it personally, she must have had an accomplice. Perhaps, it hadn't been done immediately, not while the investigation had been pending, but afterwards. She, or whoever was doing her bidding, had manipulated the recordings held at Gladestoke at some later date, when she had realised that—

167

The corner of his eye registered a bright bullet of light. That was the first warning sign. Hot on its heels came the sound of shattering glass — that was where the fireball broke through the window of Sam's study.

Momentarily paralysed, Sam stared at the flaming missile as it collided with the corner of his desk and crashed on to the floor. What seemed like blazing liquid spilled out of it in fast-travelling tongues of naked fire. They licked the papers spread on the floor and devoured them in a matter of seconds. They began to climb up the side of the shelves housing volumes of Sam's law books. His study became alive with light and the crackling noises of burning. Smoke was thickening under the ceiling.

'Sam?!' His mother's voice shook him awake from his trance. She was coming downstairs, calling out to him, demanding to be told what was going on. She gawped around her, confused and disoriented.

Sam ran across the scorching floor and grabbed hold of her on the staircase. She resisted at first, but he only tightened his grip on her arm.

'What—'

'Out!' He bellowed and led her firmly outside. He squeezed her shoulders and glared into her eyes, trying to focus her attention. 'Arson! Run to Maggie's! Call 999!'

By now she could see the fire for herself through the broken window. It was pulsing in flares of light. Sam didn't waste time explaining. He had a fire extinguisher in the hallway. It was old — he had brought it with him from London and never tested it since — but just maybe it would work.

He pulled it off the wall and aimed its nozzle at the bookcase burning inside his study. Foam burst out and began to suffocate the flames.

Chapter Twenty-five

They made a curious assembly: Maggie with her swollen feet dressed in bandages and hospital slippers, Deirdre with her wild and haunted eyes, and Sam with dusty hair and soot smeared across his forehead.

They were gathered in Maggie's sitting room, receiving sustenance in the form of hot chocolate fortified by Hobnobs. Deirdre appeared the most traumatised. Maggie had thrown a warm blanket over her nightdress and told her to put her feet up to let the blood circulate back to her brain wherefrom it had been drained by the shock. It made sense to Maggie, and Maggie alone, but Deirdre did as she was told and dangled her feet over the armrest of her chair.

It was after midnight when DI Marsh had finally graced them with her presence and an explanation. She too looked like she had just been dragged out of bed, which was exactly the case.

'I've made a provisional assessment of the cause of the fire,' she informed them, having refused an offer of hot chocolate. 'It looks like a makeshift Molotov cocktail. The firemen found remnants of a broken whisky bottle – it appears that's what was thrown through the window. Apparently, you were lucky, Mr Dee.'

Sam grunted. 'Depends on one's definition of luck, I guess.'

'Well, I'm told there was little liquor in the bottle, plus, barring your books and papers, there wasn't much fuel in your study to feed the fire. And of course, you acted decisively to put it out.'

'Oh, Samuel knows what to do. He's a hero,' Maggie gushed.

'Last year, you may remember, he didn't hesitate for one second to kill a man—'

'I do remember,' DI Marsh gave Maggie a tired glance. She then refocused her attention on Sam. 'I can't imagine you have any idea why you were targeted in this way?'

'None whatsoever.'

'Samuel is a good man. I brought him up so I know what I'm talking about. He's got no enemies. Never had!' Deirdre provided Sam with a glowing character reference.

'And he's a hero,' Maggie elaborated.

'Could it be a silly joke? A gang of local kids?' Sam asked.

'I doubt it,' DI Marsh shook her head. 'Arson isn't one of the Bishops' youths' favourite pastimes. The worst they've done so far was painting a donkey on a hill. A bit of vandalism, a bit of graffiti – yes, but not arson.'

'I really don't think that it is a donkey on that hill. If you look closely—' Maggie felt compelled to voice her dissent.

'Never mind the donkey,' DI Marsh dismissed her out of hand. 'I understand, Mr Dee, that you have prevented the vote on No Man's Land?'

'In a way – yes.'

'You have documentation in your possession showing restrictions on the use of the land. Could the attack have something to do with that? Was someone trying to destroy those papers?'

'I don't know. Possibly. They wouldn't have known that the originals are kept under lock and key at the Weston Estate. Lord Philip gave me copies of the deeds. He has the originals.'

'True, the attacker probably didn't think of that. If he had any sense, he would've guessed it and spared us this trouble . . . But what he did know was that by burning unregistered title deeds he would've effectively erased every existing record of the restrictive covenants attached to them. The fire wasn't the work of a bunch of naughty teenagers. Someone is hard at work eliminating everyone who stands in the way of the new development.'

'Just like they did Vicar Laurence!' Maggie exclaimed. 'So, you think the vicar was killed because he could block the sale to Cinnamon Rock? It's exactly what I've been contemplating – it's a strong possibility, I'm sure.'

'We have several lines of inquiry,' DI Marsh said stiffly.

'But this is one of them, isn't it? If I were you, DI Marsh, I'd be taking a long, hard look at Michelle Pike and Golden Autumn Retreat. She's in cahoots with Cinnamon Rock and she had the means and the opportunity to murder Gertrude Hornby, as you already know. The packing tape—'

'Packing tape? What do you know about the packing tape?' DI Marsh rounded on Maggie with a sharp glare. Sam's heart sunk to the bottom of his gut. Maggie had blown it big time! Gillian Marsh wasn't a fool. She would work out that Michael had told them about the packing tape link between the two murders. He had to say something significant to distract the detective.

'There could be another reason for the attack. I suppose I should tell you: I've been investigating my wife's death. It's been almost four years since Alice died . . . The coroner's verdict was suicide, but recently I've come across some information, and I began investigating it, interviewing people and so on. I may have ruffled some feathers, I guess. I'm convinced that my wife was murdered.' And from there he gave DI Marsh a tightly edited account of his suspicions, carefully circumventing the entire *informal* inquiry into the CCTV recordings that Alec Scarfe was implicated in.

To his surprise, DI Marsh nodded. 'Oh, that! I know about that – I've been brought up to speed by the Chief Super. You may be right. Forensics are examining the CCTV footage from the time of your wife's death. I'll chase that up with Riley. There may be something there. You'll have to come to the station to give your statement about the incident today, and I want to talk to you about the other matter. Tomorrow at noon. Sounds good?' She didn't wait for his confirmation. 'I'll be busy in the morning. I need time to follow up some leads before I have a word with you . . .'

'I'll be there.'

'If that's all, I'll be off.' She headed for the door. From the doorstep, she added, 'Do you have anywhere to stay tonight? You and your mother can't go back to your house until Forensics are done with the scene. It'll be some time tomorrow afternoon.'

'They will stay at mine,' Maggie declared.

Maggie had made up the bed for Deirdre in the spare room. After making Sam swear that he would not do anything stupid *like killing someone, again* – and that he'd explain everything in the morning, Deirdre allowed herself to be led upstairs and deposited in bed. Despite the excitement of the hour, she was out like a shot before Maggie had turned off the lights and left the room.

Maggie carried a duvet and pillows to the upstairs front bedroom, and informed Sam that his bed was ready when she returned to the sitting room. Sam thanked her, but was reluctant to go to sleep. It was a mixture of adrenaline and caffeine that prevented his brain from shutting down for the well-overdue rest. He also wanted to talk to Maggie. She had missed the Council meeting, and he wanted to know why.

'Ah! You've no idea what I've been through today,' she replied and relayed to him, with great exaggeration and several embellishments, all her misadventures, starting with her bleeding feet and culminating in Vesna's epileptic fit. 'The poor woman has been like that since she overdosed. They had kept her in a mental asylum until Ivo found her and whisked her away.'

'How come he didn't know where his own sister was?'

'That's the thing – they had been separated as children, soon after they'd come to this country. From the Balkans, after that dreadful war.

'In fact, it was thanks to Vicar Laurence that they were given asylum in the UK. Laurence used to be an army chaplain and he had been posted to the Balkans with the British contingent of the UN forces. As soon as he came back over here, he organised transportation of Croatian war orphans. They stayed briefly at the Folly before they went on to live with their new adopted families. The vicar's – Laurence Ramsey's grandparents were native Bishopians – he used to come here on holidays every summer when he was a boy . . . became fond of the place. Anyone would . . . He was friends with my grandfather. So anyway, when he first rounded up those poor war refugees and brought them into the country, his first thought was Bishops Well – the Folly. It had stood empty and derelict since the war when it was used as a hospital for convalescing veterans.'

'That's quite some piece of local history!'

'It was way before your time, Samuel. And mine,' Maggie added realising that even she with her long Bishopian roots couldn't possibly remember the second world war. 'But I was there when the Balkan orphans arrived. I remember those poor kids – they were so dejected, never laughed, didn't know how to play like . . . like *normal* kids. You never saw them do things that children do. They made me feel uneasy . . . No, that's not the word . . . I don't know . . . wary, I suppose. Not wary of *them*, but of the world out there, of that awful place where they came from and of how close it was to home.'

Sam shook his head in dismay. It seemed history kept repeating itself with stubborn defiance. Today it was the kids from the Middle East, traumatised by war, seeking refuge and safety. Who would be next? Where would they come from? And how soon would they come?

Maggie continued, 'So anyway, Ivo was the younger one and the luckier of the two siblings. He was adopted and took on his adoptive parents' name, Murphy. He got a decent education and made something of himself. Looking at him you'd never guess the trauma he'd been through. He's just like any other ordinary guy.

'But Vesna went from one foster home to another. She was really damaged – mentally, emotionally – she became suicidal – a danger to herself and others . . .' Maggie sighed, looking deflated. 'It's really so very sad, Sam! Vesna ended up in an asylum – what they call a Mental Health Unit these days. And that's where she met Megan and they struck a close friendship. Megan worked there as a nurse – some kind of psychiatric nurse, I presume. She became very fond of Vesna. That's how she met Ivo, by the way – when he came searching for his sister. They fell in love. And the rest is history.'

'A happy ending – a family reunited.' Sam smiled ruefully.

'Almost a happy ending. Vesna is a wreck of a human being. If you met her, you'd know what I mean. The quality of life just isn't there for her anymore.' Maggie looked pensive. 'But at least she has two people who care a great deal for her. That must count for something, mustn't it, Samuel?'

Maggie peered at Sam, pleading for reassurance. Her face didn't show much hope, however. It was shaded with sadness. Sam wished he could dispel that. It would be nice to embrace Maggie and let her embrace him in return, so that they could offer comfort to each other. There could be so much strength in physical intimacy, in feeling the other person's body heat and warm breath against your own. Words could not compete with that. But words were all Sam could come up with.

'It does matter, of course, it does – she's safe and she's loved,' he spoke with little conviction, offering nothing but empty clichés. On reflection, he added, 'We've been brought up on happy endings, Maggie. We expect nothing less than a happy ending to conclude a story. But life is much more complicated. It doesn't always present definitive answers, good or bad.'

'Well, I think Vesna is at peace. At least she's got peace of mind now that Ivo and Megan are close by and looking after her.' Maggie reassured herself even though she was addressing Sam.

'You're probably right.'

'I am!' Maggie reached for a Hobnob and crunched it between her teeth. 'I must tell you,' she was more upbeat now that the sugar rush had entered her bloodstream, 'that I've enlisted Megan to do some snooping for me around Golden Autumn. She's already given me a few nuggets of intelligence. Did you know that their new receptionist is married to a foreman working for Cinnamon Rock? His men are doing the extension to the building. The plot thickens . . .'

'The police are investigating every employee at Golden Autumn, I'm told. They'll figure it out.'

'Really? Brilliant – they're doing exactly what I would do.'

174

'Edgar told us something interesting today. We were having a pint after the Council meeting and the conversation strayed towards the murders. I can't remember how. Anyway, Edgar believes that the murderer suffers from some form of a dissociative identity disorder – a split personality, or something similar.'

'What makes him think that?'

'Something to do with the frenzy of the killing being out of step with the very methodical staging.' Sam repeated the examples Edgar had given him.

Maggie was intrigued. 'You know, Samuel, I had the same impression when we found Laurence's body, but I couldn't quite put my finger on it. It felt to me like there were two different people at work . . . Now it makes sense.'

'To me, too.'

Maggie yawned and grabbed the last Hobnob from the pack. 'Now, why don't you tell me what I missed at the Parish Council meeting. I hear you've been up to your usual heroics.'

Sam couldn't help a tiny, self-congratulatory smirk. He sat back and reported on his progress in sabotaging Cinnamon Rock's efforts to snatch No Man's Land from under the town's feet.

Chapter Twenty-six

A firm believer in punctuality, Sam reported at Sexton's Canning CID with fifteen minutes to spare. He asked for DI Marsh and listened to the desk officer as he called her extension and informed her of Sam's arrival. He was then instructed to take a seat and wait.

Noon came and went, as did two disorderly females screaming obscenities at each other. They were promptly led in two opposite directions by two officers. Sam managed to work out that their dispute was of a territorial nature.

Another incensed citizen arrived in a huff demanding to know where his car was – apparently it had been parked, *fleetingly,* on a double-yellow line in front of the bookies' in Lower Lane and had vanished by the time the incensed citizen returned from attending to urgent business at said bookies'. The desk officer struggled to establish if the incensed citizen wished to report his vehicle stolen or wanted to reclaim it from the Traffic Police Vehicle Pound at Upper Norton.

Sam listened idly to the argument and watched with interest as it escalated until the incensed citizen was removed from the premises. A lunch break followed and that was a bit less entertaining. The time was twelve twenty and still no sign of DI Marsh. She was either making Sam wait on purpose, or had simply forgotten about him. There was no one on the front desk to ask.

At long last, which occurred a few minutes later, DC Whittaker descended from the upper echelons of the police station, apologised for the wait, and invited Sam to follow him to Interview

Room Two. DI Marsh was already there, accompanied by a cup of coffee and an odorous egg-mayo sandwich. She consumed her sandwich and drank her coffee while DC Whittaker took Sam's statement about the events of the previous night.

'Do you have the feeling, Mr Dee, that the arsonist wasn't really serious about burning down your house?' DI Marsh wiped her mouth with a paper napkin and sprang into action.

'Why, no! He gave me, and especially my mother, a mighty fright. My impression was that he was damn serious!' Sam was baffled by her comment. What manifestation of evil intent did she need to witness to believe it?

'You said you were in the study when it happened—'

'I was, yes. I had a few things I wanted to research.'

'So the lights in the study would've been on.'

'Yes, my desk lamp was on.'

'And your mother was asleep upstairs?'

'She was, yes ...'

'So the whole house was covered in darkness, but the arsonist chose the one room that was lit, where he could reasonably expect someone to be still wide awake and at the ready to put out the fire ... What a waste of time and effort!'

'It's obvious he was targeting my study. It's where I keep business papers. He was after destroying the papers, wasn't he? The study was a logical target.'

DI Marsh squinted in disagreement. 'I don't think so. If he were, he would've waited until you'd gone to bed. What was the point of giving you a chance to put out the fire and save the offending deeds? If his objective was to destroy them ...'

'Point taken,' Sam had to concede it. The actions of the arsonist didn't seem rational. Unless, of course, he didn't intend to cause serious harm, but simply wanted to warn Sam off. Or unless he was a tragically misunderstood criminal.

'So, he – or she – didn't want to burn your study and your papers to a crisp. I think it was just a warning – a tokenistic warning. There was hardly any liquid in the whisky bottle, I'm told by

Forensics. The whole attack was just a firework display. The damage to the study is minimal. I know you acted swiftly, but that's just my point – they knew you would act.'

'OK, it was risky, but I can see your point, DI Marsh. I don't think I get the message though. What were they trying to warn me away from? If they didn't want to destroy the original deeds, then what did they expect I'd do next? Run? Chase them? Hand the papers over to them?'

'I'm not sure.' DI Marsh chewed on her bottom lip, deep in thought. She paged through the photos of Sam's study and showed them to him. The fire damage was indeed minimal – just a few books singed on the lower shelves; most of them were saved as they were leather-bound and not easily flammable. The wooden floorboards were blackened and all of the papers from Alice's boxes were gone, readily devoured by the initial spill of fire from the whisky bottle missile.

'What do you think, Mr Dee?' DI Marsh gazed at him with those suspicious, piercing eyes of hers that would make a saint feel as guilty as hell. 'It was a rather half-hearted effort, that arson of yours . . . It seems . . . hmmm . . . staged. No real harm intended.'

'I hope you're not insinuating that *I* staged it?'

'No, not you. Someone else, though. They didn't mean you harm – they just wanted to get your attention. So, the question is why.'

'Well, my bet would be on someone who doesn't want me to interfere in the battle over No Man's Land—'

'Failing which it could be someone who doesn't like your snooping around Gladestoke.'

'Someone like Laura Price?' Sam took the risk of mentioning the name of his prime suspect.

'But you see, Mr Dee, I've already had her alibi checked for yesterday night, and unfortunately, it is rock solid.'

'She may have an accomplice.' Sam wasn't prepared to give up without a fight. He had his convictions about Laura Price despite the many holes in the body of evidence he had accumulated so far.

'In fact, if she had planned this whole thing, she'd be particularly diligent at establishing her alibi for last night. She knows I'm on to her.'

DI Marsh dug her elbows into the table and leaned forward towards Sam in an intimidating fashion, her fists pressed against each other under her chin. 'It's not your job to be *on to her*, it's ours. I wish you'd come to me first before you started deploying my colleagues – even my so-called boyfriend – behind my back to do your bidding. You have greatly compromised this investigation and alerted the suspect.'

'I do apologise,' Sam murmured, contrite, 'but I didn't think I had sufficient evidence to make an official report.'

'So, you recruited my so-called boyfriend – and I will deal with Michael Almond in due course — and my governor, not to mention Riley, to get that evidence. Meantime, you and your sidekick, Miss Kaye, confronted the suspect and interviewed a witness. I could charge you with obstructing a police investigation, tampering with evidence, and perverting the course of justice.'

'I don't think you could.' Sam placed his elbows on the table and gazed firmly and unflinchingly into the detective's eyes. 'There was no active investigation pending when we spoke with Mr Wilkins, or indeed Mrs Price. The inquest into my wife's death was concluded with the Coroner's verdict of suicide. So no, we didn't break the law. I should know if we had.'

'Splitting hairs, Mr Dee – that's what you lawyers are so good at. You should've come to us through the official channels as soon as you uncovered new evidence.' DI Marsh didn't recoil under Sam's gaze. She was a hard nut to crack. She positively glared at him when she added, 'And you, of all people, should know that.'

Sam relented. He pulled back in his chair. 'I said I was sorry. Am I to understand that the investigation is now re-opened?'

'Yes, you are. And from now on, if in your private citizen's capacity you continue to meddle with my inquiries, I will come down on you with the full force of the law. I've just about had it with the busybodies from Bishops.' DI Marsh and DC Whittaker exchanged deeply frustrated glances. Whittaker's nose reddened with indignation. DI Marsh slammed her hand on the table. 'Whatever you do know or find out, you come to me. Not to Michael Almond. Is that clear, Mr Dee?'

'Crystal clear.' Sam maintained a serious, boy-scout expression throughout this exchange, though deep down he was punching the air – the police had re-opened Alice's case! 'Am I allowed to expect to be updated about the progress of your investigation?'

'A very slow progress, you should add, thanks to you and Miss Kaye! I can tell you this: we weren't able to restore the deleted CCTV recordings from the Tuesday. They are illegible.'

'She'd had them erased – Laura Price, I mean.'

'Perhaps yes. Perhaps the footage was erased four years ago. But perhaps, and it is likely, the perpetrator did it after you and Miss Kaye had gone to harass Mrs Price and interrogate the Station Manager just a couple of weeks ago – has that occurred to you?'

'That . . . um . . .' Sam blinked, confounded.

'Yes, exactly that. You see, I'm thinking that the tapes may not have been tampered with until you took it upon yourself to confront the suspects. That's what I mean by you obstructing us in our duties.' She sighed. 'You can go now, Mr Dee. I'll keep you informed if there is any progress. *If*, being the key word here – and that's your fault entirely. Pass my regards to the lovely Miss Kaye, why don't you?'

Sam wasn't sure whether to take that at face value as a commonplace courtesy, or to shrivel under DI Marsh's contempt. He muttered something non-committal and bid the two police officers a good day. DI Marsh snorted boorishly, but DC Whittaker reciprocated the politeness, though his sizeable nose was only slightly less red.

Chapter Twenty-seven

I called in sick. It is unorthodox for a temporary teacher standing in for another to call in sick. I could hear the unspoken condemnation in Janet's voice when she enquired about the cause of my indisposition (Janet is the sweet but deadly·receptionist at Bishops Well Ace Academy).

'I've an infected wound right across my left foot,' I informed her. 'And I had a fire last night.'

'Oh my! I hope you're all right, Maggie!' The sweet side of Janet stepped forward.

'Well, sort of,' I whinged a bit more about my swollen foot and the foreign objects presumably still lurking between my toes, and about having to shelter my now homeless neighbours. 'The fire was actually next door,' I added to clarify. 'But this house used to be a single dwelling, Janet. In fact, you can smell the acrid smoke in my bedroom . . . Well, you could smell it last night. *I* could.'

'How did it start?'

'Arson. Someone made an attempt on Samuel's life. Samuel is my next-door neighbour. And if that wasn't enough, his elderly mother lives with him – the poor lady suffered a near-fatal shock. We had a fire engine on our driveway – hoses and flashing lights going the whole hog! The police are looking into it. A full-blown police inquiry! I'm still having to pinch myself.'

'My God, Maggie! If you need anywhere to stay . . .' Janet's sweet side was firmly in charge now.

I thanked her for her kindness but said we were absolutely safe at mine, plus, of course, I couldn't travel without my foot.

When I put down the phone, I reproached myself for being a fantasist and scaremonger. I peered at my feet. The hospital slippers and the bandages were off. There was no more bleeding. In all honestly, it all appeared innocuous. My feet were back to their customary size and shape. The swelling was gone. The cut on my toe looked like child's play, as did the few scratches on my soles. The miracles of modern medicine, I marvelled and thanked my lucky stars.

I put the radio on, on a low volume so as not to wake Deirdre. Samuel was already out, running his house-fixing errands and making statements at the police station. I reclined on the sofa and immersed myself in the blissful sensation of having just thrown a sickie.

I was savouring this unfamiliar yet delicious moment – milking it with my mug of Horlicks in hand – when I heard Deirdre scramble out of bed in the room above my head. She scuttled up and down her room which she was clearly finding unfamiliar and confusing in her first waking moment, especially after the dramatic events of last night. They could have confounded a military operative with years of undercover experience, never mind an octogenarian lady brutally awakened from her sleep in the middle of the night.

'Samuel?' I heard her cry. 'Are you down there?'

I heaved myself off the sofa and hobbled to the bottom of the stairs. I called out in my most assuring tone, 'Good morning, Deirdre! Samuel's gone out to organise a glazier for later – to fix the window.'

'Oh, that!' She groaned. 'The blasted fire!'

As soon as all the facts of last night were revised and accepted, with much grumbling, by Deirdre, we sat down to breakfast. It was my second breakfast of the day, but I felt the circumstances called for it. I couldn't let my guest eat alone. I made my trademark pancakes while Deirdre engaged in her morning ablutions upstairs. She came down wearing the dress I had chosen for her from my wardrobe (she'd only had her nightdress when she had arrived on my door-step, screaming in the night). The mud-mask was banished from her face and her hair was set into an unassailable bob.

She gazed at my pancakes, accompanied by honey, lemon, sugar, and sultanas. 'You wouldn't happen to have porridge, dear?'

Of course I didn't happen to have such Spartan foodstuff. I don't consider food a form of self-mortification. Quite the opposite – it is one of my greatest pleasures. 'Sorry—' I started.

'Don't worry if you don't—'

I exhaled and sat down to breakfast.

'Because we've got it. If you trot over next door and ask the nice Forensics people to get it for you . . . It's in the kitchen cupboard next to the dishwasher. It's easy to find.'

I went next door and pleaded with a gentleman going by the name of Hughes to fetch me the porridge, which I explained was not for me but for the elderly lady taking shelter in my house. He looked me up and down quizzically but went in and returned with a bag of porridge oats. I thanked him.

Back in my own kitchen, I read the instructions and began cooking the damned concoction. Deirdre sat back, watching me.

'How are you settling into Bishops?' I asked her.

'Well,' she huffed, 'having to evacuate my bedroom last night didn't help much. But what's done is done. We exchanged contracts on my flat in London last week, so I'm here to stay.'

I congratulated her.

'It's a big step for me, Maggie,' she spoke dolefully, 'but I had to do it for Samuel. He's not how he used to be.'

'Oh?'

'He's a shadow of his former self.' She lifted her shoulders and exhaled her woes in one long sigh.

'He needs time, I suppose,' I said, just to say something.

'He's had a good few years to get over it. No, he's a broken man. And that's my son we're talking about. It pains me to watch him like this.'

I felt for her. I wished I could tell her about Alice rattling around,

183

clinging to his ankles, not letting go, that it wasn't him – it was her, but there was little hope that the old lady would understand. She would tell me to have my head examined if I mentioned Alice's ongoing presence. So I didn't. I served her porridge and dug my teeth into the now lukewarm pancakes. They didn't taste that good, but Deirdre was relishing her porridge.

'You should try it, Maggie,' she instructed me. 'You'll be as regular as a Swiss clock. I am.'

I considered that too much information and decided to change the subject.

'I think I'll put the kettle on. We could do with a nice cuppa.'

'I have coffee with my breakfast, dear. Ground coffee. I've no confidence in all that instant hocus-pocus.'

Luckily, I had ground coffee and didn't have to *trot next door*.

We decided to have our coffee in the garden. It was a lovely morning – the summer had changed its mind and decided to come back for seconds. My garden basked in dew and autumnal colours lit by the morning sun. Deirdre complimented me on my *surprisingly* well-kept garden. She sat silent for a while enjoying the morning birdsong. As did I.

Out of the blue she peered at me searchingly, pursed her lips and said, 'How do you feel about my Samuel?'

I think I may have blushed. I began to stammer and mumble about friendship and neighbourly camaraderie, and I finished on the high note of our joint business venture. All of that was true, but it felt like a lie. Was I hiding something from myself? Something I wasn't prepared to confront just yet. Something about how I really felt about Samuel Dee. He was of course my hero. He had killed a vicious criminal etc, etc, but I think I had moved on from hero worship to something else. I just wasn't ready to admit it. Probably, because I couldn't even put it into words. And then, of course, there was Alice . . .

'Because I can tell, he likes you very much, dear.' Deirdre ignored my helpless grunts. She had me pinned firmly to the spot with her sharp gaze. 'He talks about you all the time – when he talks at all, that is. But when he does, he talks about you. You're always on his mind in some shape or form.'

'Oh, we . . . I mean, being neighbours and business partners—'

'It's not business. The way he talks about you . . . well, I recognise the signs. I wasn't born yesterday. I know how men speak when it's about business, and when it isn't. And I know my son.'

I staggered inexpertly on the crutches of ums and ahs, unable to string a sentence together.

She scowled at me and my pathetic efforts. 'He is in a very delicate place, mind you. I wouldn't want you to go breaking his heart.'

'I . . . I really . . . I never . . . I,' I trudged on, deeper and deeper into incomprehensibility. My face was on fire.

'And frankly, I don't know what to make of you, my dear. You're a good-looking woman. Nothing's wrong with you . . .'

'Well, um . . . thank you.' I didn't know what to make of that either.

'But you aren't married, or with a chap . . . I'm not a prude – you can cohabit with a man without being married to him, I've no problem with that. But you're not with anyone in any way, can you see the point I'm making?'

'Well, um . . . no.'

'So I have to ask myself, *is she one of those floozy types?* What is your track record, as a matter of interest?'

Deirdre had me squirming. I couldn't make up my mind whether to get indignant, to apologise, or maybe even comprehensively explain my hazy marital status. The problem was that I couldn't explain it myself. I wouldn't know where to begin. I was . . . I was . . . I was – can you see what I mean?

So I said, 'The roses need dead-heading. I think I might do just that. It's so relaxing – dead-heading. You're welcome to join me—'

'And why would I do such a thing?'

I was hard at work, dead-heading everything I could get my hands on in my fervour to escape Deirdre's clutches. She was nodding off in the chair, having so ungracefully refused my offer to join me in my gardening endeavours. I was promising myself to give the matter some serious thought. My best time for thinking is just before bed, seated on a pile of pillows, chewing a piece of rum and raisin fudge. I would have to do that tonight: think of how I felt about Samuel Dee, and face up to it. I had a sneaky suspicion that I was out of fudge. It would have to be requisitioned from Jane and Kev Wilcox at the market today if I were to go ahead with the task at bedtime.

Alice joined me. She sat on the wall separating my garden from the cemetery. She looked serene and strangely sympathetic. For a split second, I could swear, our eyes met. I imagined she knew how I felt. She'd had dealings with her mother-in-law in the past – I wondered what her strategies of handling Deirdre had been. I wondered if she would tell me, provided she could.

'But you can't, can you Alice?' I said. 'Still, nice of you to drop by and hold my hand. I really appreciate that.' I felt we had built some rapport at long last – an understanding. Deirdre had brought us closer together.

A knock on my front door interrupted our brief meeting of minds. I guessed it was the nice Mr Hughes here to tell us that his team were done and Deirdre was free to return home (and to free me to go and buy some fudge). I was wrong. It was Samuel.

Of course, it was Samuel, I admonished my silly side. That's why Alice was here. It had nothing to do with female solidarity. She was here for Samuel, and I should have known better than to misread her intentions to suit my ego.

'Of course, it's you,' I said, deflated.

'I've got great news,' he spoke way too loudly and way too excitedly, 'the cops have re-opened the investigation into Alice's death!'

'Shhh . . .' I put my finger to my lips to calm him down. 'Your mother's asleep in the garden, poor thing. Come to the kitchen. We can have a cuppa and you can tell me all about it.'

I was amazed to discover how little I knew. Samuel hadn't updated me on anything he had done since our joint visit to confront Laura Price. And there was a lot to report! I must admit I was a trifle disappointed in him. I had relied on him to keep me in the loop. How could I help him if he wasn't sharing anything with me? I was hurt but I had to forgive him. At least he was here now, relaying every detail of his solo investigation to me.

He had retraced Alice's last journey from London to South Castle, visited the exact spot where her body had been found, and discovered that Laura Price had been busy covering her tracks the day after Alice's body had been discovered. He had even convinced Chief Superintendent Scarfe to follow a lead on the CCTV footage. Except that the footage had been tampered with! The plot was so thick that even I was finding it hard to tunnel through in order to see the light.

'Someone had superimposed the previous day's footage over the Tuesday one.'

'It could only be her!' I was surprised that I had to tell him that.

'But it wasn't, Maggie. Laura Price had no access to it, and she had no access to the IT archive in Gladestoke.'

'Then she had to have an accomplice! Someone did it. Someone who handled those tapes. An IT technician? How about that station manager you spoke to?'

'Andrew Wilkins?'

'Whatever his name, he was in charge of the station and everything else, like the cameras − he could've easily overlaid the recordings before sending them to Gladestoke.'

'Except that he wasn't in charge at the time. It was actually someone called Stan Pollock, Andrew's boss. Stan was the stationmaster. He was the man who dealt with Laura Price when she came snooping.'

'Well then?' I glared at Samuel. Did he really need me to spell it out for him?

'It's not that simple. Stan Pollock killed himself not long after Alice ...'

'Isn't that quite some coincidence?' I was growing incredulous with every new revelation. 'How did he do it? Don't tell me he threw himself under a train!'

187

'Hanged himself. I was told he'd been a compulsive gambler, lost lots of money and couldn't handle it. I tried to speak to his widow, but she wasn't there. I waited and waited – she never arrived. Anyway, it may be irrelevant.'

'Or it may not! What if he was Laura Price's accomplice? What if she killed him too? Samuel, someone tampered with that footage. We need to find out who.'

'The cops—'

'That's fine. Let the cops do their job. We must go back and have a word with the widow. You never know what we may—'

'Alec has already given me lots of grief over our cavalier handling of Laura Price. And that was before they re-opened the case. It's different now, Maggie. It's a police investigation. I'm sure DI Marsh will get to the widow in her own sweet time.'

'We could nudge her in the right direction. Come one, let's give it a go.'

'She warned me to stay away from the case. And so did Alec.'

'That never stopped us in the past. We won't be interfering. We'll just pop over and visit a poor widow. Have a chat. No one will need to know if we find nothing new. Look, Samuel, I promised you I'd help you get to the bottom of it. I've no choice – I've got to keep my word. What would Alice say if she could speak? What would you say, Alice?' I addressed the question to her. She was there with us, listening to every word. I could swear that, for the second time that day, she looked right at me. It was a conscious and focused exchanged between the two of us. Her gaze was sharp and almost real. She might not have been speaking, but she was egging me on. 'We started this so we must finish it. We're doing it, Samuel. Together, or I'll go there on my own.'

'We'll do it together, Maggie. I can't let you do it alone.' He squeezed my hand, his eyes radiant with his newly acquired resolve.

I reciprocated his grip with equal enthusiasm, and we held hands together like a pair of teenage conspirators.

That was how Deirdre found us. 'I hope I'm not interrupting

anything,' she winked. I would never put Deirdre and winking in the same sentence, but there she was – winking.

We pulled apart, blushing like said teenagers caught in the act. Immediately I began mumbling, grunting, and stammering in my well-practised fashion.

Samuel saved me further embarrassment, 'We can go home, Mum. I came to fetch you. The forensics lot are gone. I have the glazier coming in fifteen minutes to repair the window.'

'Thank you, Maggie dear, for having us,' Deirdre said imperially.

I almost curtsied in response but stopped myself half-bow. Alice, I swear it, smirked.

'Samuel, go and get our porridge back. It's in the kitchen,' Deirdre commanded her son. When he was briefly gone, she rounded on me as if I were a lost lamb, 'You really ought to give it a thought, Maggie.'

'A thought?'

'What we were talking about, earlier.'

'Oh, that! Yes, I will, Deirdre.' This time I couldn't stop myself. I did curtsey.

'Good girl,' Deirdre blinked, or was it another mischievous wink?

As soon as they were out of the door, I headed for the Thursday market to requisition the rum and raisin fudge for all the thinking I would be obliged to carry out that night before bed.

Chapter Twenty-eight

I was standing under the cream and pink awning of Jane and Kev's market stall, waiting patiently for the merchandise to be weighed. Kev, as was his custom, threw a few extra pieces in the box. I sometimes wonder why he bothers weighing them at all. He affixed a dainty label to the lid to seal the box and keep my sticky fingers out of it until bedtime.

At last the box made it into my paws.

'Rum & Raisin Extravaganza, half a pound,' he declared, inaccurately as we both knew there was much more there than just half a pound.

'Thank you, Kev!' I may have visibly salivated, just a bit, for he handed me a tissue and pointed to my face without an explanation. I licked my lips.

Jane waved goodbye to another customer and came over to say hello. We had a pleasant chat about the superiority of fudge over toffee and caramel. It was instructional. After that we veered into the subject of the vicar's death and I told them about the arson. Jane was mortified to hear about that. As was Kev. He offered me a cube of fudge to suck on, saying that sugar was the best remedy for shock. I couldn't say no. On second thoughts, I mused, I was in shock, of sorts. Not because of the fire, but because of Deirdre's revelations. I would need a lot more sugar to think those through.

I heard a curt, husky bark behind me and an equally curt and husky cry of, 'Maggie!'

I turned to face Rumpole and Vera. I hid my fudge behind my

back and dashed forward to greet them. We embraced with all the joviality of a long-time-no-see encounter. Rumpole went about sniffing my backside and wagging his tail. He made a few futile attempts to give me his paw, which I refused to accept. There would be a price to pay and I wasn't prepared to pay it – a piece of my fudge was priceless.

We decamped to the café for a cup of tea and cake. We jabbered about this and that, the usual village gossip, some of which Vera had not been appraised of and was keen to know. She had been lying low through the summer, putting up with Henry and his irrational behaviour typical of a politician with too much time on his hands. To her relief, Henry had departed for Westminster at the beginning of last week. She was a free and happy woman all over again. She prayed there would be no prorogation of Parliament. Henry's last involuntary home-stay extension had nearly led them to divorce.

Throughout our hour-long chattering, Rumpole stood by me with his snout pressed into my lap and his droopy eyes pleading with me for mercy. I did not succumb to his charms. The box housing my fudge remained sealed.

'He's awfully besotted with you for some reason!' Vera observed.

I patted Rumpole on the head apologetically. 'We are good pals, aren't we, Rumpole?' I pleaded ignorance of his ulterior motive. He licked my fingers, snuffing traces of sugar off them.

I looked at my watch. It was a few minutes past three. I had to dash home before the school rush hour started in earnest. I couldn't afford to be seen out on the town, shopping and pottering about on two perfectly healthy feet. I was supposed to be bedridden.

I said goodbye to Vera and gave Rumpole another contrite pat on the head. We agreed to meet on Sunday for lunch. I scampered home, using the back alleys.

I had hardly collapsed on the sofa in my sitting room and was still catching my breath when Cherie and Ivo bundled in, bearing gifts for *their convalescing chum* – that would be me. I was touched when they presented me with a bag of, wait for it—

Rum & Raisin Extravaganza!

'I know it's your favourite,' Cherie beamed. 'We stopped by at Jane and Kev's before coming here.'

I didn't know what to say. Internally, I thanked my lucky star that they hadn't seen me there. We must have passed by each other, literally rubbing shoulders. I felt rotten. Pulling a sickie doesn't always go without strings attached, such as the post-sickie guilt trip.

'How are you feeling, anyway?'

'Much better, to be honest.' Only I knew that my honesty was relative.

Ivo piped up, 'I really wanted to thank you for helping Megan with Vesna.'

'Oh, it was nothing.'

'Ha! If it wasn't for us, your feet would be in much better shape.'

'But they are. They are perfectly fine. It was much fuss about nothing, see?' I lifted my feet, which actually presented as angrily inflamed as they had been yesterday. It was the walk to and from the market that had aggravated them. At least their state lent some credibility to my disability claim.

'Poor you!' Cherie was a darling. 'Why don't I make us a nice pot of tea? Don't you move.' She wagged her finger as I started to heave myself from the sofa. 'You stay there. I know where everything is.' She marched to the kitchen, leaving me feeling ridden with guilt.

'Seriously, Maggie – thank you for yesterday. I should've been there.' Ivo peered at me with his mesmerising long-lashed eyes and readjusted his Harry Potter-ish glasses on the bridge of his nose. He was a very handsome young man, I reflected for the umpteenth time.

He was sitting in a chair, blissfully unaware that his big sister – her ephemeral spirit, that is – sat there with him. She was poised on the arm of the chair, leaning over him, her head tilted towards his. They looked so alike: she, as she had been in her young days, and he as he was now. Even though in reality it was Ivo who looked after his invalid, helpless sister, in the picture before me it was the other way around. She was exuding an air of tender, almost maternal, protection over him, and he seemed like a little boy lost in her arms.

I nodded and smiled. 'No problem. How is Vesna? Is she back home from the hospital?'

'No, not yet. They want her there for observation for another day or so. I think her condition has deteriorated in the last few months, although no one has told me that. She has fewer and fewer lucid moments. I think I'm losing her.' A dark shadow passed over his face. There was a twitch to his lips which he tried to contain by compressing them. But it was no good. The pain of imminent loss was stronger than his willpower. I wished I could hold the lost boy in him. He seemed like a child. I could see him through his big sister's eyes.

Cherie came back with the tea, in mugs, all ready with milk and sugar stirred in correctly. When you work with someone, you know how they take their tea. That's the first thing you learn about them. Ivo took his mug out of Cherie's hand and pressed it to his lips. It was burning hot – I knew mine was, but he didn't seem to notice.

'I can't imagine what she must've been through,' I said.

'Neither can I,' he admitted, 'though I think of it often. I try to put myself in her head. We come from the same beginnings – we've seen the same horrors. Only I was too young to understand – to really understand. And Vesna did everything she could to protect me against those memories. Until we were separated, of course.'

'How old were you?'

'I was almost seven when I left the orphanage, she would've been fourteen, going on fifteen. I remember it like it was yesterday. She stood there in the porch, waving goodbye to me. She was so beautiful!'

I know, I wanted to say because I was looking at her right now, but of course, I couldn't. I couldn't tell him that she was here with him and she looked the way she had when they had been torn apart. 'She's still beautiful,' I said instead.

'You should've seen her when she was fifteen! She looked like an angel. To me, she was an angel. If there were angels out there, they would look like my sister. In those days . . . By the time I found her, she was nothing like herself: she'd lost her mind, her looks, her whole life. That's what nine years confinement in the ATU does to you. An awful place!'

'Yes, Megan said you took her out of there as soon as you could.'

'Not soon enough . . . I know it's irrational but I've never stopped feeling guilty.'

'About what? You haven't done anything!'

'Of course I haven't, but survivor's guilt doesn't entertain logic. It's a well-known and well-documented condition. People who've been through concentration camps and watched others die suffer from it. It is irrational but very real: you feel guilty and ashamed for making it while others did not. You feel responsible for what happened to your loved ones even though you had no hand in what was inflicted upon them. Even though you were as helpless as they were . . . You blame yourself for failing them. You tell yourself it's not fair – they deserve justice and you owe it to them—'

'You owe them justice?' Cherie frowned, puzzled. So was I.

'To ease that guilt . . .' Ivo explained. 'It's justice in its most natural, primeval form: an eye for an eye. Short of gouging your own eyes out, you—'

The words withered in his throat. He smiled, an inexplicable apology swelling in his eyes. 'When I found Vesna, debilitated and damaged beyond help, I was sick with guilt. How could I have gone about my little selfish life, being loved by my adoptive parents, having friends, home, security, a future, while my sister, my flesh and blood—' He broke off again and waved his arm dismissively. 'Anyway, it's all in the past.'

'Those ATU places could be pretty grim. My mother volunteered in one of them after she retired – wanted to make a difference, I suppose . . .' Cherie said. 'Mum never stopped being a teacher, retired or not. She couldn't sit at home idly. She had to make herself useful. So it was one of those Assessment and Treatment Units for troubled youth. I remember her saying it was an awful place. She'd come home demoralised after a day in Heysham. But she kept going back, to help those kids. Some of the inmates, she said, were still only kids – they were entitled to education. She gave them what she could, though sometimes all she got back for her trouble was grief—'

'Did you say Heysham?' Ivo sat up. 'That's where Vesna was kept!'

We looked at each other, taken aback. I had forgotten what Megan had told me about Vesna's sad past. To resort to the casual saying *it's a small world* would be a serious understatement.

Finally Cherie nodded, 'Yes, the ATU in Heysham . . .'

'Blimey!' I had to chuck in my two-pennyworth because I had experienced one of those *Eureka!* moments. 'There's your connection!'

'Connection? What connection?' They both gawped at me.

'Well, the police are looking for a connection – between your mother, Cherie, and Vicar Laurence, and whoever killed them. I've heard they're checking everyone's background. Everyone who worked or visited Golden Autumn at the time of your mother's death and everyone who knew Vicar Laurence, even before he came to Bishops.'

Ivo was looking confounded, 'Why is that? Why would these two be connected? Cherie's mother died two years ago—'

'Almost three,' Cherie added. She too appeared confused.

'They think it's the same person! The same killer!' I had to enlighten them, although something was telling me that I shouldn't. There was this niggling at the back of my head that this was information imparted to me confidentially. But, since I'd started, I had to finish, 'I'd say – if I didn't know any better – that it was Vesna . . . Vicar Laurence brought you and Vesna,' I addressed the still confounded Ivo, 'to this country, so he was known to her. And then, Vesna was a patient at the same ATU where your mum volunteered.' This time I fixed my gaze on the still confused Cherie.

The fog, I could tell, was beginning to lift. Cherie frowned and asked, 'Are you trying to say that *Vesna's* the killer?'

OK, so the inside of Cherie's head was still quite hazy. I had to make myself perfectly clear. 'No, of course not. That's why I said *if I didn't know any better*! I've met Vesna. She couldn't kill a . . . a . . . anybody. She can't move very well, she's wheelchair-bound, she's — well, she's incapable . . . Physically incapable.'

'But she's the connection. My God . . .' Ivo said it slowly with such gravity that I felt the little hairs stand up on the back of my neck.

'My God,' echoed Cherie.

'It's bizarre, I realise that,' I tried to make sense of it all, 'but there's another thing. Edgar — you know, Edgar Flynn? He's a psychiatrist, and sometimes he's engaged by the police to do profiling for them. Anyway, he's convinced that the killer suffers from mental illness. What did Samuel say it was?' I searched my memory for the actual medical term.

'Dissociative personality disorder,' Ivo helped me.

'Yes, that! And Vesna suffers from—' I had to stop myself, bite my tongue and shut my mouth. It would be cruel to draw the analogy any further. But it was there, staring us in our faces! Vesna was a mentally ill woman with links to both the vicar and Gertrude Hornby!

'But I just can't imagine how she could've done it!' I concluded.

'She didn't do it. It was Megan.'

Chapter Twenty-nine

Lost for words, Cherie and I stared at Ivo. I don't think either of us was absolutely certain that he had said what we had heard him say. His words seemed to have risen from somewhere deep down beneath our feet. But it was he who had uttered them. His face was ashen-grey. He took off his glasses and covered his eyes with his hand. He clenched his fingers on the bridge of his nose.

'It was Megan,' he repeated, and this time there was no doubt in our minds that was what he was saying.

'But the killer . . . I mean, Megan isn't ill – mentally ill. She's a nurse. She looked after Vesna . . .' I tried to protest her innocence.

'Megan isn't a nurse.' Ivo shook his head while holding me with a steady, doomed gaze. 'Megan, like my sister, was an inmate at Heysham ATU. What made you think she was a nurse?'

'Oh my! I didn't—' I gasped.

'Megan suffers from dissociative personality disorder. As in most such cases there's a deep-rooted childhood trauma, in Megan's case untreated for years until it was too late . . . Megan is on medication, but . . . Damn it, it's been staring me in the face and I couldn't see it! Megan worked at Golden Autumn at the time when Cherie's mother was murdered.'

'But why kill her? And more to the point, why on earth would she want to kill the vicar?'

'Megan holds him responsible for Vesna's condition, for allowing us to be separated . . . She has said it often enough – that it was his fault, he should've fought for us to stay together. We were his responsibility – he brought us to this country and then he let them pull us apart . . . Megan blames him with all her heart. I should've listened to her, taken her seriously, talked her out of it! I thought I had her in hand . . . she was taking her meds . . . she . . . What have I done!' Ivo clamped his temples and looked to us, to me and Cherie, for something. Understanding? Denial?

We stared at him, dumbfounded. Neither of us spoke.

Ivo stood up and paced across the room. The ghost of Vesna was still and frozen on the edge of the chair. It was fainter than when it had first arrived, as if she had gone pale with shock. But she couldn't have – she would have known all along. They always know.

'Megan understood what Vesna had been through better than I ever could. Despite my useless degree in psychology! Despite everything Vesna and I had shared as children . . . They had those long talks – years of late-night talks . . . Vesna told Megan every-thing, confided in her . . .' Ivo was speaking out loud though he seemed unaware of our presence in the room. He was pacing and talking, analysing, thrusting his hand in the air, punching his fore-head. 'After Vesna's last attempt on her life, after she'd lost what was left of her faculties, Megan took on her cause. I should've seen it coming! I didn't! Idiot!' He lashed out at the wall. He hit it so hard that his knuckles bled and left a bloody mark. He hardly noticed. He just went on with his tortured monologue, while the two of us listened. 'So it was Gertrude Hornby first – one of those wretched staff from Heysham, who never listened, never wanted to, never had the time to—'

'Mother used to have this saying,' Cherie spoke hauntingly, her voice trailing, as if in a trance, '"If you don't stop telling fibs, I'll have to tape your mouth." Kids tell tall tales . . . She forever banged on about the cry wolf story . . . She didn't like liars . . . Is that what happened? Is that why Megan stuck tape to Mother's mouth? Because Mother wouldn't listen?'

This was so close to the nerve that I could feel physical pain. Of course! Megan told me that in so many words. She had repeated so many times that nobody would listen at Heysham, nobody believed them. It hadn't occurred to me that she had been talking about herself. I had thought she was talking about Vesna.

And so had Ivo. Poor, poor Ivo!

'Yes . . .' he groaned, 'that's why, Cherie, that's why she killed your mother. I'm so sorry . . .'

Cherie shook her head as if to insist that he shouldn't be sorry, that it wasn't his fault. She couldn't express that with words. She was fighting tears.

'And when I told her I recognised the vicar, that he was the man who'd saved me and Vesna . . . You see, I couldn't remember him. It'd been years . . . I was so young . . . But then at that Parish Council meeting, he suddenly looks at me and speaks of safe haven for war orphans, *like Ivo and his sister*, he says. And I remembered him! I went home and told Megan. I was so excited, such a bloody fool . . . But it wasn't the same for Megan. Vesna had told her a different story about Vicar Laurence, about the role he'd played in our childhood . . . Yes, he'd saved us but then, if you looked at it from Vesna's perspective, he'd washed his hands of her, snatched me away from her and let her perish . . . It was revenge time for Megan. I've been such an idiot!'

'Don't blame yourself,' I tried my best, but my efforts were pointless.

'She murdered two people and I stood by thinking I could control her illness, her actions . . . I'm as much to blame . . . We must call the police.'

I was relieved it came from Ivo. I had been contemplating doing just that for a while, but didn't know how to break it to him gently. The police would need to be informed. Megan would be arrested. His wife and his sister's guardian angel gone – Ivo's world would be in tatters. And how much of this tragedy would Vesna take in? What would it do to her world?

'Yes, you're right. I'll call Michael. He'll get DI Marsh. She'll be better than a . . . stranger.'

'The devil you know?' Ivo said and smiled ruefully.

Chapter Thirty

Megan was arrested the same night. The next day Cherie and I went to see Ivo after school. He had been signed off work and was home alone with his sister. He needed friends. Cherie wanted to show him that she held no grudges against him personally. I wanted to share with him that burden of guilt he had been talking about last night – and some of my fudge. I was also keen to find out more about Megan. I had totally misread the woman, which isn't like me at all.

We found Vesna in her wheelchair in the conservatory, gazing blankly at her brother who was pacing the width of their garden, waving his arms, shouting to – or at – himself. We managed to pacify him sufficiently for him to agree to sit down with us and have a cup of tea. He refused the fudge but Vesna had one piece. Her eyes lit with pleasure when she tasted it. I gave her another piece, but that one she just held between her fingers, somehow forgetting to put it in her mouth. I didn't know how to encourage her. Her hand with the fudge squashed between her thumb and forefinger lay limp in her lap. Ivo stared over our heads, not seeing any of it.

Cherie brought the tea from the kitchen. I poured it and passed Ivo's mug to him.

'When will you be able to see Megan?' I asked. 'Will they let her out on bail?'

He shook his head. 'Not a chance. She'll be taken into a facility for mental health assessment. Until that's done, they'll keep her under lock and key. Too unpredictable . . . Until they know for sure that she poses no danger . . .' He shook his head again, more vehemently. 'They will never let her out. Never! Not after what she's done . . . And I let her do it!'

That was when he lost it again. He raged as if he could not stop himself from talking. He was hysterical. Words were pouring out of his mouth in torrents. Self-recriminations. Exclamations. Curses. But we listened – well, I listened. Cherie's eyes were glazed over – she clearly was somewhere else. With her mum, I guess.

'You can't blame yourself, Ivo,' I told him as soon as I was able to get a word in edgeways, 'you aren't responsible for Megan's mental health. She was ill before you met her.'

'But she was under my care . . .' he countered, though weakly. It seemed that the surge of adrenaline in his bloodstream was rapidly receding. He looked tired all of a sudden.

'Why . . .' I started. 'What exactly is wrong with her? Did something happen to her?' I pressed on, eager to understand.

He began to explain. It was a chaotic account, but I was able to put together Megan's back story from that. I could not help but feel sorry for Megan despite what she had done. She was sick. Very sick.

Poor Megan! Since she had been a little girl she had been exposed to unimaginable domestic violence. She had watched her father beat her mother black and blue, day after day, until one momentous night her battered mother had snapped. And that was when Megan had witnessed something even more horrific: her mother had taken a meat cleaver and plunged it into the back of her father's head, nearly splitting it in half. In front of little Megan.

A couple of years later, Megan attempted to do the same to her mother, sending her to hospital with life-threatening injuries. By then Megan was on a downward-spiral trajectory into madness.

No amount of legal argument about diminished responsibility and temporary insanity could have saved Megan. She had been damaged for life. Her sentence was life. Her journey into the heart of darkness could not be reversed. And there, along the way, she had met Vesna Dobranec, and they walked together arm in arm, fending for each other.

How could I, how could anyone, not empathise with her.

'Poor Megan,' I whispered.

'Indeed,' Cherie responded.

'Dissociative personality disorder caused by childhood trauma.' Ivo sighed. 'I have transcripts of her therapy sessions. Would you like to . . . I can show them to you so that . . . you know? So that you can understand better.'

'If you're happy,' I said. 'If it helps . . .'

'Sharing always does,' he replied and left to fetch the notes.

He came back with a thick folder and handed me a couple of sheets. As he closed the folder, another loose sheet fluttered out of it. I picked it up and added it to the ones I was holding.

'Would you mind reading them out loud, Maggie?' Ivo asked.

It was a strange request but I agreed. The notes made for a harrowing reading. My voice faltered a few times, my heart going out to the poor little girl, lost and confused in a nightmare that was supposed to be her happy childhood.

Daddy and I used to go fishing together. Just the two of us.

In the Cotswolds.

There are lots of lakes in the Cotswolds – pretty lakes, some large, some small. Some are surrounded by hotels and chalets, and all that touristy stuff. But others are hidden from sight, deep in the woods, behind water meadows. You have to know where they are to find them. You may have to walk for a long time to get to them. Little, hardly trodden footpaths lead to them. It was one of those lakes that Daddy had discovered and it became our special place.

We would go fishing there. Just the two of us.

Daddy had a small rowing boat moored to a pier. It was concealed among reeds. You wouldn't know it was there unless you came looking for it. That pier was ramshackle, covered with green algae or moss. Whatever it was it was green and slimy. You could easily slip on it and break your ankle, or a leg. Daddy would hold my hand to guide

me into the dinghy. I felt like such a lady. Daddy often said I was
his little princess. That's even better than a lady.

We would row across the lake. Sometimes, droplets from the pad-
dles would sprinkle on my face or my bare arms. Sometimes Daddy
would do it on purpose. He was such a good laugh! We used to laugh
a lot together, but not while fishing – when you're fishing, you have
to keep quiet. Fish have good hearing and if they hear you laughing
or making noises on the surface, they will scatter. You will catch
nothing.

So, we would row quietly to a secluded spot and Daddy would set
the rods, one for me, and one for him. And we would fish.

Daddy would open a can of beer. It would make a hissing sound,
but not enough to scare the fish away. He liked to smoke a cigarette
with his beer. He would light one, drink from the can and puff away.
I liked inhaling the smoke that came out of his cigarette – I liked the
smell of it and how it drifted slowly away. It kept the mosquitoes at
bay. Mosquitoes don't like cigarette smoke.

If we caught a fish, we would release it straight back into the lake.
Daddy would be careful not to tear its mouth when he took the hook
out. Sometimes it couldn't be helped, but we would still let the fish
go. It would heal in the water, Daddy told me.

Daddy had a good heart. He was a good man.

DR SWANN: Did he ever do anything to you? Did he ever hurt
you?

Never. Daddy never laid a finger on me.

'Poor child, she must've adored her father,' Cherie said.

I had totally forgotten she was still around. She had been sitting
quiet as a mouse, listening.

'Probably,' Ivo said. 'It is also possible that she had blocked all the
bad memories and created a totally false image of her father in her
mind – the father she wished she had.' He shuffled papers in the
folder and passed me another sheet. 'Read this, Maggie.'

Again, I did my best to do the job, though my heart was bleeding at that point for Megan, and for her mother.

She killed him.

It wasn't cancer. Or his heart. It wasn't a car accident. It was her. She executed him.

It was done with premeditation. She had planned to do it all along. No one will convince me otherwise. It was murder. Plain and simple.

Lying, murderous witch.

She accused him of all sorts — unspeakable evil. She pointed the finger at him and lashed out — accusation upon accusation, falsehood upon falsehood, vitriol and bile. This she had planned too. It was done to draw attention away from her own crime. It was a distraction. It was a blame game.

She told so many lies about things he had supposedly done. I had never seen him do any of it. I would have done if those things were true. I am his daughter and I am not blind — I would have noticed.

But she was telling lies.

The lying, murderous witch.

She killed him and she got away with it.

I hate her.

At first, I didn't realise just how much I hated her. It had taken me a while to see through her lies —all fabrications and sick accusations . . . she was messing with my mind, everyone's minds. Everyone believed her, even I did, at first. Though something was niggling at the back of my mind, that tiny voice whispering into my ear, telling me it couldn't be true. Daddy wouldn't hurt anyone.

Daddy was a good man.

She was a lying, murderous witch playing the innocent victim. As if!

She murdered Daddy and made me mad with grief — insane.

I am insane, they say and they're probably right. That's what you think, don't you?

DR SWANN: Let's not talk about that. Let's talk about her. Where is she now?

She is dead. Good riddance.

'Did the mother die?' I asked. 'I thought you said—'

'No, she survived, but she was dead to Megan,' Ivo told me. 'In fact, she's still alive, living somewhere in Surrey, but she never tried to contact Megan. And as far as Megan is concerned . . . well, she has no mother.'

'Do you know,' Cherie spoke in a soft, resigned voice, 'my mother knew what she was getting herself into when she volunteered to work with those damaged young people at the ATU, she wasn't stupid . . . And I think, even if today she knew what would happen to her all those years later, she would've still done it. That's the sort of woman she was.' Tears glistened in Cherie's eyes. She blinked them away. 'Anyway, I'd better be going. Lisa must be wondering where I am.'

'Me too,' I thought I should come with her. 'Thank you, Ivo, for sharing this with us.' I folded the sheets of paper and absent-mindedly shoved them in my pocket.

'Yes, me too.' Cherie said.

'If it helped . . .' Ivo saw us to the door. He seemed calm. Our visit and being able to talk must have done the trick.

Cherie and I walked back home in silence, each dwelling on what we had found out in our own way. We reached Priest's Hole first, Cherie's house being further down the road. I hugged her on my doorstep and she disappeared into the night, on her way to cuddle her lover and cry on her shoulder, and maybe feel a little bit better afterwards. I glanced at my neighbour's windows. They were dark. Samuel and Deirdre had to be fast asleep. It wasn't surprising after last night's dramas.

I withdrew into my house, slumped on the sofa, and scoffed the rest of the fudge.

Chapter Thirty-one

It was unclear what they would achieve, but if nothing else, they would enjoy a day trip to South Gloucestershire. It would be just over an hour of companionable chatter with Maggie (or rather *by* Maggie). One way, and back again. Sam was looking forward to it. His mother was not – well, not entirely.

Deirdre had spent the whole of Friday preaching about the superiority of one bird in hand over two in the bush. She had been making thinly veiled allusions to Sam *still pining for Alice and missing what was right under his nose*. It didn't take a genius to work out that she was referring to Maggie. When Sam had informed her that he was taking Maggie to South Castle, she had looked as happy as a cat that had stolen the cream. But the cream went sour as soon as the purpose of that trip was revealed.

'When will you let Alice rest peacefully in her grave, tell me!' Deirdre lamented. 'When will you start living your life again? It'll pass you by . . . And you can't go back, I should know!'

No amount of explanation would get through to his mother, so Sam didn't waste his breath trying. On Saturday morning he and Maggie waved a cheerful farewell to Deirdre (who didn't wave back, but just stood on the porch, looking glum) and drove into the sunrise. As soon as his mother's stern glare was out of sight, Sam's spirits lifted. If nothing else, this would be a welcome break from his mother's nagging.

Maggie wore a tweed jacket and a matching hunter's hat with the flaps tied up on top. Sam wondered whether it was her way of getting in touch with her inner Sherlock Holmes, but he dared not ask. The fact was that she looked nothing like the spidery, sour Holmes. She looked delightful. It was to his unspoken regret that she had elected to take the back seat. Apparently it was due to Alice occupying the passenger seat next to Sam.

'She's not shifting and I can't sit on top of her, can I?' Maggie shrugged and sprawled in the back of the car. 'Anyway, we have to give it to her – this trip is all about Alice. You won't believe, Samuel, how excited she is. If only you could see her! She's ready and raring to go!'

'As long as she doesn't insist on driving,' Sam quipped.

Maggie chortled. 'That'd be the day!'

Sam located her eyes in the rear-view mirror. 'And we're safer with you in the back seat too,' he added unwisely. Maggie scowled.

Unlike his first foray into South Castle, this time the day was crisp and sunny, the sky blue and bereft of clouds. A prime example of an Indian summer. They pulled up in the car park at South Castle train station. Sam paid at the meter and displayed the ticket on his dashboard.

'Stan Pollock's widow lives in that bungalow, over there,' he pointed at the tiled roof to Maggie. 'There's a footpath leading to it. It's only a five-minute walk. Are you OK to walk?'

'Why wouldn't I be?' Maggie gazed at him, genuinely baffled. And so was Sam. She had taken two days off work due to an alleged foot injury. Only yesterday she had been showing him the supposedly festering cut under her toe. It didn't look painful, in fact it looked like nothing at all, but – as Maggie had put it – appearances could be misleading.

They proceeded along the path which wound under heavy foliage on one side and an assortment of dilapidated fences on the other. Maggie led the way, her backside wiggling determinedly and with brisk energy.

'We have to handle the conversation sensitively,' Sam attempted to warn Maggie.

'I know, Samuel. Of course, we do! That's why I intend to do the talking. Leave it to me.'

'What exactly are you going to say to her?'

'I don't know yet. It depends. I'll know when I see her. It'll come to me.'

Sam sighed, resigned to the possibility of being thrown out of the bungalow in a matter of minutes and having yet another complaint made against him to the police. The only consolation was the perky bottom jiggling in front of him like a juicy worm on a fishing hook.

They arrived at the doorstep of the bungalow and rang the bell. While they waited, Maggie admired the fairy tale garden with its white picket fence, green pond, and an assortment of wildly colourful gnomes. As soon as Marion Pollock opened the door, Maggie let her know how impressed she was.

'Lovely garden, Mrs Pollock!'

'Um, thank you,' the woman responded, looking both pleased and suspicious. She was in her late forties, of stout stature, regular features, and electric mousy hair that hadn't seen a stylist's scissors in a long while. That didn't make her appear scruffy, but slightly on the wild side.

'My name is Maggie Kaye and this,' Maggie gestured towards Sam, 'is Samuel Dee. May we come in?'

Marion Pollock looked them up and down, without surprise but with curiosity. 'You're the husband of that journalist that killed herself,' she told Sam. 'I was expecting you. Andrew Wilkins said you were wanting to talk to me.'

The inside of the bungalow was spacious and airy with large windows. From outside the bungalow was deceptively small. On entering, you felt as if you had just opened the door to the Tardis. The view of the huge and green back garden pouring in through the sliding doors reinforced that impression.

Maggie and Sam were invited to sit on a cream leather sofa while Marion Pollock disappeared into the kitchen to get tea and biscuits. She returned with a mouth-watering offer of homemade fig rolls. She was a woman after Maggie's heart.

'So what do you want to talk to me about?' she enquired.

Unfortunately for Maggie, her mouth was full of fig roll and she was in no position to *do all the talking* as she had threatened to do. Sam had to take the reins of this interview into his hands.

He said, 'Mr Wilkins may've told you what we'd found out when I was here last.'

Marion Pollock raised her eyebrows and remained silent in an encouraging sort of way.

'That your husband was interviewed by . . . by the police,' Sam chose to avoid bringing Laura Price's name into the conversation, 'regarding my, my wife's death. She—' He swallowed, momentarily, too emotional for words.

Maggie jumped on the opportunity between her last fig roll and the next, 'But there's no record of your husband being interviewed anywhere in the police files. The policewoman who spoke to your husband, DC Price, well . . . where do we start? We suspect she may've been involved in Alice's death. We just can't prove it.' Maggie peered at Sam, feigning frustration.

'But how could I help you prove anything? I don't know anything. And Stan is dead, as you know. He killed himself not long after your wife, as a matter of fact—'

'That's what made us think,' Sam explained, having regained his composure. 'South Castle is a small place and suddenly, within six months of each other, two people commit suicide. It may look like the two are totally unrelated, but now we know, they had something in common. My wife had travelled to South Castle – to the train station, as it happens – on the day of her death, and your husband was interviewed by the police the next day about the CCTV recordings at the station. No record was made of that interview and the CCTV footage is missing, but—'

'But you think my husband was somehow mixed up in your wife's death. And he killed himself out of guilt?' Mrs Pollock stared at Sam incredulously. 'That is poppycock!'

Sam was at pains not to lose her goodwill. He had warned Maggie to tread carefully but it was he now who was struggling to keep his temper at bay while Maggie was merrily polishing off the fig rolls.

He spoke calmly, 'No, not mixed up. I think he knew something perhaps, and someone silenced him.'

'Laura Price did,' Maggie added helpfully.

'Who is this Laura Price,' Marion demanded. 'You've mentioned her twice now.'

Ever helpful, Maggie hurried to clarify, 'She is the daughter of that high-ranking police officer, John Erskine.'

Marion's eyes rounded with disbelief. 'The one that was involved in that child sex scandal?'

'The same one!' Maggie nodded in ominously slow motion.

'Blimey! But what did my Stanley have to do with that?'

'Probably nothing.' Sam had to control the direction of this conversation. It was beginning to take a detour into uncharted territory, and the possibility of another complaint to the police seemed too close for comfort. 'It's just that he may have stumbled on some information . . . I mean, we realise it's a long shot. Your husband's suicide – that was all gambling debts, I am told.'

'Well, you're told wrong. I don't know where people got that idea from. People don't know what they're talking about at the best of times! Idle gossip, if you ask me!' Marion Pollock growled. 'Let me tell you this: Stanley was a small-time gambler, that much is true, but when he hanged himself, there were no debts. He was riding the wave – one win after another! I wondered myself how he came into so much money. He never bet more than a tenner. And then, out of the blue, he goes and gets himself that Audi – says he got lucky . . . I got twenty-two thousand pound for it when I sold it! And even the day before he hanged himself, he was on about another windfall coming his way. He kept on about his lucky streak. When he hanged himself, whatever it was that was eating him, it wasn't money troubles.'

'That's what I suspected, and—' Sam inhaled deeply before continuing.

'We suspect your husband was killed, just like Samuel's wife, Alice,' Maggie waded in, boots and all. 'Either he was in cahoots with Laura Price or he knew too much . . . Did he say anything to you about Alice's death? Did he make any comments?'

'No more than what others were saying around the town. But one thing is for certain, and I can tell you this for nothing: Stanley was in cahoots with nobody. He may've been a gambler but he wasn't no killer, or—' Mrs Pollock pursed her lips angrily. 'Don't go around blackening his name.'

'No, we wouldn't do that. I've lost my wife, and you your husband. I think they were both victims in all of this. He knew something. If only . . . There's a CCTV recording missing—'

'Would Stanley have left any work papers lying around?' Maggie asked her first sensible question.

'Why, yes . . . There's plenty of his junk in his desk, with bills and bank statements, and such . . . I never got down to clearing it.'

'I know how that feels,' Sam empathised.

'Let's have a look at what's there. You never know.'

Marion led them to a small box room with nothing but a tiny skylight, a desk with an ancient desktop computer, a chair and an electric guitar propped against the wall, with an amplifier next to it.

'Stanley was in a band,' Marion said, a note of pride ringing in her voice. 'So, there. The drawers are full of his junk. Be my guest.'

They dived into the drawers, chaotically at first, but soon they divided their labour and began working their way through the contents of the drawers methodically. It was Sam who found the memory stick. It wasn't labelled in any way, but it was in a small re-sealable bag hidden under a wad of invoices.

'Could we possibly see what's on it?' He asked Marion Pollock.

'Go ahead.'

'Does this computer work?'

'Yes, I'm still using it. It's in perfect working order. No password to get in.'

The computer took a little while to come on, exuding strange whistling noises and displaying a couple of security alerts before it finally settled into action. Sam inserted the USB stick. It contained a video file. He played it.

Chapter Thirty-two

Alice.

He recognised her car as soon as she pulled into the car park and clumsily manoeuvred it into a free space with what looked like a five-point turn. The clock at the bottom of the recording showed TUE 10:47:34. It was the missing Tuesday's recording.

Alice emerged from the driver's side.

Sam felt his breath halt in his windpipe. His blood went cold and trickled away from his brain. He could feel the bristling current receding from his face, along his arms and down to his fingertips.

Alice.

On her thumb dangled her childish cat-face purse (he remembered it so well! It had a missing eye and the zip was broken, stuck halfway between open and closed). She approached the car park ticket machine and dropped a coin into the slot. She removed the ticket and took it back to her car. She fetched her case from the back seat.

She used to carry her entire office in that case. All her tools of trade were packed in there: her Dictaphone, her camera, a notebook, and of course the indispensable kitchen sink – he would laugh at the idea of it. That case had never been found.

Not that anyone had looked for it. Sam had forgotten all about it. But now it came back to him: Alice's portable office.

She pressed a button on her remote to lock her car and dropped the remote and the key into the case. She headed for the platform. The clock now read 10:53:08.

Sam watched the clock for another twenty-three minutes – every twitch of every second and every flip of every new minute. Nothing happened. The car park remained deserted: no one arrived and no one left.

He began to feel an acute sense of loss. It occurred to him that she may not be coming back. Those six precious minutes of her parking her car and paying the fee could be all he would get. He waited for her to burst out of the station building one last time. She had to come out. She had to drive to that lay-by by the railway tracks where her car had been found abandoned. Surely, she was coming back.

Maybe she would look up and he could catch the expression on her face, the last blink of her eyes.

It was just a recording, it wasn't life, it wasn't contemporaneous, it had occurred four years ago – he knew that, of course, but it didn't seem to mean anything. Sam wanted to look Alice in the eye one last time before she died.

Alice did not come back. At 11:16:45 Laura Price ran out of the side passage leading from the platforms. She was carrying Alice's case. She was in a hurry. There was something in her hand. She was pointing it away, directing it at random cars. Alice's car key with the remote. Price was searching for Alice's car.

It responded with a triple blink of the hazard lights.

Before getting inside, Price scanned the car park. There were no people present. Sam could picture her sighing with relief, though of course he couldn't see that from the footage.

At 11:22:09 Price drove away in Alice's car.

There was an apparent stillness to the recording until, at 11:26:17 a corpulent man in a black uniform hurried across the car park and entered the station building.

'That's my Stan!' Marion Pollock cried. She leaned heavily on the desk, suddenly out of breath. It didn't occur to Sam to give her the chair to sit in.

'He always came home for morning tea at half ten. His shift started at five. By ten he was famished.'

11:30:06 marked the end of the video.

Sam sat in front of the now empty screen, staring at it and waiting for it to somehow spring back into action. Alice was still there, on the platform – she had to come out.

Only he knew she wouldn't.

She was dead.

He couldn't explain how her body had travelled several miles along the tracks to end up near that pedestrian bridge, in the middle of nowhere. Laura Price had not carried it to the car, alone or with anyone else's help. Stanley Pollock had not been her accomplice – he hadn't been at the station when the two women met. Sam couldn't explain anything but he could tell that Alice had not come out of the station. She had died there.

'She killed her,' Maggie's voice seemed distant. It seemed to Sam that it had arrived from a different dimension. Sam wasn't in the here and now – he was there and then, stuck in stopped time. He was waiting for Alice even though he knew that she wasn't coming.

'We've got the evidence,' Maggie went on. She grabbed his arm and shook it. 'We have got irrefutable evidence against Laura Price!'

It took him a while to internalise what she was saying and to pull himself out of the time vortex, back to reality.

'Yes, Maggie, we've got it. Let's go and get the bitch.'

Calm and collected, he copied the content of the USB stick on to the desktop computer and then safely removed the device from it. He slid it in his pocket.

'I'll need to hang on to this,' he told Mrs Pollock.

Maggie had given up trying to reason with him. No, he wasn't going to sit back and wait for the cops to arrive in order to hand them the evidence. He had every intention of getting to *that bitch* before the police charged in to protect her. She was one of them. They would let her get away with it, like they had done in the past. Samuel wasn't going to let that happen. He was burning with white hot fury.

Maggie was rattling on the back seat, flying from side to side as he took sharp corners without slowing down. A couple of times she had dropped her mobile, but at last she managed to hold on to it for long enough to make a call. Samuel wasn't listening to her conversation though he heard the name DI Marsh mentioned twice. He knew he had to hurry if he were to get there before she did.

He slammed on the brakes to bring the car down from sixty miles per hour to a screeching halt in the street outside Price's house. He sprinted out, leaving his door open and Maggie picking herself up from the floor. He pressed the bell and held it down with all the impotent violence brimming in his gut. Laura Price opened the door, retreated and made to shut the door in his face. He applied his whole weight to push it back at her.

'What do you want?' she snarled.

'It's about what you want.' Sam felt for the USB stick in his pocket. He shoved it in her face. 'It's all here – the car park footage. Pollock kept a copy.'

She let him in. Just as Maggie had succeeded at pulling herself out from the back seat and approached the house, Sam flung the door shut behind him. He didn't want her there. He didn't want her to witness what he was about to do, and he didn't want her to stop him.

She banged on the door, screaming, 'Samuel, don't do anything stupid! The police are on their way! You won't be my hero if you harm her, do you hear me! You can't go around killing people! One was enough! Open that door this minute!'

Price gazed at him, hoping that he would relent. He said, dangling the USB stick in front of her, 'You want to see it, to be sure?'

She whisked her head away from him, her nostrils flaring. 'I've seen it.'

He let her talk. He wanted to know how she did it, what were Alice's last words, every detail – everything except the soap story about her wronged father. She probably thought she could distract him until the police kicked the door down and rescued her backside. But Sam would only let her speak until he got all his answers. Then he intended to stop her once and for all.

'Pollock was blackmailing me. He saw me drive away in . . . in *her* car from the top of the footpath. Later, when they found her body and it was all over the news, he recognised the car and checked the CCTV. When I came back asking about the coverage from the platforms, he had me. He knew who I was. Coming back to the scene was a mistake, but I wanted to be sure I had disabled the camera on the platform. I was worried about it. I didn't know about the other one.

'He said he'd erase the car park footage – it'd be all gone for a mere fifty thousand quid . . . He said he understood why I did it. He knew my father. Everyone in these parts knew my father. He was a good man—'

'You told me that before. About your father. I don't want to hear it again.'

Her eyes shifted nervously from Sam to the window. It was dark. Apart from a street lamp shedding feeble orangey light on the driveway, there were no lights, no sirens, no activity of any kind. The police cavalry had not materialised. Not yet. Even Maggie had gone quiet.

Her gaze returned to Sam. 'So what do you want to know?'

'All there is to know about Alice. You lured her there, offering information. We have that from your texts. And then what?'

'I deleted them.'

'They could be retrieved. You used to be a copper. You should know it can be done.'

'I didn't think anyone would be looking for them.'

'Alice,' Sam rounded on her. 'Tell me about Alice, or we can end it here.'

Another anxious glance at the window, and a pleading one aimed at Sam, 'I have a child – a young boy who—'

'I used to have a wife. She was the love of my life. Two children . . . Tell me about Alice,' Sam growled. His jaw was locked. The pressure from his clenched teeth radiated to his temples.

'OK.' She was going to tell him. Of course – she had no choice.

★

'South Castle station is deserted most of the time. It's mainly freight passing through it, just a couple of commuter trains in the rush hour. I checked the timetable. A freight train was scheduled to travel through the station at eleven. I sent *her* a text and told her I was ready to talk about Dad. He was dead. He wouldn't mind me coming clean on his behalf. She bought it, like any other scandal-mongering journo would. They thrive on tearing people's lives to shreds—'

'Get back to the point.'

'This is the point,' Price barked back at Sam.

'How did Alice die, not why.' He spoke calmly.

'I couldn't drive to South Castle – my car is fitted with a tracking device. I couldn't take public transport for obvious reasons. So, I went on my bike. I cycled to the pedestrian bridge crossing in Middle Holding and hid my bike in the bushes by the lay-by. I walked from there. I had ample time – I arrived at South Castle just after ten.

'I watched Pollock leave at half ten, which was my first stroke of good luck.'

Sam cringed at that turn of phrase, but didn't interrupt her. He wanted her to get to the end of it as quickly as possible.

'*She* was dead on time. I had to hold her attention for just a few minutes before the train approached. It didn't slow down, or if it had, not by much. It was easy – I grabbed her bag and pushed her. She was light. She didn't put up any resistance. I think she was too surprised. The front of the train snatched her and carried her on. It happened so quickly the driver didn't even register it. That was my second lucky break.'

'Because the body was found miles away from the crime scene?'

'Precisely. And not only that. It was found not far from where I'd abandoned *her* car. I couldn't believe my luck! I drove to the lay-by where I'd left my bike. I parked there, left the door open and the key in the ignition. I checked her mobile – it was in her case. I deleted our text messages and whacked the phone with a rock for good measure. I scrambled over the bank covered in

218

brambles – scratched my legs and arms raw – and hurled her mobile over the tracks. Little did I know, the ruddy train had carried her body all the way to that very location. I couldn't believe my lucky stars when the body was discovered there the next day! The suicide verdict was inescapable. I hadn't counted on that . . . It was poetic justice.

'But it did surprise me – the body turning up where it had. I investigated it. You see, there's a sharp bend in the tracks before that overhead bridge crossing, then single tracks become double before Gladestoke station. Trains often have to wait there to pass. There's a signal controlling the traffic. I gathered that the train had carried the body at speed until reaching that point. That's where it had to slow down or come to a standstill, and that's where the body was finally dropped. In the exact same spot where I abandoned *her* car! Poetic justice . . .'

Price smiled dreamily at the memory of her lucky break. That smile made Sam's skin crawl. The woman didn't understand the first thing about poetic justice, but she was about to find out all about it—

'Mummy, when are you coming for the story?'

The figure of her little boy stood in the doorway. He must have climbed silently down the stairs from his bedroom. This was the time for tucking him into bed, with a story and a glass of warm milk, Sam realised. He wondered, briefly, if Laura Price loved her son as much as she loved her father.

The boy whined, 'I been waiting and waiting,' and yawned.

219

Chapter Thirty-three

I had been waiting, and waiting. There was very little else I could do. Samuel had shut the door in my face. I don't believe for one second that he realised that at the time – he was so charged! I was concerned for him, and especially for Laura Price. He would be capable of killing her, I was sure of that. It was that despair to exact justice that Ivo had spoken about . . .

I was on my own, sitting on the doorstep, listening to the faint voices inside. Alice, naturally, had gone in with Samuel. I had nobody to share my fears with and no way of preventing the unspeakable from happening. I had little confidence that the policeman I had spoken to had taken me seriously.

He'd sounded dismissive when I had mentioned Samuel having tasted blood before and that he wouldn't flinch before throttling someone just like that. Especially if that someone was Laura Price, the woman who he now knew for a fact had murdered his wife. Thinking back to my conversation with the doubting policeman, I was convinced that he had hung up on me before I finished speaking.

I jumped to my feet when my phone lit up and sang its jolly tune of an incoming call. My fears were unfounded. It was DI Marsh. She had been contacted after all.

'Are you with him?' she asked without any ceremony, not even a polite introduction. She was lucky I had recognised her snappy tone at the first note.

'DI Marsh, thank God! No, he's shut himself inside the house, with Laura Price as his ... hostage. I've no way of finding out what's going on! How far are you?'

'We're on our way. Stay put. Is he armed?'

'Only with a memory stick.'

I could hear her speak to someone else in a car; her voice seemed muffled, 'This'd better not be a bloody hoax.' She rang off before I had the chance to express my moral indignation at even the idea of this being a joke.

The whine of a police siren drew my attention to the flashing blue light growing in the distance. They were almost here!

I scrambled off the steps and ran to the street. I stood in the circle of the street lamp, jumping and waving my arms, 'Over here! Over here!'

They nearly ran me over.

Two police cars pulled up. Two uniformed officers sprang out first, followed by the waspy silhouette of DI Marsh flanked by the bulk of DC Whittaker. They headed for the house.

I followed closely behind.

DI Marsh let one of the uniformed policemen bang on the door after her ringing of the bell proved unsuccessful.

'Mr Dee!' She had a surprisingly powerful voice for a woman of such tiny stature. 'Mrs Price! It's the police. Open up or we'll break the door!'

At that point, I spotted the battering ram – well, it was a small-scale ram, rather like a cylindrical fire extinguisher with handles. One of the uniformed policemen was poised to use it.

He didn't have to. The door was opened and Samuel stood in it. He told DI Marsh to keep her voice down.

We pushed by him. DI Marsh demanded to know where Mrs Price was, but she didn't wait for his answer. The officers dashed from door to door, diving in and shouting *Clear* from the inside.

'What have you done to her, Samuel?' I whispered to him in sheer horror. 'Please tell me you didn't kill her ...'

He smiled ruefully – he looked like he was sorry, only I couldn't distinguish at that point whether he was sorry for killing the woman, or for failing to kill her. I feared the worst.

'Where is she?' DI Marsh snapped.

'Upstairs. Putting her son to bed.'

Samuel, Alice, and I sat in Samuel's car, watching the goings on: Laura Price's mother arriving – distraught and hysterical (she had been asked to stay with the boy), Laura Price's lawyer arriving – cold and tight-lipped, none too pleased about this overtime opportunity, and finally Laura Price led in handcuffs to the police car; the cavalcade of the two police vehicles and the lawyer's black BMW finally departing and leaving the three of us in the car.

Alice leaned in her seat and put her head on Samuel's shoulder. He twitched slightly at that. Perhaps on some level he had felt it.

'Alice is happy you didn't hurt that woman. And so am I, if it counts for anything,' I told Samuel from my back-seat vantage point.

'I realised that would only compound the evil,' Samuel spoke to the rear-view mirror, looking me in the eye. 'Anyway, I didn't care for revenge. I only wanted to know for certain that Alice hadn't left me.'

'No, of course not. That's what she wanted you to know, too – that she wouldn't have.'

'No, she wouldn't. And I should've known that. There was no note. She wouldn't have gone without at least a goodbye.'

'Quite right.' I sighed, glad that it was all sorted, out in the open and crystal clear. Deirdre would be pleased.

Alice lifted her head and kissed Samuel on the cheek. She turned to me and we looked at each other for a few eerie seconds. I mean it when I say she was looking at me – not through me, as she had done in the past. It was a benign, I'd even venture to say, *friendly* look. I knew what she was trying to say to me. I nodded to reassure her. She nodded back.

She gazed at Samuel again – a longing, doleful gaze. Her fingertips touched the back of his neck.

'It's a chilly night,' he shuddered.

Alice was gone.

Just like that.

She didn't get up and go. She didn't do the slow vanishing act: the fading into the night thing. She was just gone.

I left my back seat and relocated to the passenger one next to Samuel. 'OK, let's go home. I'm knackered.'

He stared at me.

'What about Alice? You're sitting on top of her—'

'I wouldn't dream of doing that! She's gone, Samuel. She told me to say goodbye to you – she didn't want you to think, again, that she would leave without a word. But she's gone now. I don't think she'll be coming back.'

His face dropped. His lips went white with emotion. A sob shook his body. He gripped the steering wheel and thrust his forehead against it.

I let him cry for a bit. It is a form of release when you cry. I have tried this on many occasions and it's never failed me.

He raised his head, still looking as pale as the ghost of his now truly departed wife. He said, 'I don't think I can drive. My hands.' He extended his quivering fingers towards me. 'Would you like to drive, Maggie?'

'If I must,' I reined in my enthusiasm.

We swapped seats. I started the engine and felt Samuel's Jag come to life under my foot. I actually relished it, for I knew it was probably my last time driving the beast.

Chapter Thirty-four

It wasn't a large crowd, but then on this frosty December morning and with only two weeks until Christmas, people had other, more pressing, things to do with their time. We huddled together, our bobble hats pulled down over our ears, our hands buried deep in our pockets and our breath rising out of our chests like white smoke clouds out of chimneys.

Vera had brought Rumpole with her, but Henry was conspicuous by his absence. He had already returned home from Westminster, however – Vera told us while rolling her eyes – he was concerned that supporting *this refugee hullabaloo* could harm his community standing and re-election prospects. Aaron Letwin & Co had been planning to be here too, but with intentions diametrically opposite to ours: they had been concocting a protest march. Despite it being advertised on social media, it had not gathered momentum and they lacked the numbers to get noticed. Like I said, in this busy festive season people had other things to do. As the ancient tradition dictated, most Bishopians were having predominantly charitable thoughts in the spirit of Christmas. Objecting to a bunch of traumatised ten year olds taking shelter in the old folly didn't sit well on people's consciences. On the whole and with few exceptions, Bishops Well is inhabited by a decent lot.

The ghost of Vicar Laurence was presiding over the proceedings. I do mean that literally. I hadn't seen him anywhere near the church since his untimely departure. I had been convinced that his spirit had lost interest in earthly matters and gone straight to heaven. I had been very wrong. The Folly Orphanage was Laurence's baby – he wouldn't abandon it. I guess he was here to stay until Judgement Day, overseeing, rejoicing and doing God's bidding even from beyond the grave.

Quentin Magnebu, our new vicar, had been installed at St John the Baptist two weeks earlier. He was running around like a headless chicken – or, his size considered, like a headless ostrich. He had unwound a reel of bright-red ribbon and attached it to the entrance to the folly, ready for an official opening ceremony later on. Whilst chatting with the *Points West* TV reporter he was also nodding his thanks to Agnes Digby, who was arranging gifts and cakes on a foldable table. A lot of us had brought little somethings for the children – it was Christmas after all. I had made double chocolate muffins and Deirdre had sent a homemade fruitcake via Samuel (although she herself had stayed at home for fear of *civil unrest and bombs going off*). Vanessa and Mary had thought of putting their creative talents to good use and together made some thirty-odd snowman baubles to present one to each child. Cherie pointed out that the idea of snowmen may be alien to those children, but Edgar said that it would grow on them in no time. Or fall on them, Michael added. It was indeed a chilly day.

James had flown his whole family in from the south of France: Letitia and their two boys. The boys, albeit with poorly concealed reticence, parted with an enormous Lego box, almost as big as them. They dragged it to the table laden with gifts and shoved it as best they could underneath, out of sight, hoping perhaps that it would be somehow overlooked when the gifts were dished out to the war orphans. The younger boy snuffled back tears when he returned to his parents, without the Lego set.

'It was your choice, man up,' James rebuked him. 'You could've sacrificed the console.'

'We couldn't of! Not the console!' Both boys looked mortified.

'So there – no regrets!'

I smiled at the scene. The Weston-Joneses had more than one reason for celebrations this Christmas. Lord Philip's dispute with

Daryl Luntz over No Man's Land had ended in an undisclosed financial settlement, but I had it on good authority (from James's mouth after a couple of sherries at mine) that because the land had not been rezoned it had failed to acquire commercial value and therefore the reimbursement Lord Philip paid to Mr Luntz was a negligible fraction of the original purchase price.

We stood and we waited, and we were killing time with idle chatter. I asked Ivo about Megan.

'They're assessing her,' he told me. 'I don't think they'll find her fit to stand trial. She's regressed a lot, withdrawn into herself. She's like a scared and angry five-year-old . . . Sometimes she'll lash out at people, wildly and violently, like she used to when I first met her at the ATU — she was nothing short of a caged animal then.'

'It may sound insensitive, but experience tells me that she'll be back in another mental establishment at Her Majesty's pleasure. And that's for an indefinite period, I'm afraid,' Edgar pointed out.

'Another incarceration in one of those will kill her.'

We all looked at each other helplessly. We had no words of consolation or hope to offer.

'How's Vesna taking it? I bet she misses her . . . Do you take her to see Megan at all?'

'I visit Megan alone. I can't imagine it'd do her or Vesna any good if I brought Vesna to see her.'

Vesna was seated in a wheelchair, her legs covered with a tartan blanket. She was staring blankly into space and didn't as much as blink at the mentions of Megan's name. Ivo bent over and kissed her forehead. 'We're coping just fine on our own. We'll manage, won't we, sis? It's not the first time.'

'At least you've got each other,' Samuel reflected, a shadow of sadness crossing his face. He was still missing Alice, perhaps now more than before. Because now he knew that she had never intended to kill herself and leave him on his own, that she had never stopped loving him. I wanted to squeeze his hand or pat his back, or do something tactile and friendly to let him know I was here for him, but I refrained. That could send a mixed message.

The coach arrived.

We started waving, calling out and grinning, a couple of us clapped our mitten-clad hands for some reason. You never know what gestures are best suited to make someone feel welcome. We wanted those kids to feel at home even though this wouldn't be their home for long. It was only a halfway house, after all. From here, they would go to live with their new adopted families at best, or to permanent orphanages all over the country.

The pneumatic door opened with a hiss. George Easterbrook descended first and then our refugee charges started alighting. Two older ones stepped out, a girl and a boy aged somewhere between thirteen and eighteen, it was hard to tell. They were wrapped in oversized coats and scarves that clearly hadn't been bought with them in mind – they were handouts. There were three younger ones too, looking even smaller in the cocoons of their winter gear. Their ages ranged from five upwards.

They stood bunched together, reluctant to abandon the proximity of the coach.

We kept smiling and now all of us were clapping.

We were waiting for all of them to come out of the bus. But no one else had. That was it – the five of them. That was the whole lot.

They were peering at us timidly and with suspicion, uncertain of our intentions, and probably frightened by the racket we were making.

I heard Ivo speak to Vesna, 'Remember, sis? The beginning of our nightmare . . . it all started here. Poor bastards, they don't deserve this . . .'

His comment took me aback. I had assumed that he and Vesna would be celebrating, cheering for these children. After all, just like Ivo and Vesna all those years ago, these kids had escaped war, death, misery and been given a second chance. Their arrival here should mark the end of their nightmares, not the beginning.

Bearing gifts, Vicar Quentin and Agnes Digby raced towards the knot of little people to welcome, embrace and untie them from each other. The vicar broke into a God-praising sermon, filmed by the TV crew. I wondered how many of his many biblical references would make it to our screens – probably none.

From the corner of my eye, I saw Daryl Luntz and Hannah arrive by car and hurry across the field towards us. They looked flustered and bothered, probably because they were late. They were laden with shopping bags, and that explained their lateness. I must admit I didn't have Daryl Luntz, the horror master, as the charitable type. And yet, appearances can be so blisteringly deceiving!

I had to chuckle at the memory of my spying mission and my madwoman's accusations of murder that I had thrown in his face based on the passages from that book of his . . . what was its title?

Dying at the Altar.

But at the time, to be fair to myself, that conclusion was inescapable. The whole stage around Vicar Laurence had been set up with a faithfully macabre attention to detail as described in that book. The murderer had been hard at work, creating an illusion, trying to frame Luntz, no doubt about that . . .

That was the exact moment when I saw the light. I had been feeling my way around in the dark, bumbling about like a blind woman. How come I had not seen it before! It had been staring me in the face all along! Of course, Megan wasn't capable of such premeditation, of framing Luntz using his own book!

In Ivo's own words, Megan *was like a five year old lashing out wildly and violently — a caged animal* . . . She could well have delivered all those multiple stabs and frenzied slashes to Laurence's body – just like the self-inflicted cuts on Vesna's arms and thighs, something that must have driven Megan to white fury – but she was not the one who had painstakingly set the crime stage at the altar in order to point a finger at Daryl Luntz.

She was not capable of such rational, calculated thinking.

And then there was that attempted arson. Someone tried to cleverly divert everyone's attention towards Samuel and the debacle over No Man's Land. That someone wanted the police to think that Laurence's death and the staged arson were linked. Megan couldn't have possibly acted with such premeditation.

My first instinct was correct: there had been two people involved in the vicar's death, one of them had been Megan, and the other—

'Samuel, you have to take me to Sexton's library!' I shouted in Samuel's ear, over the cacophony of Vicar Quentin's speech imbued with the humming of the small crowd.

He gazed at me, puzzled. 'OK. I will, no problem. Let's just, first—' he said and switched his attention back to the preaching vicar.

I pulled his arm by the sleeve, rather aggressively. 'Now!' I shrilled at him.

'Can't it wait? We're in the middle of—'

'No, it can't! I must check something this very minute. It's a matter of—'

'Don't tell me! I know – a matter of life and death. It always is with you, Maggie.'

Chapter Thirty-five

In the library, it took some skilful convincing to get the librarian to reveal the names of the borrowers of Daryl Luntz's *Death at the Altar*. Well, at least the names of all the other borrowers. Once Samuel understood what I was trying to achieve, he came to my way of thinking. He was much better placed to talk reason to the lovely but rather obstinate librarian who was quoting some crazy data protection compliance rules at us as if they were the Ten Commandments and we were about to transgress all ten of them at once and go to hell, dragging her with us.

I was frantic with anticipation and just shouted and talked over the two of them, so I couldn't tell what arguments Samuel used to persuade the stubborn woman. Whatever they were, they were good. Together, we looked at the electronic records on the librarian's computer.

And there he was – the last person to have the book before I took it out to confront Daryl Luntz was Ivo Murphy. Borrowed *Death at the Altar* at the beginning of July. A month later Vicar Laurence had been murdered at the altar of St John's church, and the scene of crime had been staged accordingly.

'He can't have done it!' Samuel was aghast. 'He couldn't have killed Laurence – he was with us that morning, helping at Badgers' Hall! Maybe,' he gave in to idle speculation, 'maybe Megan read the book and used it to stage the scene of her crime ...'

'Megan?' I would laugh at that if the situation wasn't as grave as it was. 'Megan is incapable of acting with premeditation. You should've read the transcripts of her therapy sessions. In her mind she is still a young girl, just trapped in a woman's body . . .' Suddenly, I remembered Megan's therapy notes Ivo had given to me to read and I had inadvertently stuffed in my anorak pocket. 'Come, Samuel, I've got something to show you. You'll see that Megan couldn't have possibly planned Laurence's murder or staged the scene afterwards.'

From the library, Samuel drove us back to Priest's Hole where I retrieved the notes (thank the Lord Almighty that I hadn't washed the anorak!). I handed them to him and told him to read.

'You'll see what goes on in Megan's head,' I informed him. 'She's totally absorbed in her own world, in Vesna and Ivo. Nothing else is real to her. She certainly wouldn't have read and re-enacted some horror book for the fun of it.'

While Samuel read, I retreated to the kitchen to make hot chocolate (the day was frighteningly cold) and open a pack of Hobnobs. When I returned to the sitting room with the goodies, Samuel stared at me, frowning.

'Why has nobody given these to the police? The last document constitutes a confession of guilt – she as much as admits to killing Cherie's mother,' he said, mysteriously.

I gawped at him in genuine consternation. 'I don't recall there being any confessions amongst those notes, just ramblings of—'

'Oh, come on, Maggie, surely even you . . . Have you really read these? This in particular,' Samuel thrust a sheet of paper at me.

I put down our hot drinks on the table and grabbed a Hobnob. I slumped next to Samuel on the sofa and began reading: at first, just scanning the document for familiar phrases, then realising I had not seen it before, and finally taking every word in slowly, my eyes misting with great big sorrow for poor Mrs Hornby.

How would she feel if I told her I'd tape her mouth?
   For fibbing.
   She was the fibber. She had lulled us into a false sense of security.
We trusted her. She had made us trust her. We thought she was

different – kind. We thought we meant something to her. She had us fooled right from the word go.

We knew not to bother telling the others. They were the reason we were unhappy – of course, they wouldn't listen! They wanted our bruises and their finger marks on our arms to disappear – fast. They'd put Vesna in isolation, and then they would put me there too, so that they could shut the door on us and not hear a word of what we had to say. And for no one else to hear it. We knew that. There was no point in reasoning with them. They'd only say we were nothing but trouble. The moment we opened out mouths they would have us restrained, gagged and isolated from the rest. Especially from each other.

We thought she was different. A sweet and nice old lady with grey hair in a bun. She was like the granny I'd never had. Neither of us ever had a granny.

She was our teacher, our light shining in the darkness. She was gentle and kind, but I think I've already said that. She was our inspiration. Sky was our limit, she would say, even for the likes of us. We read together – books she would bring for us from the outside. Books about reversals of fortune.

We sat on either side of her, Vesna and I. Sometimes, when the book was at that point where you clench your fists and bite your lip, and wish for the pages to turn faster and faster, we would reach out to each other over her lap and hold hands, squeezing hard. I would read on over her shoulder, run ahead of her, and then I would have to wait at the bottom of the page for her voice to catch up with me. Vesna wasn't as good at reading as me. She had to listen all the way. She was good at listening. I may have said that already too. Previously. But that's the first thing about Vesna – she is a good listener. Even now.

Little good did that do her! No one would listen to Vesna, not even our dear old lady with all the time on her hands, but no time to listen to us.

But she was a great reader. She read those stories with feeling and expression. Her voice was soft and deep, grown-up, reliable. I think the two of us had come to associate her with some of the characters, the good ones, the ones you could trust. We were desperate for her to be part of the stories she read to us.

She read Rebecca first, then Wuthering Heights. And Austen. Both Vesna and I loved Jane Austen. Because everything would always come good in the end. Happy endings — we started believing in them. It was thanks to her in all fairness.

So, we started talking. We were telling her of the injustices and the abuse, and the nastiness that went on. We hoped she would sort it out for us, bring on our own happy ending. But she wagged her finger at us and peered at us from under her reading glasses, and with that spark of amusement in her eye told us to stop fibbing, we could get innocent people in trouble, it wasn't nice to make up stories like that, and if we didn't stop she would have to seal our mouths with tape.

The next day, or maybe it had taken Vesna longer than that to pilfer the dispensary for pills —maybe it was three days, maybe a week, but it was after that that Vesna had overdosed. I nearly lost her. Well, in many ways I did lose her. She is lost now. There is no finding her even though she sits right here, next to me. Just look at her. All we have is a shell of Vesna —her exoskeleton.

When I found our dear old lady —not that I had been looking for her, but faith had brought her to me —I knew what had to be done. I gave her a taste of her own medicine. It's called justice.

I made her feel comfortable in death. I am not a monster. I puffed her pillow and put her head gently on it, tucked her in. She was, after all, a nice lady — kind.

IVO MURPHY: Maybe she didn't have to die. Have you ever regretted it?

No. If only she had believed us, none of this would have happened. She brought it upon herself.

'Oh my!' I gasped when I finished.
'She confesses to killing Gertrude Hornby, and you're carrying

233

this vital document in your anorak pocket,' Samuel looked at me, mortified at my recklessness.

'I didn't know I had it . . .' I tried to remember back to that day when Ivo had given me Megan's therapy notes to read. Now I recalled him dropping a sheet of paper – it had fluttered out of his folder and I had picked it up, and put it with the other papers. Then, by total fluke, I swept all the notes into my pocket. Ivo had never intended to disclose this confession to me. In fact, he pretended he had only just realised that Megan may have murdered Mrs Hornby, and by implication, Vicar Laurence, with the packing tape being the common denominator. 'Clever bastard,' I whispered, my voice heavy with the horror of my discovery.

'Who?' Samuel asked.

'Ivo, of course! It was he who killed Vicar Laurence. He used Megan – the knowledge of her killing Mrs Hornby, her use of the packing tape . . .'

'What are you saying, Maggie?'

'You see, Ivo Murphy killed the vicar the same way Megan had killed Mrs Hornby. But he went further than Megan – he slashed the old man's thighs and forearms, just like his sister had done when self-harming . . . Megan had made Mrs Hornby, um . . .' I searched for the right word, 'comfortable before committing the deed: she had puffed up her pillow and drawn her duvet to her chin. Not Ivo! He mutilated Laurence's body with hatred and white fury. Two distinctly different perpetrators using the same symbolic weapon: the packing tape . . .'

'But Ivo was with us the whole day,' Samuel argued. 'Remember? The day of the vicar's death we were renovating Badgers' Hall.'

'Yes, but he was late!'

Samuel nodded slowly, the ghost of realisation passing through his face.

'He must've killed Laurence in the morning, then had to go home to change – he must've been covered in his blood. Ivo arrived at Badgers' Hall late – an hour or so, I remember that clearly. He must've been thinking about it all day while working with us,

234

establishing his alibi. Perhaps it was only then that he decided to stage the scene of his crime in such a way as to incriminate Daryl Luntz . . . Luntz had a motive to murder the vicar, and he wrote a book about a death at an altar . . . We know Ivo had read it. So later, when we finished at Badgers' Hall and Ivo said he had to rush home, he crept back to the church to set the stage and put on that dreadful CD. Remember, that music started later, when we were at mine having supper,' I whispered. I don't know why I was whispering. I think I was in awe of the evil that I had never suspected Ivo capable of. He came across as a benign and wise young man, the same man who had taught the incorrigible Thomas Moore to do no harm. 'He's a psychologist. He knows how to play with people's minds, how to manipulate them—'

'But why?'

'Why, oh why . . . I only realised it today. When he said something about a nightmare beginning for the refugee kids here, at Bishops . . . He must be blaming Laurence for what happened to Vesna, for her breakdown, self-harm, her suicide attempts . . .'

Samuel frowned, still confused. 'But Laurence saved them. They were orphans. They'd have perished in that war on their own. Laurence gave them a chance—'

'It looks like Ivo has a different take on it,' I said. 'Why don't we ask him?'

Samuel stiffened. 'I think we should take this confession to the police and share your suspicions about Ivo with them. We should let them talk to him.'

I cocked my eyebrow at Samuel defiantly.

'Why do I have the distinct feeling that we won't get the police involved until—'

I smiled. 'Let's go. Let's have it from the horse's mouth. Then I'll leave it to you to contact Ms Marsh.'

Although it was dark outside, the soft confetti of snow, arriving unexpectedly to cut the autumn short, brightened the evening. The snow was setting on the ground determined to bleach it white. It was slowly succeeding, but there was no bleaching of Ivo's crime notwithstanding the fact that the consequences for his sister would be dire. He would go to prison for a long time, and she would return to the mental health facility where she would wither, alone and unloved. It was a heart-breaking but inevitable perspective.

Ivo opened the door to us. His smile died on his lips when I shot from the hip: 'You made a mistake, Ivo – two mistakes, in fact.'

He didn't try to argue when I laid our evidence out for him. He simply hung his head and said, 'Yes . . . I see.'

'But why?' Samuel demanded impatiently. 'Why would you want to kill a man who saved you and your sister from the bloody war zone, brought you to safety and gave you a second chance?'

'*Saved* Vesna?' Ivo gave a contemptuous snort. 'Look what became of her since Laurence brought her to this country and tore her little brother away from her!' He pointed to Vesna who was slumped in her wheelchair, a dribble of saliva trickling down her chin, an expression of nothingness in her eyes. 'Vesna swore to protect me, to keep us inseparable, but he gave her no chance, no choice to keep her word. The only thing she could control was whether – and when – to die. And even at that she failed—' Ivo's body shook with emotion. Something rumbled inside his ribcage like a rolling thunder.

'I'm sorry about Vesna,' Samuel said. I couldn't speak – I understood what Ivo was saying and didn't need to ask any more questions. Samuel however struggled to comprehend. 'But you've got a good life here: adoptive parents, good education . . . Why—'

'Survivor's guilt,' Ivo shrugged, 'a bit more than that. As a psychologist, I know – I can self-diagnose – I am damaged goods. War, loss, death – they do that to you . . . You can't heal by sticking a plaster to your head filled with ghastly images. Those images stay there and fester under the surface. Let me describe it to you. You may just get an idea . . .'

And he began while Samuel and I sat speechless, listening and weeping helpless tears.

'There was a shot – a dry, hollow bark of a pistol. Vesna put her finger to her lips and shook her head slowly from side to side. She looked ghoulish: our mother's blood had seeped through the floorboards and dripped on Vesna's head, and travelled in her hair and down her forehead in fast-drying rivulets.

'I wanted to scream but she had asked me to be quiet, so I held that scream back. I've been holding that scream inside me for so long. It's still burning in my lungs.' Ivo rubbed his chest, screwing up his eyes and face in the pain that he was obviously still feeling.

'We waited for those men up there, above our heads, to leave. Our mother was dead, there was nothing we could do for her. And those militia men were still in the house. We could hear their heavy boots pounding against the floorboards. We waited for a very long time. Just in case.

'When darkness came and we couldn't see each other or the slightest intimation of light coming from above, and the silence was as still as death itself, we clambered out of the cellar. It wasn't the kind of cellar you would know – with its own electric lights and walls and the floor, a place where you could stand up. It was just a small hole in the ground where we stored potatoes – cold and dark. So when we crawled out of there, it felt like coming out of a grave. Our limbs had gone to sleep in there. We stretched and marched up and down to get rid of the pins and needles.

'We didn't put the lights on. Just in case someone was out there, watching.

'It turned out that I had pissed myself so Vesna changed my clothes. She said it was nothing to worry about. She said we had to leave that night, we couldn't stay at home, but we would come back when it was all over. She had packed bread and whatever food she could find for us to eat later. I wasn't feeling any hunger anyway. I had a lump in my throat and that scream was lurking there too. There was no room for food.'

Ivo paused. He sat there silent for a couple of minutes. I thought he had finished talking and was waiting for us to react. I didn't know what to say, or do next. Samuel was also silent, his shoulders hunched and lips pursed. Ivo took a deep breath.

'Our mother's body was just a bulge on the floor. I was subconsciously aware of her being there, but I didn't look. I couldn't look. Vesna said not to. She said that would give me nightmares. She knelt by Mama's body and mumbled something, maybe a prayer, maybe an oath. She covered the body with a blanket. I gathered it was to keep Mama warm.

'We slipped out into the night. We would creep carefully, avoiding light and people. We didn't speak at all. Vesna was holding my hand really tight. We kept going until we reached a wood. Even then, we kept going. Only when we were out of breath and it seemed like we had gone several times in a circle did we stop. We ate food. I can't remember what I was putting in my mouth. It didn't taste like anything I knew. We slept.

'Over the next few days, we found our way around the wood. It was big enough to swallow us and keep us out of sight. Vesna sat me down on a log and explained everything. She said she had promised Mama that she would take care of both of us until the war was over. She was in charge. She was almost an adult – fourteen – she knew what to do to keep us alive. I wasn't to worry about anything at all. I wasn't to leave the safety of the wood. I wasn't to talk to anyone. If I saw people, I was to hide. I understood all of that. It made sense. I remember feeling better.

'The UN soldiers found us within a week. We were exhausted by then, starved and no longer alert. We hadn't seen them coming. We could have been asleep when they did. They promised us the world. They were kind, attentive. They fed us well. Gave us warm clothes, a bed to sleep in, all that and more. Their chaplain, Laurence it was, though I'd forgotten his name until now, came to talk to us. He was good at talking, which was an icebreaker because we weren't saying anything. He said we were lucky. He would take us to a safe place – a new country, give us a new start with a lovely new family, new Mama . . .

'We weren't given a choice. We would have preferred to spend the war in the wood. But, all being well, we would have to endure it in that new country of his, in England. Vesna said not to worry – as long as we stuck together . . .

'We tried, but we were only kids . . .

'When my new parents came to the Folly to take me away, we thought they'd take both of us. We only realised when we were told to give each other a hug, to say goodbye. Vesna didn't say goodbye. She was crying and saying how sorry she was that she couldn't keep the promise she gave Mama. She said she would find me as soon as she was eighteen. She told me to wait.

'She never came for me. I had to find her. And when I did, it was too late.' Ivo lifted his eyes and glared right at us. 'Do you understand? Laurence had promised us the world, but he had lied. He should have let us stay in the wood near Kijevo, near our real home – together. Vesna and I were all that was left of *our* family, and we were torn apart! It was his fault. Nobody else's. His fault. He was responsible and he had to pay. Simple as that.' Ivo closed his argument.

'And the whole charade of staging the crime scene?' I asked.

'Oh, that,' he smiled ruefully. 'The idea of the parcel tape came from Megan, you see . . . Her act of revenge inspired me. It followed that I would use her method on Laurence, but then I realised I would be implicating Megan if a connection was made between Gertrude Hornby and Laurence. It was really an afterthought to point a finger at Luntz. The fire at your house, too,' Ivo glanced at Samuel apologetically, 'was to keep everyone focused on the dispute over No Man's Land. If the cops believed someone was running around eliminating people who could block the housing development . . . I'm sorry, Sam, for any damage . . . Anyway, I made sure you'd have a chance to save yourself.'

'I know, the cops told me it was a half-hearted arson attempt,' Samuel said. He reached to his pocket and took out his mobile. 'I'm going to call DI Marsh.'

Ivo gazed at Vesna with such sadness, and dare I say guilt, that my heart broke in half. 'What will happen to my sister?' he asked.

Of course, he didn't need an answer. He knew.

Chapter Thirty-six

Badgers' Hall was a sight to behold. The restorative works were now (more or less) complete. Everything looked fresh, inviting and clean (and any offending items not meeting the criteria of loveliness had been swept under the carpet).

The B&B boasted five en-suite guest bedrooms, each with its own unique character and named after a local landmark: Stonehenge, Avebury, Barbury, Cherhill White Horse and finally, with Maggie's reserved blessing, Bishops' Mule. The last one was the 'presidential suite' sprawled in the loft, formerly known as Maggie and Andrea's bedroom. It featured a view of the actual 'mule' carving on the hill, to which some ill-informed Bishopians erroneously still referred to as the 'White Donkey'. That however was done infrequently and only out of Maggie's earshot.

A tall and dense Christmas tree had been installed in the reception room at Maggie's insistence. The tree had brought with it the distinct scent of the so-called *real Christmas*. Sam had a lot to learn about that concept, apparently. Being a born and bred Londoner, he was used to the good old artificial tree, complete with all the decorations and flashing lights affixed to it permanently. However, outside the bubble of London, he was reliably informed by Maggie, people made most of their own Christmas decorations and recycled those passed down from generation to generation. Trees were real and smelt – Christmassy.

Maggie was positively glowing. Sam had caught her a few times wiping away an unruly tear of joy. For the first time in over twenty years she was surrounded by all the people she loved, though some of them she hadn't met before this moment. Her sister Andrea had arrived from New Zealand with her husband Elliot and son Jack. They took the presidential suite, from where they could admire the Bishops' Mule at every sunrise and sunset of their stay. Even Will relented and agreed to celebrate Christmas at Bishops. He and Tracey took up residence in Cherhill while their two girls shared Stonehenge, which once upon a time had been Maggie's parents' bedroom.

Sam had his own share of family togetherness this Christmas. His mother was of course at hand and wasn't going anywhere. She had taken charge of Christmas cooking and reduced Maggie to the inferior position of waitress and Sam, to a dishwasher. Sam didn't mind this relegation but Maggie pulled a squinty face and made a loud disclaimer that *next year things would be done her way.* To which Deirdre simply snorted her disdain and got down to business with a turkey that needed marinating. Campbell arrived by train with his girlfriend, Rosamunde – a fresh-faced redhead. She was in the final year of Journalism and Media studies and dreamt of becoming a reporter.

'Like Campbell's mother,' Maggie chimed in.

The reference to Alice provoked a tightening in Sam's chest. It didn't help when Deirdre sagely pointed out that sons often looked for their mothers in their life partners. Alice had been dragged into this Christmas in spirit, if not in body, although only Maggie could tell that even the spirit was no longer present *in person.*

Abi descended upon Badgers' Hall last, on the morning of Christmas Eve. She had come by car, alone and full of ideas of feminism and with a pinch of Extinction Rebellion activism thrown into the mix. Sam was proud of his girl, of her independence and verve, and of her strong opinions which she had defended with gusto over a glass of punch. She, too, had brought a tiny bit of Alice back to life.

After the Christmas dinner, Sam took his post by the sink and Maggie began her jolly rounds, bringing empty dishes to him.

She'd had quite a few sherries by then and with every new load of dirty plates she seemed to be one sherry up on her previous intake. At some point she had burst into an unwieldy but enthusiastic rendition of *While Shepherds washed their socks by night* . . . and attempted to relay to Sam a couple of jokes Andrea had shared with the company in the dining room. Unfortunately, Maggie had lost the punch-lines somewhere between the dining room, the hallway and the kitchen.

Undeterred, and by then seriously inebriated, she pulled Sam by his apron and dragged him towards the door, where under the mistletoe, she planted a hearty and rather lengthy kiss on his lips. As their bodies crashed against each other, Rudolph the red-nosed reindeer came to life on Maggie's Christmas jumper, flashed his antlers and broke into *Jingle Bells*. That startled Maggie and shook her out of her drunken stupor. She peered at Sam sheepishly and began to apologise for her . . . well, her absolutely unacceptable behaviour for which there was no excuse and no reason, and she would forever regret it, and—

Sam stopped her half-senseless sentence, and planted his kiss on her lips.

They stared at each other gobsmacked, in more ways than one following those fervent kisses.

'I didn't mean- It wasn't – I . . .' Maggie stammered.

'I did – I meant it.' Sam said. 'And I've also been meaning to ask you—'

'My God, Samuel!' she flapped her arms and staggered, briefly losing her balance. She found support in the wall by pressing her back into it. 'You mustn't make any rash decision! Because you're not ready and I – I certainly am not ready. And you'd come to regret it because I would have to say no. At this stage, I would have to say—'

'Maggie, stop. Just listen for once in your life. I wasn't proposing to you, or anything as life-changing as that—'

'That'd be the day!' She laughed a little too loud. She pulled herself away from the wall and thrust her chin forward. 'I need a drink.'

Sam stood in her way, between the wall and the bottle of sherry. 'But I was thinking that we could go away for a while. After all our hard work on this place, and everything we've been through, we deserve a holiday. You and I. What do you say?'

She beamed at him and Rudolph on her jumper did too with his flashing antlers. 'You mean a cruise? To a distant, exotic location?'

'Well, I wasn't—'

'What a brilliant idea! I always wanted to go on a cruise.'

THE END

DISCOVER MORE FROM ANNA LEGAT . . .

IN CASE YOU MISSED IT . . .

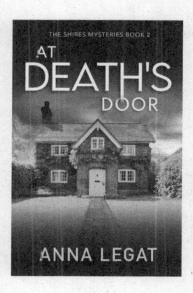

Discover the first two addictive novels in
the Shires Mysteries series

Available to order from

HAVE YOU MET DETECTIVE INSPECTOR GILLIAN MARSH?

It begins with holiday of a lifetime. But paradise is easily lost . . .

When a woman goes missing in the Maldives,
DI Gillian Marsh is assigned the case.

Gillian is a good detective, but her life back in England is
dysfunctional to say the least. And as the investigation gathers pace,
she realises that she may be out of her depth professionally too.

**With twists and turns that lead the reader to shocking
and unexpected conclusions, don't miss this thrilling
series of murder mysteries by Anna Legat.**

All five books in the DI Marsh series are available to order from

ACCENT

THRILLINGLY GOOD BOOKS
FROM CRIMINALLY
GOOD WRITERS

CRIME FILES BRINGS YOU THE LATEST RELEASES FROM
TOP CRIME AND THRILLER AUTHORS.

SIGN UP ONLINE FOR OUR MONTHLY NEWSLETTER AND BE THE FIRST
TO KNOW ABOUT OUR COMPETITIONS, NEW BOOKS AND MORE.